THIRD WEST

H.H. VANGH

Third West by HH Vangh

Cover Design by Lao Lao
Interior design by Patti Frazee

Edited by Sally Heuer

ISBNs:
978-0-9960806-0-6 (print)
978-0-9960806-1-3 (ebook)

Clairvoyant

Clairvoyant Publishing Inc.

To the men and women in law enforcement.

Proudly you stand by honor and your oath. The work you do is often overlooked and underappreciated. Those who criticize you will never be able to walk in your shoes. You are the real heroes. God bless you. And may you always go home safely to your families.

To Jerry Vick.

Not only that you were a great cop, but you were also the greatest human being I've ever known. You will be missed. May God be with you on your journey.

To my mother,

You have been through so many adversities. But never once did you thought about giving up. Your sheer will and tenacity has inspired your children to become better people in society.

THIRD WEST

H.H. VANGH

CHAPTER 1

A voice is calling to me. It sounds faint, like it's calling from a distance. I can't make out what it's saying. But my heart longs to hear it again.

"Honey!" the voice calls. I can hear it clearly now. That sweet, angelic voice is familiar and comforting.

"Honey!" the voice calls again. Now I recognize it! It's my wife calling to me!

I slowly open my eyes. The beams of light are already piercing the cracks in the curtains, illuminating my bedroom. It is morning in Rover, the city where I live. I have awoken from my slumber.

"Honey!" my wife calls.

"Yes?" I reply. "What is it?"

"Come eat!"

"I'll be down in a couple of minutes!"

I take a deep breath and sink my head back into my pillow as I bask in the moment. What a wonderful life I have lived so far! Although I have never prayed to God, I silently thank him every morning for such a blessed life.

Then a touch of sadness comes to me as I glance over at the clock on the nightstand. It is almost noon. I have slept through the entire morning. Now I won't have much time to spend with my wife before I have to leave for work.

I swing my legs over the edge of the bed and instantly cringe. The aches and pains never cease to go away. My knees are stiff and sore. The dull, perpetual sting in my neck and back are a constant irritant. Waking up feeling this way has become a regular routine. I often wonder how long I will be able to perform my job as effectively as I want to.

My job…Yes, my job… My name is John Hua. I am a police officer for the city of Riverdale, Minnesota. I was once a great street cop. But now, I'm just a shell of my former self. I no longer have any interest in chasing down bad guys. My arrest record has become nonexistent. At this stage of my career, I'm content to just write police reports until I retire. Five more years doesn't seem that long to most people. But if they did what I do every day, those five years couldn't come fast enough.

After my usual wash-up routine, I go down to the dining room and settle myself across from my wife at the dining table. A curious frown flashes across my face when I notice some of my favorite dishes displayed on the table. I know whenever she does something special like this, she is trying to ease me into something dreadful she is about to reveal. But it doesn't matter how bad it is, I can never be mad at her, and she knows it. This is her way of expressing her gratitude. *She probably went to the store and spent an ungodly amount of money on something already*, I tell myself.

"What did you do?" I ask, half-teasing with one brow raised.

She giggles softly. She doesn't respond, but she seems pleasantly amused by my curious inquisition. Obviously she is trying to prolong the suspense. Or she is trying to figure out how to gently break some news to me.

"What did you do?" I ask again, being a little persistent this time. "How bad is it?"

She finally bursts out laughing. "It's your birthday today, silly," she says, chuckling.

My eyes widen in full circles at the unexpected surprise. A warm flush of blood immediately fills my cheeks. I glance at my watch to confirm the date. Yes, *it is* my birthday today. I was born forty-five years ago on this date.

I sigh deeply as I think about how quickly the years have gone by. Even though I don't want to be forty-five, my aching body won't let me forget. "Thank you for reminding me that I'm old," I say teasingly.

"Well, at least one of us still remembers our birthdays," she blurts out.

Although she giggles after she says it, I know she means it. I really don't know how to respond. It's a justifiable statement. I completely forgot her birthday a few months ago, and she won't let me forget about it until her next birthday comes around. An embarrassed smile spreads across my face as I start in on my meal.

As I watch her watching me enjoy the dishes, I've never felt so lucky. Although time has altered my own appearance quite a bit, she is still the same beautiful woman that captured my heart over twenty-five years ago. I have to admit that I haven't been the easiest person to live with. But she has stood proudly by my side after all these years. Together, we've raised five wonderful children, three of whom have left home to begin their own lives. I could never thank her enough.

After the meal, she surprises me again by bringing over a huge piece of cake. She smiles delightfully as she watches me eyeing the mouthwatering strawberry whipped cream topping. I know it pains her to do this. She would prefer that I eat healthy.

"Honey, you don't have to do this," I say gratefully.

"It's OK," she replies. "You just have to go to the gym later."

I give her a faint smile and say nothing. I have no intention to go to the gym tonight. I have no intention to go in the near future either. It has been such a long time since I've actually done a workout. In fact, I don't even remember the combination to my gym locker anymore.

"Why did you come home so late?" she asks.

"I had to book someone. It took me longer than I expected."

"You should have called me. I was worried."

"I didn't want to wake you."

"Well, call me anyway. Because when you don't come home at the usual time, I get worried."

She is right. Being the wife of a police officer has never been easy for her, even after all these years. "I promise I will call you from now on," I assure her.

I glance at my watch: two o'clock. I am deeply saddened that my time with her was so brief. I feel even sadder knowing that it's my birthday and I have to leave her. "Maybe I'll call in sick and spend the rest of the day with you," I hint.

She quickly puts an end to the idea. "Use your sick time when you are actually sick."

"I know. But I just don't feel like going to work today. I feel like I will never see you again if I—"

"Don't say that," she interrupts. "It is bad luck to say something like that."

She pauses for a moment, as if she is trying to come up with something to help ease my despair. Then she smiles sweetly. "You're going to be off tomorrow anyway," she says. "We'll go shopping for a gift for you."

She presents me with a gift card to my favorite computer store. She knows I'm a computer geek. So the gift card couldn't be more perfect.

As I look at her lovingly, she winks and cheerfully adds, "I wasn't supposed to tell you this, but I can't hold back any longer. The kids are planning to take us out for your birthday dinner tomorrow evening."

I can't find the right words to say to her. It amazes me how she always manages to find the right words to say to me. I'm truly happy and content with my life.

As I say good-bye to my wife, an overwhelming feeling of sorrow engulfs my entire being. As a police officer, I am never certain if I'm going to be able to go home at the end of my tour. So leaving my wife for work has always been very emotional to me. But for some reason, this time it's heartbreaking. I cry as I embrace her. I feel as if I am embracing her for the last time.

CHAPTER 2

The city of Riverdale was located inside the Minnesota River Valley. To the east flowed the Mississippi River, the Moran River to the north, and the Fargo River to the west. All three rivers converged at the valley and surrounded a unique tract of land. It was on this land that Riverdale was set.

The ways in and out of Riverdale were either by boat or by one of the fifteen bridges that connected it to the surrounding cities. The population of Riverdale was a little over a hundred thousand and growing. The housing prices in Riverdale were a lot higher than those of the surrounding cities. Of course, Riverdale did have its fair share of ghettos and public housing or "the projects." I grew up in the projects. My mother was living there until recently when I finally bought a house for her and moved her out to the city of Oakdale.

It was another hot, humid day. The temperature outside was peaking at a blistering ninety-five degrees. This particular summer had been unusually hot. For the third week in a row, temperatures had reached well over the nineties.

The walk down the driveway to my truck was intentionally slow because I was dreading being in the cab. The air conditioner in my truck hadn't been working for at least two years, and I knew it would feel like being inside an oven. I thought about driving my wife's car. But she had to pick up our two youngest at school that day. I didn't want them to be roasting in my truck.

The drive from my house in Rover to the police station was nearly thirty-five miles. I was doing fine on the freeway with the windows down. But after approaching the Riverdale Bridge, traffic was at a standstill. The rest of the drive was bumper to bumper. I was getting exhausted and frustrated with the slow pace. With no breeze coming into my truck, the sweat was oozing out of my pores, gluing my clothes tightly to my skin. I thought about turning back several times. But I was almost in the city. I didn't want to be roasting for another hour on the drive back home.

I finally made it to the Western Sector Office or "West Team." I was mildly irritated after pulling into the parking lot and noticing that every parking space near the rear entrance was taken. I had no idea what was going on inside the community room. I just wished some of the citizens who attended the meeting in there would have some respect for the "Police Parking Only" sign that was clearly posted at the entrance to the parking lot.

After parking my truck in the last remaining spot, I walked thirty yards in the scorching heat to the entrance. Still drenched with sweat, I decided to go into the sergeant's office and chat with my buddy Nick for a little while.

The large room was surprisingly empty. Nick was at his cubicle. His spectacles were resting comfortably on top of his shiny bald head. His hands were constantly rubbing his rough, rugged cheeks as he stared intently at the computer monitor. He was clearly flustered with the new electronic time system that the city so graciously bestowed upon the department.

Nick Mueller and I went way back, back to the time when all police reports were handwritten. We went back to the time when we could actually touch someone and didn't have to write a "Use of Force" report to explain our actions. We went back to the time when criminals actually respected us for standing up to them and giving them a justifiable ass whooping—unlike the current pansy thugs who talked tough, but immediately cried "police brutality" as soon as you laid a finger on them. Nick and I were dinosaurs in this new era of policing, and we would always be impervious to the change.

A silly grin flashed across his face after noticing my drenched T-shirt and the sweat that was still trickling down my forehead. "I take it that you didn't find a parking spot near the entrance?" he chuckled.

"Yeah," I replied, wiping the sweat from my forehead.

"Well you should've waited. They're almost done down there in the community room."

"What's going on down there?"

"They made seven new sergeants today."

I rolled my eyes. "Wow, that's what we needed. Make more specialty units and take more bodies off the streets."

It was so frustrating. We were always at a minimum, playing defense almost every night. I could never get the days off that I wanted because we were constantly short-staffed. Now it was going to get even worse with seven more bodies off of patrol.

"Well, I got more bad news for you, my friend." Nick said, adding more drama. "One of the new sergeants is your old pal, Paul."

I took a deep breath and slowly let it out. I was completely flustered at how this department had skipped five people to get to Paul. "Well, I guess life is great when you're the golden boy. They practically gave him the answers to the sergeant's exam, and he still placed way in the thirties. Who knows how many asses he had to kiss. But for them to skip five spots to get to him, it's got to be an enormous amount."

Nick laughed. "I know what you mean. To get anywhere in this department, it's not about intelligence. It's always about how good you are at kissing ass. And he is very good at it."

"Isn't that the truth," I quickly added. "I bet that dipshit already called the Hmong newspapers to be here for the crowning of the first Hmong sergeant in this department, didn't he?"

"He sure did. Everyone who claims to be someone important showed up for this historic event."

I let out a deep, painful sigh as I thought about my own career. I had done so many good things. But they were always overlooked and underappreciated. It just sickened me that those insider-good-ol'-boys had done nothing of any significance on the streets. But yet they were highly praised for all the public-relations bullshit that they claimed to be doing for the department. I knew I would never be of any significance to the department. The only thing I had done so far in my career was to go out there, put my life on the line, and serve the public honorably. *I guess that's not what the department looks for*, I told myself. I wasn't the right candidate to be groomed.

"Well, at least I can proudly say that I have real police stories to tell," I said, smiling.

Nick laughed. "Well, it gets worse my friend." *Oh, no. Here comes more drama.*

"What is it?" I asked, bracing myself.

"He'll be working on this tour. He's going to be your boss too. As a matter of fact, he will be working with me tonight."

I didn't want to ask any more questions. I was pretty sure the answers would only get worse. I just wanted to go home right now. At least I'd have a few days to get over it. "How's the map looking for tonight, Nick?"

Nick let out a sigh. He knew I was hinting about going home. "We're way under the minimum again," he replied. "And to make matters worse, I have to detail five guys to Central Sector for that abortion protest at the Riverdale Hospital. Everyone else is on standby."

"Shit, I'd completely forgotten about that protest today. Is anything happening over there so far?"

"It's been relatively peaceful. But they are expecting some problems later on tonight." He let out a sigh again. Then he gently added, "I really wanted to, but I can't give you the day off."

"I know," I said. "Well, since we're under minimum, we're going to play defense again. I'm just so sick of playing defense every night. And it's going to be one hell of night, too."

"I know," he said. Then he quickly chuckled. "Well, if it's any consolation to you, I couldn't give Liam his usual Monday off either."

It wasn't a surprise that Liam had called to ask for the day off. He had been doing that ever since the beginning of the year. I rarely saw him on his Monday, the first day of his work week.

"So, was he pissed?" I inquired. Not that I was worried. I was just so sick of Liam's attitude.

"Yup, he's pissed."

"You should have given him the day off, Nick. I'm tired of his Monday rages." I really meant what I said. Whenever Liam had to come in on his Monday, he was unbearable to be around.

"Believe me, I thought about it. But we're so understaffed, I couldn't do it. Besides, once you're out on the streets, you don't have to see him again for the rest of the night."

Liam Hirsch had been with the department for five years. But he acted as though he had been there for twenty years. He was one of those one-uppers who had to be better than everyone else. If only his work ethic was as good as his mouth, his heroic fictional stories would be a little bit more believable. His mood swings were erratic and unpredictable. He was the only cop that I always tried to avoid.

"Hua!" Nick called to me while I stood in the doorway. "I'm sorry to do this to you. But if the shit hits the fan at the hospital, you and Tim are going to be the only west cars until everything is resolved."

"That's fine with me. I just hope that Tim will actually exceed his usual three calls a night."

"I will make sure that he does."

Ever since I started the job, everyone has been referring to me by my last name, because there are just simply too many "Johns" in this department. I was annoyed at first. But now, I preferred it. John wasn't the name my parents gave me. My real name was a mouthful to say, and no one could ever say it correctly. So I chose the name John to make it easier for people.

I entered the locker room and saw the five new recruits at their lockers. It was their first day of training under an FTO (Field Training Officer). Their uniforms were neatly pressed, and their buttons and boots were polished to a glistening shine. I chuckled as I watched them carefully inspecting each other's uniforms. I knew that Nick had something planned for them. Someone was going to get punked at roll call later on.

A touch of sadness came to me as I continued staring at those energetic, spirited, and motivated young men. I was sure they wanted to go out there to protect, serve, and make a difference. But they had no idea what they were getting themselves into. The bullshit that they would be dealing with would chip away at their morale for the next thirty years. I just hoped they didn't end up like me—a tired old man who didn't give a shit anymore.

"Good afternoon, sir!" they shouted simultaneously as they spotted me.

I smiled amusingly. "Are you guys ready to go out there and make a difference?"

"Yes sir!"

"Good, let me know if you guys make a difference. I still haven't made any difference after twenty-five years on this job."

Maurice "Mo" Barnes had just stepped out of the shower when I approached my locker. A soft-spoken guy with a huge, intimidating body, Mo was one of two African American officers working in the Western Sector. He and his partner, Teng, worked the University Boulevard beat, the toughest beat in the Western Sector.

"That's a great idea, Mo. I should have come in earlier and taken a shower, too."

He smiled. "Hello, old man," he said. "Hey, I heard that Bradley was yelling at you all day at training last week. What did you do?"

"I didn't do anything wrong. Bradley was just being Bradley, the super cop. But I didn't make the situation any better when I told him in front of everybody to go fuck himself."

Mo chuckled. "Did you remind him that you're a twenty-five-year vet?"

"I sure did. I also reminded him in front of everyone that what we do on the streets now is a lot different from fifteen years ago when he was working patrol."

Mo burst out laughing. "I got to hand it to you, old man. You got balls. No one would have the balls to say that to a commander, especially to Bradley."

"Well, what are they going to do to me? Put me on patrol? I'll be extremely happy if they put me behind a desk for the rest of my career."

Mo continued laughing. "That guy is so full of shit," he said. "I'd like to see him go out there and handle some 911 calls or take a couple of domestics. He'd probably shit himself."

I laughed. "Well, when a guy spends two years on patrol and then sits behind a desk for the next fifteen years, he really has no credibility. Still, he never stops trying to prove to everyone that he is the best of the best. His one and only police story about shooting that emotionally disturbed guy for trying to attack an elderly woman was told at least five times at training."

"That is exactly what's wrong with this department," Mo started in. "I mean, we all swore an oath to put our lives on the line. And then you have those guys who immediately go into specialty units as soon as their probation is over. Then they sit behind their desks and try to climb the ladder. Once they make the command staff, they come up with training protocols that make no sense for what we do out there on the streets. They're so far removed from the streets. They have no clue. It's just ridiculous!"

"You're preaching to the choir, Mo. But, you and I are just bottom feeders. We have no control over what the gods at HQ bestow upon us. But remember what they've always said to us: 'Patrol is still the backbone of this department.'"

I was struggling with my uniform pants when Liam walked in and sat on the bench behind me. I chuckled at his black skintight nylon T-shirt. It was nearly a hundred degrees outside. I just couldn't understand how he could be comfortable in that shirt, especially with all that body hair. I mean, even if he managed to take off that shirt, he'd still look like he was wearing another shirt underneath.

I could tell that he was still pissed about not getting the day off. I tried ignoring him. I knew he was waiting for me to say something. But I kept quiet to piss him off even more.

"Go ahead and say it!" he finally blurted it out.

I turned to him and smiled. "Thanks for being here, Liam," I said. "Your divine presence will give us the much-needed uplift for tonight."

He gave me a huff. Then he got up and walked over to the toilet to do his usual routine of taking a crap before work.

• • •

I was adjusting my duty belt when Kevin and Tommy came into the room. It seemed they had been out patrolling for a while. "Did you guys come in early?" I inquired.

"Yeah," Kevin replied. "Day shift needed help because of that protest at the hospital. We got the call and we came in at noon."

"This is *bullshit!*" Tommy spat angrily. "As soon as we put ourselves in service, those day guys headed straight to the gym. I was like, what the fuck? Did they just call us to come in early so that their guys could go work out? I'm not doing this shit again!"

I laughed. "That's why I never answered the phone when they called me, Tommy."

Kevin Yang was a straight-arrow kid who grew up in the city of Woodbury. He was twenty-five years old and already had his master's degree. I always encouraged him to climb the ranks so that one day he could be the city's first Hmong chief of police.

Tommy Lor was a troubled youth from the ghettos of the Charlestown neighborhood. He was a personal project of the beloved Commander Thelon of the Western Sector. Thelon took Tommy under his wing and guided him through high school. He cleared Tommy's juvenile records so that Tommy could get hired on with the department. Tommy earned the nickname "Charlestown Tommy" because within a year, he'd already managed to get himself in trouble three times.

I laughed quietly after entering the roll call room. The recruits were standing in line at the front of the room. Paul was walking down the line, trying to look important as he carefully inspected their uniforms. I smiled amusingly as I caught a glimpse of Nick winking at me. The new sergeant had just been punked in front of everyone.

After inspection, Paul conducted roll call. He was humble at first. But it didn't take long before he began patting himself on the back as he exaggerated about his experiences as a patrol officer, and praised himself for his great achievements as a detective. He might have been able to impress the younger guys who had never seen him in action. But I wasn't impressed. Everything he talked about completely contradicted what he'd actually done. He was a cowardly patrol officer who was afraid of his own shadow. He stayed on patrol for a year. When his probation was over, he immediately went to a specialty unit and sat behind a desk for the next ten years. I had never heard of anything he had accomplished as a detective either, except that he spent most of his time in "deep undercover."

Jack Lefebvre was sitting at the other end of the room. We kept rolling our eyes at each other. We were both Paul's FTOs, and we both knew how incompetent Paul was. I smiled amusingly as I thought about how I'd teased Jack over the years. Although he had a French last name, he always insisted that he was English. He got very angry every time I teased him about his French last name and then called him "Jacques." He was as stubborn as a mule. He would never compromise if he thought he was right about something.

Bobby "Crash" Jay was sitting next to me. He was a big, overweight, goofy-looking white guy who claimed to be Native American. I didn't know how that could possibly be. He had blond hair and blue eyes, and was as white as a ghost. He was very impulsive and prided himself on his mouth not having any filtration. I figured that his brain was just too slow, and by the time it caught up to his mouth, he had already said things that he shouldn't have said.

I could tell that Bobby was dying to say something to the new sergeant. So I quickly reached over and slapped him on the back of his head. "Bobby, you better keep your inner voices inside," I said half-teasingly. "If you prolong this roll call any longer with any of your stupid comments, I'm going to shoot you right here."

CHAPTER 3

The Riverdale Police Department divided the city into three sectors: Eastern, Central, and Western. I worked as a patrol officer assigned to the Western Sector, which I'd been working ever since I started my career. The shift or "tour of duty" that I worked was the afternoon shift, which was referred to as "Third West."

The Western Sector was also the largest sector in Riverdale. Because of this, it was divided into two districts: Northern and Southern. The Northern district was by far the busiest because of the strip malls, shops, restaurants, and markets alongside University Boulevard. Also within the Northern district were two of the most populated and crime-ridden neighborhoods: Sims City and Charlestown. Sims City was the name given to the neighborhood south of University Boulevard. Charlestown was the neighborhood to the north. Together, these two areas accumulated over seventy percent of the calls for services.

Right after roll call, Tim immediately put himself out on an investigation at the area of Hershey Avenue and Central Street. There was a small pizza shop over there. Everyone knew he was going over there to eat. *What a worthless asshole!* I thought. I often wondered how he could go through life being that worthless. He obviously didn't care or he was impervious to what people thought of him.

With Tim doing that, the dispatcher knew that roll call was over. I was quickly dispatched to a domestic in the Charlestown neighborhood. Angie, our dispatcher, still hadn't fully grasped the concept of north and south—even though she had been dispatching for the Western Sector for over a year. The reason the department established the two districts was because it would take a lot longer for a south patrol officer to make his way up north and vice versa.

• • •

As I drove east on University Boulevard, approaching Orbit Parkway, I saw a little boy at the bus stop near the southwest corner of the intersection. He looked so cute standing there chomping on an ice cream cone. I smiled and waved at him, expecting him to do the same in return. But he gave me the middle finger instead. A man I assumed was the boy's father was standing next to the boy. He was smirking at me as he patted the boy's head. What a proud father he was!

I wasn't surprised. I wasn't mad either. I actually felt sorry for that little boy. *Just look who he has as a role model,* I said to myself, shaking my head. That little boy did not have a promising future. I knew the cycle would repeat itself all over again—job security for the cops.

It was hard for me to believe how much society had changed. There was no gratitude for what the police did anymore. It was amazing how those idiots hated us so much. They didn't want us to be in their neighborhood. But yet, we were the first people they called when they needed help. Then they complained about us not getting there fast enough. It was laughable when they told me that I didn't understand their situation because I didn't grow up in the 'hood. What a bunch of bullshit! I grew up in the projects! I knew what it meant to be poor. I also knew that in order for me to get out, I would have to make the effort. It sickened me that so many idiots wanted to live that kind of lifestyle and dine on a steady diet of government cheese. Then they blamed everyone else for their pitiful situation. We had become a society of entitlements, where people refused to make the effort, yet they felt entitled to the rewards. I was so happy to be at the tail end of my career. I felt so sorry for those young officers who still had so many years ahead of them.

I finally made it to my call and immediately recognized the dump of a house. *The Drunken McCoys,* I said to myself.

Bo McCoy and his wife Tammy were habitual drunks. Besides being drunk and dim-witted, they were also hoarders. Their tiny house was filled with junk that they had accumulated over the years. The only thing positive about the two of them was that they didn't have any children. Those poor things wouldn't have a chance. They'd be screwed from the moment of conception.

I opened the front door to a mountain of garbage inside the hallway. With junk on both sides, stacked from floor to ceiling, there was barely enough room for me to squeeze through. The familiar and pungent stench of booze, cigarettes, and body odor became more potent as I inched closer to the living room. As bad as the smells were, they were actually a welcome relief. They helped nullify the unbearable stench from the kitchen.

I smiled amusingly when I heard the usual nonsensical, slurred voices coming from the living room. I often wondered how those two could actually understand each other. I couldn't understand a single word they were saying. And I was sober.

"Guys, what's going on today?" I said as I entered the room.

As I spent several long minutes listening to Bo and Tammy argue over who drank the last can of beer, an epiphany hit me: no matter how bad my life might get in the future, it couldn't possibly get any worse than theirs.

After the situation was resolved, I was immediately dispatched to another call in the Charlestown neighborhood. I sighed deeply as I looked at the dispatch screen on my computer and recognized the name of the caller. *Candice*, I said to myself. *She's off her meds again.*

Candice Norwood was a paranoid schizophrenic who called the police at least twice a month to report that she had been raped. She was by far the most raped woman in the city.

Candice was standing outside her apartment building when I arrived. I quickly stopped my squad car upon seeing her. She was wearing a blue T-shirt and nothing else from the waist down. It was a disturbing sight to anyone in the immediate vicinity, because she stood less than five feet tall and weighed about two hundred and thirty pounds. I quickly jumped out of the car and ran to the trunk to get a blanket before approaching her.

"Candice, what are you doing out here, honey?" I said, wrapping a dirty blanket around her waist.

"I've been raped!"

"Who raped you this time?"

"Sweeney did it," she replied. Then she looked over her shoulder and started in on her usual conversation with herself. "Yes, you did, Sweeney! No! I told you I didn't want to have sex. You raped me! Yes you did! Don't you be lying now, Sweeney! You did!"

As I watched Candice having a heated argument with one of her three imaginary boyfriends, my mind was focusing on something else: *Only five more years until retirement.* How I wanted to get away from all of the madness and move to a wilderness somewhere in Alaska. I would never miss my job! I would never miss society!

"Sweeney, get out of here before I arrest you!" I sharply interjected, trying to appease Candice.

After a brief silence, I asked Candice if Sweeney was leaving. "Yes," she replied. "He's walking away, but he's still yelling at me."

"Keep walking, Sweeney!" I shouted as I stared in the direction she was staring. "Candice, did you take your meds today?" I gently added.

"No, my meds make me sleepy."

"Honey, you have to take your meds every day so that those guys don't come back and bother you again."

After I finally convinced Candice to go back into her apartment and take her medication, I was pretty much done with taking any more crazy north calls. I wanted to go down south and be among normal people. I wanted to be among the taxpayers who still had a healthy respect for cops. But I didn't even make it to the freeway before Angie sent me another call up north again—an aggressive panhandler at the area of University Boulevard and Miller Street. "It's Larry," I muttered.

Larry Folk was a habitual drunk and a complete dirt-bag. He had been panhandling in that area ever since the small strip mall at the southwest corner of the intersection added a liquor store.

Larry was standing at the entrance of the small Asian grocery store at the southeast corner when I arrived. He usually blocked the entrance to the store and demanded money from people who were looking to go inside. The store owner, Mrs. Lee, was too afraid to tell him to leave because of his aggressive behavior toward her. I felt sorry for her because her business was greatly affected by him scaring off her costumers. I had arrested Larry many times in the past for doing that. But the City Attorney's Office refused to prosecute him. They claimed that I was harassing him. *I wish those assholes were here to see this*, I told myself as I got out of my squad car. *Maybe they'd have a little bit more compassion for the poor lady.*

Larry had his eyes fixed intently on me as I started toward him. He had both hands at his side, clenched tightly into fists. Obviously, he was trying to give me his most intimidating look. I knew he was all bluff. Like all bullies, he'd cower as soon as someone stood up to him.

"Man! I ain't done *shit!*" he shouted angrily.

I went up to him and looked him straight in the eye. "You better let some air out of that chest!" I said sternly. "Look at you, acting all tough as if you're going to scare me. You know you ain't got shit to scare me with!"

"I ain't done *shit!*" he shouted again, acting as if he was going to hit me.

"You better quit playing!" I said, moving a little closer to him this time. "What are you gonna do? You gonna hit me? You got your chance right now! I'll even let you have the first shot!"

He quickly backed down. "I ain't done nothing wrong!"

"You playing me for a fool? You know why I'm here! You know you got a stay-away order!"

"But I ain't at the liquor store!"

"Man, you stupid! All this time you thought it was for the liquor store? The stay-away order was for this store, you dumbass!"

I couldn't arrest him for violating the order. It had expired two months ago. But he didn't know that. I was just going to use it to scare him away.

"I ain't stupid! I'm a *fifty-year-old man!*" he roared loudly.

"You're not a fifty-year-old man. You're a fifty-year-old boy. A man wouldn't be hanging out here every day, drunk, acting a fool and hassling people for money. A man would be home taking care of his sick wife like he was supposed to do."

"Man! Fuck you!" he shouted. "A black man ain't got no right to be out here, huh?"

My mind went straight into overdrive after hearing that. "Don't you fucking pull the race card on me! Take a good look at me! What the fuck do I look like to you? I'm a Chink, a fucking minority just like you! But unlike you, I don't constantly use my race as an excuse for being a fool. You have a choice with your life and you choose to be an uneducated, ignorant bigot! You have no fucking idea what racism is, yet you bring that shit up every time you don't get your way! *I know what racism is! My people were exterminated because of our race!* You have no fucking clue what racism is and how dare you bring that shit up with me!"

Larry remained surprisingly quiet as I continued to vent. "Obviously the booze destroyed the few brain cells you have left. Race isn't the issue here! The issue is your *stupidity!* You stand out here every day. You threaten people for money. You use the money to buy more liquor. You get drunk and stupid. And then you do that shit all over again. You have nothing to offer society except your stupidity. You better get the fuck out of here or I'll whoop your ass!"

Larry was defeated and he knew it. He continued running his mouth off as he walked away. I wasn't bothered by it. He was leaving, and that's all I wanted. I didn't want to take him to detox because his wife, a very nice woman, had cancer. She needed him home with her. How she ended up with that loser baffled me.

Larry was about mid-block and still running his mouth off when an angry voice shouted from behind me, "What's your fucking problem, asshole? Come back here and say it like a man!" I quickly spun around and saw Liam behind me.

As Larry and Liam shouted profanities at each other, I could tell that Liam was getting really hyped up. People were now stopping to gape at them. So I quickly interjected, "Larry you better get out of here or I'll arrest you for the stay-away order! You won't see your wife again for a long time!"

After Larry finally left the area, Liam directed the rest of his anger at me. "Why did you let him talk to you like that?" he shouted.

"What do you want me to do?" I calmly asked. "You want me to kick his ass for running his mouth off? As long as he is leaving, I don't care what he has to say."

"You shouldn't let him talk to the police like that! Now he's going to be like that to the police every time!"

"He's been like that to the police ever since I've known him. I'm pretty sure he got his ass kicked many times for it. He didn't learn then, and he will never learn now. He is a lowlife! Why would I want to kick his ass for running his mouth off? I'm above that. I'm better than that."

"Well, he still needs to go to detox!"

"If you want to take him to detox, then be my guest."

Without even glancing at me, Liam went back to his squad car and sped away. I knew Liam was right. I shouldn't have let Larry talk like that to the police. But society had changed. And so we had to change too.

As I drove down University Boulevard, I noticed Bobby out with a lady in the parking lot of an auto shop. They were standing face to face with their arms repeatedly flapping up and down. I knew they were having an argument. And knowing how impulsive Bobby was with his mouth, I decided to stop by. I wanted to save him from getting his ass chewed out by the commander the next day.

"What's going on, Bobby?" I asked, pulling him aside. "Hi, we'll be right back," I said nicely to the lady.

"That crazy woman wants to report that her tire was slashed," Bobby said. "The damage on her tire wasn't consistent with it being slashed. Obviously, she ran over a curb and caused the tire to pop."

"So how long have you been arguing with her?"

"I've been trying to explain it to her for thirty minutes. She was arguing with me the whole time."

"So, instead of taking fifteen minutes to write a bullshit report for her, you argued with her for thirty minutes? Have you resolved the issue yet?"

"It's bullshit! I'm not going to write a report for her. She's a lair."

"So, is the department paying for the damages?"

"No. But—"

"Write the report, Tubby!" I interrupted. "She is going to complain about you if you don't. Then the sergeants will have you come back here and take the report, after they've chewed your ass out!"

Bobby took a deep breath. "I suppose," he said. "Hey, Jack, Liam, and I are going to Morrie's for coffee after this. Do you want to come?"

I didn't mind having coffee with Jack and Bobby, but I didn't want to see Liam again, especially after what had happened. He was going to bitch about it again, and I didn't want to hear it.

"No," I replied. "I have to get down south before I get stuck up here all night."

CHAPTER 4

The pending queue in my computer was stacked with north calls. None of them were of any interest to me. After twenty-five years of dealing with domestics, fights, and disorderly calls, I was tired of it—sick of it. I just wanted a south call so I could write the report and rest for a while.

Tim had been out eating for more than two hours. The worthless piece of shit couldn't care less that we were getting our asses handed to us while he wolfed down pizza. I wished he would go to another sector. Everyone tried to encourage him to do so. But the other two other sectors already had their share of worthless people.

After a while of constantly checking for pending calls, a south call finally popped into the pending queue. The comments on the dispatch screen stated that a small Asian male was hiding underneath the Pine Street Bridge. I knew it had to be Robbie. *He's probably drunk again*, I thought. I immediately got on the radio to take the call before Tim did. He also knew Robbie. And he would milk the call for the next two hours if he got it first.

"Do you need a squad to assist?" Angie asked.

"Negative," I replied. "I'll advise for now."

"Show me en route to assist," Tim suddenly said on the radio.

"I can handle Robbie by myself, Tim," I quickly responded. "You can finish your pizza."

"Copy that," Angie interjected, chuckling.

I'm sure everyone else was chuckling too. It was wrong of me to say that on the air. But the worthless asshole needed to take at least one real police call before he put himself out on some fictitious calls and milked them for the rest of the night.

I was actually excited about seeing Robbie again. He was a childhood friend of mine. We grew up in the same public housing complex. I hadn't seen him around for months. My mother was constantly pestering me about him. Now I'd have an answer for her. Maybe our encounter would help ease some of her worries about him.

After arriving at the bridge, I went to the south end and ascended the hill. A curtain was covering the small opening of the crawlspace. I knew Robbie placed it there to be inconspicuous to passersby. As I gazed down at the old, musty curtain, a deep rush of sorrow came over me. It pained me to see that he was still living like this. I was hoping that his life would get better. But I knew he would continue to live like this until he died.

"Robbie! It's me, Hua," I called. "Come out, buddy. It's time to go to detox."

I was expecting him to come out and cheerfully greet me as usual. But all I got was a low, raspy growl coming from behind the curtains. I wasn't sure what to make of it. So I slowly backed away.

I was thinking about calling for backup. But I was embarrassed at the way I'd acted earlier. Tim was probably the only available officer now, and this was his chance to get back at me. I wasn't going to let him have the gratification. I could handle Robbie by myself. He had never posed a threat to me before. Besides, he stood about five feet tall and weighed less than a hundred pounds.

As I pondered how I was going to coax Robbie out, I heard moaning sounds from behind the curtains. "Robbie, if you're hurt," I said, "I'll get medics for you! Just come out, buddy!"

Again, I didn't get any response, except for a growl. After a minute went by, the moaning finally convinced me that Robbie was probably hurt and unable to come out. I had to go check on him.

My nose caught a whiff of a pungent mixture of odors as soon as I poked my head through the curtains. The darkness inside the crawlspace was nearly impenetrable. "Robbie, where are you?" I said, reaching for my large metal flashlight.

Suddenly, a pair of hands grabbed onto my head and began pulling me through the curtains. "Robbie! Let go of me!" I yelled out as I instinctively swung the flashlight forward. The hard impact caused him to let go and I quickly backed out.

I was a little shaken. So I went down to the small grass field at the bottom of the hill to collect myself. I knew I'd struck Robbie. But I wasn't sure where. Then the blood and the huge dent on the metal handle of the flashlight confirmed it—I'd probably struck him in the head. I knew I had no other choice but to go back up and check on him.

I walked back and stood a few feet away from the curtains. The moaning inside told me that Robbie wasn't dead. But he was probably badly injured. "Robbie, if you're hurt, I'll call medics for you," I said. "You're not in trouble, Buddy. Just come out, I'll get some help for you."

I tried to remain calm as I spoke. But my eyes were focusing on the field. If someone else besides Robbie came through that curtain, I was going to run down to that field and maybe straight into my squad car.

Then a head suddenly poked through the curtains. Startled, I jumped back a step. It was definitely Robbie. His head was drenched with blood. I gasped as I noticed his eyes. The familiar bloodshot eyes that I was used to seeing weren't there. It seemed as if his eyeballs had ruptured and blood had spilled out into the white part of his eyes. The corners of his eyes were also leaking with blood.

I was completely mystified. I never thought I could do that much damage to him with just one blow to the head!

Robbie's irate face was beginning to concern me. I'd never seen him so angry before. I knew he was mad at me for hitting him. But this was still way out of character for him.

"Robbie, please calm down," I said, as I slowly backed away. "I'm sorry for hitting you. You were holding on to my head. I was only defending myself. I'm really sorry for hurting you."

My apologies didn't make any difference. He was still furious. Now he was crawling toward me! I had to get down to the field. The unlevel terrain where I stood would put me at a disadvantage.

I made it to the field and stood in the middle. The space would give me enough room to maneuver. There was probably going to be a fight. I didn't want to hurt him even worse than I already had. But I wasn't going to lose this fight!

Robbie made it out of the crawlspace and began crawling down the hill. His fiery eyes were fixed intently on me the whole time. When he reached the bottom, he slowly stood up. His face was covered with blood. His mouth was slightly open and pinkish foam was oozing out of it, trailing down to his chin. His old, raggedy white T-shirt and blue jeans were soaked with blood. Some brownish stains were plastered all over his shirt. I was staring at him as if I was in a trance. Again, I just couldn't believe that I'd caused that much damage with a simple blow to the head.

As I wondered about the stains on his shirt, a sudden downward wind blew by me and I caught a whiff of the odor. I couldn't believe that I'd hit him so hard he shit himself!

Robbie was badly limping as he began moving toward me. I cringed as I looked down at his right foot. His ankle was bent outward and his foot was flopping loosely. His ankle was obviously broken. Every step he took was just too painful for me to watch. I couldn't believe he wasn't affected by it.

I knew if Robbie continued putting weight on his ankle, he was going to cause permanent damage to it. So I decided to stop backing away. I was hoping that he would stop too. But he didn't.

"Robbie, please stop walking," I pleaded. "If you keep putting weight on your ankle, you're going to make it worse. I'm so sorry I've hurt you. Look, I'm not going to arrest you. I'm just going to take you to the hospital to get help for your injuries. Please, sit down and don't put any more weight on your foot."

Robbie paid no attention to my desperate pleas. He was determined to get to me. I had no idea what was going on in his mind right then. But I knew that after all the years of heavy drinking, paint sniffing, and drug using, his mind was probably gone.

Robbie got within a few feet of me and abruptly stopped. Then he opened his mouth and let out a low, angry growl. His badly decayed teeth were clenched tightly together at first. But after another growl, he began snapping his teeth together.

The teeth snapping really scared me. I immediately withdrew my pistol and held it at my side. I was thinking that I might have to shoot him to protect myself. But I couldn't do that. He was my friend—someone that I'd grown up with. He needed help. He needed to be hospitalized. He didn't need to die.

I placed my pistol back into the holster and I took out my expandable baton. After extending it to full length, I raised it over my shoulder and waited for whatever he was going to do next. I was planning on knocking him down with the baton, and then secure him until medics arrived.

Robbie suddenly let out a high, screeching scream and lunged at me. I reacted by swinging the baton as hard as I could. The tremendous impact from the baton sent a stinging sensation that started at my wrist and rippled throughout my body.

I knew I'd connected. When I opened my eyes, I saw Robbie down on the ground. He was on his back and was motionless for a moment. Then his body began twitching. The huge indentation across his forehead was evidence that I'd struck him in the head—again!

I felt even worse now. With him twitching like that, I knew I'd caused permanent brain damage to him. I didn't know what could be worse for him: being dead, or being alive with brain damage.

Robbie slowly came to and began flailing his arms. He was trying to roll over. I didn't want to hit him again. So I waited until he rolled over on his belly. Then I quickly jumped on him and handcuffed his hands behind his back.

Medics arrived about thirty minutes later. I was pissed that it took them so long to get there. I wanted Robbie to get to the hospital as soon as possible. But after seeing the expression on the medic captain's face, I could empathize with him. They were probably having one hell of a night too.

After Robbie was strapped down onto the stretcher, I briefed the medic captain. I told him about the nature of the call and what had happened. I also told him briefly about Robbie's drinking and drug use.

"So this guy was the one that bit all those people," said the captain.

"What?" I inquired. "How long ago was that?"

"A couple of hours ago," he replied. "Within the past five hours, we've taken twelve people to the hospital because of him."

"How do you know it was him? Why didn't any of those people report it to the police? I only got this call a little over an hour ago."

"Well, most of those people were homeless. I'm pretty sure it was him because they said that a guy named Robbie bit them." He laughed as he continued, "A big guy told me he was out walking his dog on the trail earlier when a little Asian guy ran up to him and bit him in the arm. He said he beat the shit out of the Asian guy and then he went home. He didn't report the incident to the police because he was afraid he might be in trouble. Anyways, he felt really sick later and called us."

"Well, that explains some of Robbie's injuries," I said.

"I think he bit a lot more people than just the ones that we took to the hospital," the captain continued, "because when we were at the hospital earlier, a lot of people showed up at the lobby with similar illnesses. The other hospitals are swamped with sick people, too."

We were still conversing when we were startled by a loud yell. I quickly turned and saw big Tony Swede, the other medic, covering his left forearm.

"What happened, Swede?" I asked.

"I was trying to start an IV," he replied. "Then he lifted his head up and bit me!"

"Spray some antiseptic on it. We'll have a doctor look at it when we get to the hospital," said the medic captain.

As I watched the medics leave with Robbie, I was saddened by what I'd done to him. He'd already had such a rough life. And now, I'd just made it even worse for him. Although he was never what you'd call a normal person, I doubted that he would ever be himself again.

CHAPTER 5

The thought of Robbie was the only thing on my mind as I headed to the hospital. I wanted to be there for him. *I'm the closest thing to family for him,* I told myself. *I just hope that he'll forgive me.*

After the Pine Street Bridge was a few blocks behind me, Angie radioed to ask if I was still at the bridge. "Negative," I replied. "I'm en route to the hospital. What's going on at the bridge?"

"We got a call of a man down."

"Medic is transporting him to the hospital," I said, thinking it was Robbie. "Clear it out as a dupe."

"Negative," she replied. "The caller still has eyes on. The man is lying in the ground."

Freddie, I said to myself. *I should have checked for him when I was over there earlier.* "Copy, I'll go back," I said. "He might be a detox candidate. I'll advise on another squad."

Freddie Bluebird was an old Native American guy who had been a drunkard before I was born. He had been admitted to detox more times than the total population of some of the small towns in the state. He and Robbie were drinking buddies. They usually drank themselves to the point of unconsciousness.

I was hoping that Freddie wasn't as crazy as Robbie. But I wasn't too concerned about it. Freddie was well into his seventies. He also couldn't walk without the use of his cane. Besides, he'd probably be unconscious by the time I got back to the bridge.

As I approached the area where I was out with Robbie earlier, I spotted a shirtless guy standing in the middle of the field with his back toward me. *Probably not Freddie,* I thought. *He doesn't have a cane.*

I parked my squad car at the small service road and started down to the field. I was a little hesitant to approach the guy. He might not be Freddie, and I might end up fighting with him. But after seeing the grayish ponytail in the back of his head, I was relieved. He was definitely Freddie. No other person would tie a distinctive blue feather to their ponytail.

I didn't want to surprise him, so I called out to him as I approached. "Freddie! How much did you have to drink today? Obviously it's not enough because you're still standing. It's time for detox, buddy!"

I paused when I noticed that he was slowly turning around. Then, my eyes widened. My mouth dropped. How could this be possible? How could he still be alive?

Freddie's belly was ripped open. His entrails were dangling from his waist. His chest was covered with deep bite marks. His pants were drenched with blood and something that resembled feces. Chunks of flesh were missing from his right forearm. His head hung low and was tilted to one side. His eyes were half-dazed as he gazed at me. I immediately noticed their distinctive similarity to Robbie's eyes. But Freddie's facial expression was different from Robbie's. Freddie didn't have that enraged look. His expression was emotionless, almost peaceful.

After a moment of gazing at me, Freddie slowly opened his mouth and let out a low, raspy growl. A foamy mixture of blood and saliva began oozing out of it. *Ah, shit! Not this again!* I said to myself.

As I watched Freddie slowly stagger toward me, my body began to tremble. I tried to comprehend what I was seeing. But I still couldn't believe it. With those injuries, he should be dead. *Could he be a zombie?* I wondered. *Could he really be a freaking zombie?*

Approaching me, Freddie lifted both arms and tried to grab me. I quickly pushed him away. He stumbled a few steps backward, but then he regained his balance and started toward me again. After noticing how slowly he was moving, I realized that he wouldn't be able to catch me. So I decided to just keep moving away from him until medics arrived.

Suddenly, a loud scream alerted me to someone behind me. Two women were standing by my squad car. One of them seemed horrified and was freaking out. The other, a heavy-set woman, began walking toward me.

After noticing that her eyes were fixed on Freddie, I instantly knew what her intentions were. The crazy do-gooder yuppie was going to get herself killed! "Stay back!" I shouted.

"He's hurt!" she shouted back. "He needs help!"

Grabbing a hold of her arm, I sternly warned her, "Listen to me! He'll kill you! Go back or I'll arrest you!"

"I'm a nurse!" she said defiantly. "I have to help him!"

With that, she jerked her arm free from me, ran toward Freddie, and took his arm. As she attempted to direct him to the ground, Freddie immediately latched onto her. She let out a loud, painful scream as she tried to push him away.

I quickly ran over to them and tried to kick Freddie away from her. But I ended up sending them both tumbling to the ground. Freddie landed on top of her and was chomping on her neck. I grabbed his ponytail and pulled him off of her. Then I dragged him about twenty yards away and left him there.

I went back to the woman. Freddie had bitten off a chunk of flesh from her neck, and she was losing a lot of blood. I ripped off her shirt and placed it on the wound as her friend came over to assist.

I was so focused on saving the woman's life that I was oblivious to my surroundings. Then a scream from her friend quickly alerted me to Freddie. He was up and was moving toward us. I knew I had to kill him before he reached us. Withdrawing my pistol, I aimed it at him. But I was reluctant to shoot. I had never killed anyone. Now I had to kill someone I knew.

"Freddie, if you come any closer, I will shoot!" I said, trying desperately to make him understand.

But just like Robbie earlier, my pleas to Freddie were unheeded. He continued to advance toward me. I had to shoot him to save the woman's life. But still, I was reluctant. "Freddie! I'm going to shoot you if you don't stop!"

To no avail, I closed my eyes and fired off a round. When I opened my eyes, he was still standing there. I must have missed, I thought. I fired another round at him. This time I had my eyes open the whole time. The bullet struck him in the chest. But it didn't seem to faze him at all. *He has to be a freaking zombie!* I said to myself, on the verge of panic. *What do I do? What do I do?*

Then I decided to shoot him in the head. I remembered that after watching countless zombie movies: A zombie could only be killed with a shot to the head. I quickly fired two rounds at Freddie's head. But it wasn't as easy as in the movies—I'd completely missed! I was rushing too much. I had to slow down and aim carefully.

I fired off another round. The impact had caused him to turn his face away from me. He took a few steps backward to regain his balance. Then he turned his face toward me again. I was completely stunned! The entire right side of his face was gone. But he was still alive!

Noticing that he was having trouble directing his remaining eye at me, I took the opportunity and quickly ran up to him. Aiming the gun directly at his forehead, I squeezed the trigger. The bullet went into his forehead, taking out a huge chunk of his skull as it exited on the other side. He slowly went down to his knees. Then he finally went down to the ground and lay motionless.

Medics arrived a short while later. The woman was in shock from the massive blood loss. I doubted she would survive. I felt bad for her. She was doing what she was trained to do. But the cynical side of me was saying, *She got what she deserved.* She defied my warnings. She had killed herself. She also made me kill another person!

Freddie was dead—a victim of deadly force by the police. I didn't want to radio that in to Angie, because I didn't want the whole area to be crawling with people and reporters. So I discreetly informed her that I needed a supervisor and another officer to assist me with the scene.

As I set up the crime scene tapes to establish a perimeter, I couldn't help but stare at Freddie's body. The small white blanket that medics had placed over his body was now stained with patches of blood. A sudden chill ripped through my body and I began shaking uncontrollably. Then, my knees buckled beneath me. I dropped down to the ground and began vomiting. *So, this is how it feels to kill someone?* I wondered.

CHAPTER 6

It felt like a dream—a horrible nightmare. Everything was spinning wildly around me. Yet I was moving in slow motion. I felt as if I was trapped in a world of illusion. *This can't be real*, I thought. But everything in front of me said otherwise.

I didn't know how long I'd been in this trance. It seemed for just a minute, but my watch indicated that an hour had passed. I'd completely lost track of time. I had no idea what had happened within that hour.

A crowd had gathered around the scene. The only thing keeping them at bay were the thin strips of crime scene tape. With cameras and cellphones directed at the bloodstained blanket, arguments broke out between some of them as they jostled for a better position.

I was getting concerned that I might lose control of the scene if a fight broke out. I tried calling for an ETA on the assisting officer. But the radio traffic was dead silent. *Why isn't Angie monitoring?* I asked myself. The battery level on my pack set still indicated one bar left.

After another unsuccessful attempt to get a hold of Angie, I switched over to the Central Sector channel to speak to their dispatcher. My ears were immediately bombarded with the frantic voices of officers. The noises in the background sounded as if they were in the middle of a war zone. I instantly knew it had to be the protest at the hospital.

I felt extremely conflicted as I pondered what to do. *I should follow protocol and stay at the scene*, I thought. But I couldn't ignore the cries for help any longer. I had to go to the hospital!

As I sped away from the scene, there was no doubt in my mind that I would lose my job. And along with that, my pension. I would lose everything I'd worked for over the past twenty-five years. But in my heart, I knew I was doing the right thing.

By the time I reached the intersection of University Boulevard and

Morris Street, I could no longer continue. Hundreds of people filled the streets and sidewalks, frantically running in all directions. Fires arose from some overturned vehicles, filling the entire area with thick, dark smoke. *The protest is completely out of control*, I thought.

I sighed deeply as I took the shotgun from my squad car. I knew I might have to use deadly force to defend myself. I just hoped I didn't have to kill anyone else.

I went to the trunk and took out the box of shotgun shells that I'd stashed away behind the spare tire. My old backpack was still inside. After I dumped out the contents, I placed the box of shells, a dirty towel, a bottle of hand sanitizer, and the first aid kit inside the backpack. I was ready.

But after walking a block or so, I began to question whether I should continue. The thick smoke was hindering my vision. The noxious rubbery fumes were burning my lungs. The sweltering heat from the fires had turned the sweat on my face to a dry, salty residue. My body was also lacking the energy to maneuver around vehicles and dodge the people that were running in my direction. It was exhausting. But I pressed on.

After another block, the scene got worse. Some of the crashes were horrendous. Body parts were sticking out of the car doors and windows. The ground was scattered with dead and dying people. Those people were lucky, I thought, compared to the charred people who were still inside the fiery vehicles. The smell of burning flesh was nauseating.

When I finally made it out of the smoke, I realized that I was at the northern border of Central Park. The hospital was five hundred yards away at the southeast corner of the park. But I was right in the midst of the chaos. It was going to be a lot tougher and longer process than I'd originally thought.

Thirty yards into the park, my lungs could finally breathe in fresh air. My body was revived, but not my spirit. The noises had amplified to a deafening level. People were still running in every direction. Fights were breaking out everywhere. Everything was happening all at once, and I couldn't figure out where to go or what to do.

Suddenly my ears were drawn to the blood-curdling screams of a woman. Looking in her direction, I spotted a group of people huddling together on the ground. From twenty-five yards away, I couldn't tell what they were doing. But after seeing a pair of legs kicking out from under them, I knew they were attacking someone. My instinctive reaction was to go over and stop them.

By the time I reached the group the screaming had stopped. I froze as I saw what they were doing. It was something straight out of a horror movie. A young woman was on the ground, twitching and barely moving. Her belly had been ripped opened. They were pulling out her insides. I almost fainted as I watched them devour her entrails.

The woman was still alive as they continued ripping her apart. I wanted to leave before they noticed me, but for some reason I couldn't. My soul was screaming from within for me to avenge this wrong! *Those bastards need to pay for what they've done to her!*

The perpetrators still hadn't noticed me standing behind them with my shotgun aimed at them. They had no idea what was coming. I had no hesitation for what I was about to do to them. I began firing, blasting every one of them away from the woman.

After it was over, I went over to the woman. She was still alive and gasping for air like a fish out of water. She was too far gone, and I knew that. All I could do was to help end her suffering.

As our eyes met, I knelt down in front of her. I managed to give her a warm smile, assuring her that I wasn't going to hurt her. Although she couldn't speak, through her teary eyes I understood what she was saying. I gave her a slight nod and withdrew my pistol.

As I aimed the gun at her forehead, she slowly closed her eyes. "Go in peace now," I said quietly. With a squeeze of my trigger, she suffered no more.

CHAPTER 7

An intense battle was brewing between my rational mind and my conscience. My rational mind was screaming for me to turn back. But my conscience kept urging me to press forward. I really didn't know why I kept going. Was it for my pride, or my honor? Maybe I was still searching for an excuse to succumb to my cowardliness.

After another thirty yards, I found that excuse. The severed head of a young girl inside a small flower bed finally convinced me to turn back. I would share the same fate if I continued on. I had a wife and children that I needed to go home to.

I made it back to the squad car to find it had been completely wrecked by another car. The driver of the other car was still inside. He was bleeding and barely conscious. Dark fumes were coming out of the hood of his car. It would start on fire at any moment. I had to get him out!

The driver was still strapped in by his seatbelt, and I couldn't get the buckle to release. As I searched for my pocketknife, I saw a group of people quickly approaching. I could tell by their high-pitched screams and their wild facial expressions that they were not coming to help. It was too late to run. They were almost upon me, and I would have to shoot them.

I aimed my shotgun and fired off a couple rounds. They went down to the ground, but they were still alive. As they were trying to get back up again, I fired the remaining rounds and they finally stayed down. Within seconds after the shooting, my ears were bombarded with the heavy sounds of footsteps and high-pitched screams. The gunshots had alerted everyone in the vicinity to my location. I had to get out of there quickly!

As a police officer, it was very hard for me to leave that guy behind. That action would weigh heavily on my conscience for a long time. Sadly,

I also realized that I would probably have to do it again. *I can no longer afford to be thinking like a police officer if I am going to survive this,* I told myself. *I will have to give up my pride and honor. Self-preservation will be the only thing on my mind from now on.*

The giant mob was following me as I ran west on University Boulevard. I was getting tired. But the distance I was putting between me and them encouraged me to keep going. I had no idea where I was going. All I knew was that I needed to get away from them.

After a while, I was feeling dejected. I was exhausted and could barely run anymore. But every time I looked behind me, the mob was still there. Even with the distance between us, they were still determined to get to me.

I knew I had to find a place to hide soon. I wouldn't have the energy to fend them off if they caught up to me. As I scanned my surroundings, the Thao Oriental Market, kitty-corner from where I was, caught my eye. I'd been in that store numerous times. I was also familiar with the external layout.

The narrow driveway between the store and a large office building led me to a private parking lot at the rear. A dumpster was at the end of the driveway. A huge concrete wall stood between the lot and the alley. The area between the dumpster and the wall had just enough room for me to sit and stretch out my legs. From there, I also had a full view of the driveway and the street at the front.

Although I was content to stay there until the mob passed, I was also greatly concerned about being trapped there. The sight of the wall was comforting. But it seemed too high for me to climb over to the alley. I tried reaching to the top of the wall. But I couldn't do it. I was still about a foot short.

Desperate, I looked around for a way out. The empty lot seemed to have enough room to fit four or maybe five cars. There was a large flowerpot behind the rear door. To the east of the flowerpot were several large cardboard boxes.

I thought about checking the door to see if it was unlocked. But then I remembered that the store closed at five o'clock. My watch indicated that it was past eight o'clock already. Then I thought about stacking the cardboard boxes together at the wall. I could use the boxes to help me reach the top. It was the only option I could see at this point—I had to go over there and try it.

I was just about to step away from the dumpster when the heavy sounds of footsteps quickly alerted me to the front of the driveway. The mob had finally arrived. I ducked behind the dumpster and froze. My mind was telling me to peek out and observe the mob. But I lacked both the strength and the courage to do so.

As the sounds of the crowd drew nearer, my heart was creeping up into my throat. My breathing was rapid and irregular. It was just a matter of time before some of them would decide to come down the driveway. Anxiety was taking over my body, and I could barely concentrate on anything.

It was when the sounds of footsteps subsided that I could finally breathe normally again. But as I stood up to check the driveway, I immediately crouched back down again. A large guy had come into the driveway. My anxiety was out of control now. Although I was hesitant to check, I had to find out how far away he was from me.

Peeking around the side of the dumpster, I noticed the guy had stopped halfway along the driveway. He was just standing there, sniffing the air and staring at the large window of the office building. *Can he smell that someone is in there?* I wondered.

I held my breath as I noticed that he was now staring at the dumpster. As I pondered what I should do if he decided to approach, I began to dread the idea that I might have to fight him. Shooting him was not an option, because the noise from the gunshots would bring more of them over. But after seeing how big he was, I thought shooting him might be the only option.

As I continued observing the guy, I was getting increasingly desperate. I was really hoping he'd lose interest and leave. But his eyes were glued to the window. He seemed fixated on whatever was inside the building.

After a while, I knew I would have to get rid of him. If he continued standing there, the others would see him. And if they came into the driveway to join him, then I would be trapped. I had to get rid of him!

My choice of weapons was down to the expandable baton now, because I couldn't use my guns. *I might not be able to kill him with it*, I thought, *but at least I'd have an advantage*. Maybe I wouldn't survive the fight. But I was going to give it everything I had.

I took several deep breaths and slowly stood up. The guy was still fixated on the window and hadn't seen me yet. I swung the baton forward to full extension. The loud click finally alerted him to me.

With his attention focusing on me now, I walked away from the dumpster to the middle of the lot. I wanted to be behind the building so that no one else could see us. I also wanted to have plenty of room to maneuver when the fight began.

Within seconds, the guy appeared at the end of the driveway, but he abruptly stopped when he saw me staring back at him. As we sized each other up, I didn't feel anxious or scared anymore. I was actually calm and relaxed. I didn't know what his plans were. But my plan was simple and definite: I was going to aim for his head and hit it as hard as I could.

Without a word, I slowly got into a defensive stance with the baton raised above my shoulder like a baseball player. As we continued eyeing each other like two warriors about to duel, he suddenly let out a loud screeching sound and took off running toward me. I waited until he came into range, and then I swung the baton as hard as I could.

The tremendous impact sent a rippling wave of pain from my hand all the way down to my feet. I quickly spun around for another strike. But he was already on the ground. I was a little bewildered by what I saw. The skin on his forehead was ripped open, revealing his severely fractured skull. Brain matter was oozing out of the cracks. The blow to his head should have killed him or knocked him unconscious. But he was very much alive and was thrashing about. After several more strikes to his head, he finally stopped moving.

Darkness was looming, and I could barely see the dumpster from where I was. I went over and checked the door. Just as I expected, it was locked. The door was one that opened outward, so I couldn't kick it in. The boxes were emptied and couldn't support my weight. Now I had a huge dilemma! If I stayed there, I would have to fight a lot of the same battles. I might be able to defeat one guy, but I would not be able to defeat a group of them. But if I left, I would be running around in the dark, searching for another place to hide.

As I gazed down at the flowerpot, I remembered what the store's owner, Mr. Thao, had said to me the day after his store was burglarized. Three years earlier, I had been dispatched to his store on an alarm. After arriving I checked the doors, and both the front and rear doors were still locked. There were no signs of forced entry, so I cleared the call as a false alarm.

The next day, I went back and spoke with Mr. Thao. He told me his store had been broken into and all the money had been taken from the cash register. Apparently, someone snuck inside from the rear door and stayed in the basement. They waited until the store closed. Then they went back up and set off the alarm. They knew the doors were locked and the police couldn't get inside. They waited for the police to leave, and then they cleaned out the register. Ever since the incident, Mr. Thao left a spare key inside the flowerpot for the police.

I was amazed I still remembered after three years. I just hoped the key was still inside the flowerpot. Rummaging inside it, I felt a small object and held my breath as I brought it up to my eyes. The key!

"Thank you, Mr. Thao," I said silently.

CHAPTER 8

Sitting on a smelly, dirt-filled carpet, I watched as the sunlight slowly peeked through the three small basement windows. I took a deep breath and I leaned my back against the wall. *Morning has come and everything will be back to normal*, I thought.

As the light steadily illuminated the room, I finally got the chance to explore my refuge for the first time. The basement was crammed with hundreds of cardboard boxes, stacked from floor to ceiling. Cockroaches were scurrying about. Mouse droppings littered the floor, piling up at the northwest corner where the bags of rice were stowed. The potent smell of mildew, stale food, and mouse urine was nauseating. But I couldn't complain. I was lucky to be there.

I really didn't know how much sleep I'd gotten, having been constantly awoken by the horrific screams outside during the night. The distant rumbling sound of gunshots was the only thing that brought some comfort to me throughout the night.

I had tried calling my wife off and on all night. But for some reason, the cell phone signal was disrupted. My police radio was dead. That was completely my fault, since I'd neglected to swap out the old battery with a recharged one during the start of my tour. That left me clueless, helpless, and hopeless.

As the seconds turned to minutes and then to hours, my desperation finally reached a tipping point. I had to do something or I would suffer a mental breakdown. I needed to go upstairs. I needed to go into the shopping area to find a TV or a radio to help alleviate some of my distress.

I ascended to the top of the stairs and stood by the door, where I hesitated: I had no idea what was waiting for me in the shopping aisles. Carefully, I put my ear to the door and listened for the slightest bit of noise from beyond it. The continuous silence finally convinced me.

With the sunlight pouring in from the small windows near the ceiling, I was able to see inside the gloomy room. The stillness around and between the shopping aisles was reassuring. The curtains at the front windows were still closed. Both the front and rear doors were intact and tightly secured.

Rummaging around, I found a small flat-screen TV behind the front counter, as well as a large machete and a baseball bat tucked between the counter and the display case. The baseball bat seemed ordinary to me. But the design of the machete amazed me. I'd never seen anything like it before. It looked like a large, elongated kukri knife with a sharp tip. The impressive two-foot-long titanium blade was thick and razor-sharp. The extended full tang handle was designed for comfort and for a two-handed grip, if need be. A thick black leather sheath with snap button closures lay underneath it.

I let out a slight chuckle as I imagined Mr. Thao holding the machete to scare off an assailant. *Asian people are nuts,* I said to myself, *especially when it comes to protecting their livelihood.*

I turned on the TV to see that the city of Riverdale was on the national news. The governor and the president of the United States were addressing the media. The president had declared a national emergency, saying that it was a "Pandemic of epic proportions." Several prominent doctors also came on and tried their best to answer questions from the media.

As I continued watching the news, a loud scream alerted me to the front of the store. Peeking through the blinds at the small window behind the counter, I spotted a woman on the other side of the street. She was running from shop to shop, frantically trying to open the doors. Then she looked behind her and let out a quick scream as she took off running across the street. I looked past her but didn't see who or what she was running from.

Glancing back at her, I froze for a moment as I noticed that she was looking directly at me. I quickly backed away from the window. But it was too late. We'd made eye contact, and she knew that I was in the store. Seconds later she was pounding on the front door, desperately pleading to be let in.

I tried ignoring her like I'd done with all the other voices the previous night. But it was more difficult this time. Those voices didn't have a face to go with them. I'd seen the woman's face. It had become personal.

The woman's cries became more frantic, as if she was about to be attacked. I couldn't stop myself from looking back outside. Noticing that she was looking behind her, I shifted my eyes in that direction and spotted who she was running from. A huge guy was on the other side of the street. He had seen her and was making his way toward the store.

Her desperate cries were overwhelming me, calling to every shred of moral and ethical decency within me as a man, a police officer, and a human being. My conscience would never let me forget it if I allowed her to die out there. I would not concede to my cowardliness this time!

I knew that if I let her in, the guy would be pounding at the door and more of them would follow. I couldn't risk being trapped in the store. I'd have to get her to go to the rear. And I'd have to kill the guy chasing her, or we would never be safe.

I lifted the blinds and tapped on the window. As soon as I made eye contact with the woman, I motioned her to the driveway. Although she couldn't hear me, she seemed to understand. She left the door and quickly ran toward the driveway. Taking the machete, I ran to the rear door.

I was conflicted when I shut the door after I stepped out into the lot. I wanted the woman to be safe inside the store while I fought with the man. But I didn't want her to lock me outside. She would need to stay outside with me while I fought him.

I went to the middle of the lot and set myself in a fighting stance, holding the machete above my head, ready to swing. I was going to use the same tactic I'd used the previous day. But as I stood there anxiously waiting, I noticed something missing. The man that I'd supposedly killed the day before was gone. He was nowhere inside the lot. Now I was getting concerned. He might have gone back to the window. If two of them were coming, then I might not win the fight. *I might have to leave that woman to her demise*, I thought.

As I seriously pondered that idea, the woman suddenly appeared at the end of the driveway. Seeing me, she stopped abruptly. She seemed afraid of me and unsure what to do. I was bewildered for a moment. Then I realized that she was afraid to come over because of my aggressive stance. I lowered the machete and motioned her to come over. She let out a scream after looking back at the driveway. Then she took off running toward me.

"Go hide behind those boxes!" I said, directing her to the cardboard boxes.

Moments later, the huge guy appeared. He, too, abruptly stopped when he saw me. My heart instantly sank when I realized who he was: It was Tony Swede! He was still in his medic uniform. But he was no longer the gentle giant that I'd known. His face held the same crazed expression that I'd seen on Robbie's face. I knew then it was Robbie's bite that had caused Swede to turn like this. *It was probably Robbie who caused this pandemic.*

Swede's expression was getting more intense by the second. It was just a matter of time before he would attack me. As I braced myself for the fight, sadness swept over me: how could I kill someone I knew and respected?

"Swede, please go away," I pleaded.

He quickly let out a loud, shrieking scream and charged toward me. I could feel my heart racing and my body shaking as he got closer. Taking a deep breath, I held it as I swung the machete forward. Silence immediately followed.

I didn't have to look behind me to see what I'd done. Half of his head was on the ground a few feet in front of me. Then a loud thud from behind me assured me that he had fallen. "Goodbye, Swede," I said.

CHAPTER 9

The woman's name was Kara Rose. A well-spoken girl from the city of Woodbury, she was about the same age as my daughter. Her brown eyes were stunning, and her long, black hair was a perfect complement to her pretty face. Her clothes were not skanky or distasteful. But they provocatively revealed parts of her attractive twenty-year-old body that as a father, I did not want my daughter to be revealing.

Kara told me she and her friends had gone to the hospital to counter-protest against the massive Pro-Life rally. Thousands of people were already there when they arrived. The police were also there.

She said that as the crowds shouted at each other from their respective sides, another crowd came out of the hospital and began attacking everyone, and mass chaos soon erupted. Then the police began shooting tear gas into the crowd. Everyone scattered in different directions. That was when she lost sight of her friends. She ran to the park and started up the hill. When she made it up the hill, she looked back at the hospital and saw that the crowd was also attacking the police.

She said that she had been running around and hiding all night. Every person she encountered was trying to kill her. Then this morning, Swede spotted her and she ran from him. When she saw the blinds moving in the building I was in, she ran over. She knew that someone was inside.

"Did you see any police officers in the streets when you were out there earlier?" I inquired.

"No," she replied. "Everyone was insane. I couldn't tell the difference between the good guys and the bad guys."

I slumped back into my chair. My co-workers were probably all dead or had turned into those monsters. I would have shared the same fate if I had continued to the hospital. Although I felt ashamed because of my cowardliness, I also felt fortunate that I'd become a coward. But I could never reveal it to anyone. And I didn't want to be reminded of it again.

I was still deeply engrossed in my thoughts and didn't realize Kara was saying something to me. After she quickly stood up and walked to the stairs, I finally snapped out of it. "Hey!" I shouted. "What the hell are you doing?"

"My sister!" she said frantically. "I just remembered that my sister and her husband were planning to go to the protest, too!"

"Listen to me," I said calmly as I approached her. "Your sister and her husband are probably dead."

"They're *not!*" she shouted. "They're out there, and we have to go save them!"

"Look, I'm not—"

"Go with me!" she quickly interrupted. "You're a police officer. It's your duty to go out there and save people!"

That statement hit me deep to the core. I'd hated myself for ignoring all those people the night before. Now she was scolding me for it. And reminding me of my cowardliness again!

"Listen, lady!" I said angrily. "I don't give a rat's ass what my duties are! All I care about right now is staying alive and going home to my family. I don't care about your friends, or your sister and her husband. You guys chose to go to the protest and put your lives at risk. If you want to go back out there and die with them, then be my guest!"

Kara was a little shaken by my harshness. But she was still persistent. "Please," she begged. "Please help me find them!"

Clearly she wasn't getting it. I took a deep breath to compose myself, trying not to blow up again. Then I calmly said, "Do you remember that big guy that I killed earlier?"

She nodded.

"Well, his name was Swede. He was a friend of mine. He tried to kill me, and I had to kill him to protect myself. If your sister and her husband are not dead by now, then they probably turned into something like him. You better be able to kill someone if you want to go back out there. You might see your sister again. And when you do, you better kill her first before she kills you."

I left Kara and went upstairs to gather up some food. The TV was still on, and the news was still going. I watched in dismay as a barrage of activities around the city was being displayed. Giant concrete walls had been placed on the bridges, blocking access out of the city, the reporters said. The entire city was besieged as hundreds of small lookout posts were being set up on the other side of the rivers. Armed boats were patrolling the rivers with orders to shoot anyone who tried to swim across.

"It's a necessary precaution we have to take to ensure the safety of all the citizens," said the president when the camera shifted to him. "Governor Matthews and I agreed that until this pandemic is under control, the city of Riverdale will be under quarantine. The military will use whatever means necessary to enforce the order." Then he turned to the reporters. "I understand that you have a job to do. But we also have a job to do. Therefore, the military has established a no-fly zone within fifty miles of the city. The military will use whatever force necessary to ensure that the order will not be violated."

"Is the military actually going to shoot anyone who tries to get out of Riverdale?" asked one of the reporters.

"Let's make it perfectly clear," the president sternly replied. "This is a *pandemic of epic proportions.* The safety and wellbeing of the entire nation will be affected if anyone gets out!"

"Mr. President!" a reporter shouted. "What about all those people in the surrounding cities that have to be evacuated? When will they be allowed to return to their homes?"

"I'm not sure at this time. As of today, no one is allowed to return to their homes. If anyone sneaks back in, they will be arrested and quarantined inside the city of Riverdale."

"Where will all those people go?" asked another reporter.

"They were transported to an emergency campsite about sixty miles away. I will personally see to it that they have all the supplies they need."

"Mr. President! Mr. President!" a chorus of voices shouted.

"That's enough questions for now," said the president. "I want to say a few words to the residents of Riverdale." Looking straight at the camera with an empathetic expression that only a master politician could muster, he began. "Citizens of Riverdale, I can't possibly understand what you're going through right now. It must be harder than anything anyone could ever imagine. I want all of you to know that we will not leave you. We will not rest until all of you are safe. Please stay in your homes and do not try to leave the city. I promise that we will all get through this together."

A deep feeling of uncertainty engulfed me as I turned away from the TV. I had been somewhat optimistic this morning. But now, I wasn't sure if I would ever get to go home. I didn't know what the government was planning to do. But after watching the images being displayed all over the city, all I could think of was that something catastrophic was going to happen.

• • •

When I came back to the basement, Kara was a lot calmer. She seemed to have an understanding of what I'd told her. "I'm sorry, but this is dinner," I said, handing her a package of beef jerky, some rice cakes, a mango, and a bottle of water.

"Thank you," she said quietly.

She took out a strip of dry meat and began chewing on it, swallowing it down almost immediately. "Slow down or you'll choke," I said. "I don't remember how to do CPR."

She grinned at me and gulped down some water. "I'm so hungry," she said. "I haven't eaten anything since yesterday."

"Well, you have to eat slowly and chew thoroughly before you swallow. Especially with that hard, dry meat."

"It tastes like crap, but it's so satisfying," she said, smiling.

"From now on you'll have to get used to eating anything you can find. No matter how disgusting it is."

She smiled again and gulped the rest of the water. "So, what is your name?" she inquired.

"My name is John," I replied, "but people called me by my last name, Hua."

"Thank you for saving me, Hua," she said sincerely.

I gave her a slight nod and continued eating. I didn't want to tell her how appreciative I was to hear those words. She had given me an opportunity to regain my honor, and maybe even save my soul from condemnation.

After a moment of silence, she asked me what my plan was. "What plan?" I asked, glancing at her.

"You know…do you have a plan for how to get out of here?"

I let out a deep sigh. "I was planning on staying here until help arrives," I replied. "There's plenty of food and water in here to sustain us for a long time. I don't want to go back out there again."

"Sounds like a good plan," she said with a satisfied grin.

I chuckled. This young lady had a sense of humor. Although I was in despair from what I'd seen on TV earlier, she was cheering me up. My decision to save her was the right and honorable decision.

CHAPTER 10

I would love to say that I woke up the next morning in my comfortable bed, to the wonderful melodies of the birds outside, and to the sweet aroma of my wife's cooking. But none of that was true. In fact, for the next seven mornings, I woke up lying on a dirty carpet, with a smelly old blanket covering me. The noises outside were not birds singing, but the distant sounds of gunshots and screams. And the pungent odor of mildew, stale food, and mouse urine was the only thing that I smelled.

Still sleeping a few feet away from me was the young lady who had been my only source of comfort for the week. As heartbroken as I was about not being with my wife, I was thankful to have another person with me so that my days and nights weren't so long and lonely.

I tried many times to make sense of what I was seeing outside. But my mind was filled with only unanswered questions. It was beyond the realm of realism for the dead to come back to life! There was no logical explanation for any of it, and trying to make sense of it only filled my heart with more despair and hopelessness.

I thought about what the president had said a few days before. I didn't recall him mentioning anything about sending help. If he did, I must have missed it. I really didn't know how long I could continue to hold on to hope. No matter how much I tried to remain positive, I found it increasingly difficult. I'd been inside the store for more than seven days, and still there were no signs of help coming. It seemed the writing was already on the wall. My cell phone was dead, and Kara's cell phone still had no signals. The service was cut off to the store phone. The power to the city had been shut off for six days. I wondered if the government was planning on something catastrophic for the city. I would have done the same thing if I was in their shoes. If I was going to stop a plague from growing out of control, I would have it contained and then destroy it. The city of Riverdale was already under quarantine—the government already had the plague contained. I dreaded what was going to happen next. And I didn't want to be there when it happened.

• • •

After an hour of letting my mind run rampant with that theory, I found it nearly impossible to keep my sanity. I had actually thought about leaving three days earlier. But I wasn't as desperate then as I was now. I had to leave now or I'd go completely insane!

I thought about going to headquarters. There had to be some survivors there. They were probably in communication with the government already about evacuation protocols. Then, I thought about Kara and I didn't know what to do with her. She was too much of a liability to me. I didn't want to be worrying about her when I was fighting for my life. She should stay here, I thought. *She'll be safe until help comes for her. There's enough food and water to sustain her for the duration.*

I thought about leaving her while she was still sleeping. But my conscience wouldn't let me do it. I couldn't bear the thought of her waking up to that dark, empty room, alone and scared. As a father, I would never do that to my daughter; I couldn't do it to her. At least I'd let her know what I was planning to do. Maybe then, my conscience would leave me alone.

"Wake up, Kara," I said, gently nudging her.

"I'm still so tired," she murmured. "Please let me sleep just a little while longer."

Glancing at my watch, I saw it was already past nine o'clock. Although HQ was less than three miles away, with everything that was going on outside, it'd probably take me all day to get there.

"You have to get up now," I said. "I'm leaving today."

"What?" She immediately sat up. "Where are you going?"

"I have to leave this place. I have to find a way out of this city."

"Why?" she asked, puzzled. "Help is coming, right?"

I sighed deeply. "It has been quite a few days now. I really don't think help is coming."

"How do you know that?"

"I don't," I replied. "I really don't know what the government is planning to do. But I have to get out of here. I have to look for a way out of this city."

"Please don't go," she said in a desperate tone that made me want to look away from her.

"I *have* to go. I'm going insane in here with all this uncertainty lingering within me."

"What about me?"

"I'll come back for you when I've found a way out," I assured her. I knew I was only trying to ease her mind. In truth, I wasn't sure if I'd ever see her again.

"I don't want to be alone," she cried. "I'm really scared."

With that being said, and the way she said it, I was extremely conflicted. Although I initially didn't want to take her, I wasn't sure what to do. *She will be a hindrance to me*, I thought. *She will put both our lives at risk with her screaming.* But I couldn't just leave her. At the very least I needed to let her decide what she wanted to do. Maybe then, I could live with myself, knowing that it was her decision.

"Then you have to make a decision," I said. "You can stay here and wait for help. Or you can come with me."

"I'm so scared to be out there," she said faintly.

"I know," I said. "I'm scared too. But I want to go home to my family."

I gave her a moment to decide. Then she surprised me by saying that she wanted to go with me. *Why does she want to go back out there?* I wondered. *I guess she is even more afraid to be left alone in here.*

After a meal of canned sardines and crackers, we went to the shopping aisles and began gathering up supplies. Using an old backpack that I'd found in the basement, I began filling it with as much food as I could fit. Then I handed it over to Kara.

"Where are we going?" she asked.

"We're going to police headquarters," I replied. "We'll be safe over there."

My initial plan was to head to HQ. But as I planned out a route, I realized that going over there might not be a viable option. We would have to go back to the hospital. There was a huge public housing complex behind the hospital that we would also have to go through. Then we still would have to get by the homeless shelter complex after that. If all those people over there were infected, we wouldn't stand a chance.

The only option now was to head to West Team. At least there we'd be among my co-workers, if any were left. And it was still a police station. There had to be some sort of communication with the government over there, too.

"Change in plans, Kara," I said. "We're going to go to West Team instead. We'll meet up with more police officers over there. They're probably in communication with the government already. We can stay there until help arrives."

"What's West Team?"

"It's the police station I work out of."

"Where is it?"

"It's a few miles west of here."

CHAPTER 11

My weapons were the shotgun, the pistol, and the baton. I also had a baseball bat and a heavy-duty machete. I still had two full magazines inside the pouches on my duty belt, as well as a full box of shotgun shells. I topped off the magazine inside my pistol with the loose rounds in my pockets. Then I loaded the shotgun to capacity and slung it over my shoulder. I took the machete out of the sheath and attached the sheath onto my belt with a rope. I gave Kara the baseball bat and instructed her to swing toward the head if anyone attacked her.

The rear door was still tightly secured. I stood by it and listened for any noise or movement outside. After a few minutes of silence, I was satisfied. Then I slowly cracked it open, just enough to peek outside.

Swede's body was still there, lying motionless on the ground. The stench from it was overpowering and unbearable even from where I was. I could tell that Kara was also struggling with the smell. "Breathe through your mouth and not through your nose," I said.

Taking a small ladder with me, we took a few steps into the lot. I tried not to look at Swede's body, but we had to go by it to get to the wall. I couldn't help but take a quick glance. No words could properly describe what I saw. It was beyond grotesque. The body looked like it had exploded. The entrails had burst through the bloated belly and were sticking out of it. Fluids had leaked out from the body, encircling it in a pool of dark, yellowish liquid. Hundreds of maggots were squirming all over the body and covering most of the head. Flies were hovering overhead like a swarm of bees.

The stench was so extreme that even though I was breathing through my mouth, I was getting overwhelmed and dizzy. Kara dropped to her knees and began vomiting. Her loud gagging enticed a sudden movement from Swede's body, and I instantly jumped into a defensive stance.

As I gazed at the body, my mind was telling me, *That's not possible.*

But my eyes could clearly see. Even with half his head chopped off, there were definite movements from his left side. But a faint moan quickly assured me that it wasn't him. Someone else was lying beside him!

The face of an Asian woman slowly appeared from behind Swede's huge, bloated belly. Kara screamed, and I immediately reached over to cover her mouth. "Control it or I'll leave you here!" I said sternly but quietly.

I could feel Kara's trembling body behind me as we watched the woman slowly stand. I was no longer surprised at what I saw. Just like the other victims, this woman's belly was ripped open. Some of her entrails were dried out and dangling from her waist. Her right arm was missing. Her left leg was badly mauled, with the majority of the flesh missing. It was obvious that she was attacked right there while I was inside the store. She was probably one of the many voices that I'd ignored for days.

After seeing how debilitated the woman was as she slowly staggered toward us, I knew she wasn't much of a threat. I wanted to walk around her and get to the wall. But I couldn't bear to watch her in that state. If she could speak, she probably would have wanted me to end her suffering. I had to do that. I had to put an end to her misery.

I was thinking about chopping off her head. But then I decided to let Kara kill her instead. The woman was extremely weak and slow, and Kara wouldn't be in any danger. *Kara needs to learn how to kill*, I told myself. *She needs to know how it feels. If she can kill this woman, then she will probably be able to do it again when her life is in danger.*

I turned to Kara and directed her to the woman. "I want you to kill her," I said.

Kara's eyes widened. "I can't do that!"

"You better do it!" I said sternly. "From now on, it's either you kill them or they'll kill you!"

"No! I can't do it," she said defiantly. "Look, we could go around her."

I grabbed Kara's arm and looked her straight in the eye. "If you want to stay alive, you better be strong! If you can't kill this woman, then you better go back inside. You're only going to be a liability to me, and I will not take you with me!"

After those strong words, Kara reluctantly went up to the woman. She whimpered as she held the bat over the woman's head. "Now swing down on her head!" I ordered.

Kara hesitantly swung the bat onto the woman's head. The impact was minimal, and the woman was still standing. "What the hell is *that*, Kara? You better hit her harder than that!"

"I can't!" she cried.

"Just do it!" I warned. "She'll kill you and eat you if you don't kill her!"

Just then the woman lunged at Kara, who responded by striking the woman repeatedly, sending her down to the ground. After it was over, Kara looked like she was in a trance as she gazed down at the woman.

I walked over to Kara and gave her a hug. She was trembling and unresponsive to my touch. I knew it was very hard for her to do that. She seemed like a very gentle person who would never harm anyone. But this was survival. Her life depended on her courage.

"I've never killed anyone," she said weakly.

I looked down at the woman. The blows had stunned her, but she was still alive. I took the bat from Kara and ended the woman's suffering with two hard blows to the head. "You haven't killed anyone yet," I said. "But I know that you could do it if you had to."

After a while of sneaking from one garage to another, hiding, waiting, and running from one side of the street to the other, I was feeling increasingly dejected. It was already two o'clock in the afternoon, and we were only a few blocks away from the grocery store. My anxiety was also working against me, making me unusually jittery. I kept jumping into a defensive stance at the slightest bit of noise. And to make matters worse, the stench of death was everywhere. I felt as though it was all around us and we might meet our demise at any moment.

A short time later, I spotted something lying inside a grassy area several yards away from a blue detached garage. After Kara hid between two trash bins, I went ahead to inspect it.

From a few yards away, I could see a man's body. Like I had seen in others, the man's belly was ripped open. His internal organs and entrails were pulled out, chewed on, and scattered around him. I guessed the insides were the first things the monsters ate. As gruesome as that was, it made sense to me. The monsters were behaving like wild predatory animals. When predators eat their prey, they almost always start out with disembowelment. They eat the insides first before moving on to other parts.

I also noticed another body a few yards away. The only things left on that body were an arm, a leg, and a partially eaten head. Everything else was just bones, with bits of flesh still attached to them. What I could tell from the decapitated head was that this person was a woman. *She was probably attacked first*, I reasoned. *The guy was attacked while trying to save her.*

My heart sank. It saddened me to think that these two people were probably a couple. It seemed so unfair that they were parted in such a violent and horrific manner.

I waited for a while to see if the perpetrators were still around. But I didn't see or hear anyone. Then I went back to Kara. I knew she would scream if she saw the gruesome sights ahead. So I told her to close her eyes and hold on to my backpack. I would lead her away from the bodies.

We made it past the first body when Kara let out a loud scream. I quickly spun around and covered her mouth. I took a deep breath and shook my head. I worried she would attract attention. *I shouldn't have brought her along*, I thought.

We froze for a moment. I was hoping that no one had heard the scream. But that hope was quickly shattered. The sound of footsteps alerted me to the houses east of us. *They're coming!*

"Run!" I whispered to Kara.

I had cleared three city blocks before I realized that Kara wasn't behind me anymore. I stopped and turned to look for her. She was down on the ground about a block away. I could see that she was trying to get up but kept falling back down. She was obviously injured.

As I frantically pondered what to do, I noticed that the situation was getting worse. The infected were arriving! Two people were moving toward Kara from the opposite side. They were still a block away, but they were closing in on her. Kara hadn't seen them yet. She was still looking at me while trying to get up.

My mind was screaming for me to escape. Kara was injured and wouldn't be able to continue on anyway. *She's a lost cause*, I told myself. *I have to leave her. I have to save myself.* But I had to go with my conscience this time. I had to go back for her!

With the machete held in front of me, I ran past Kara and headed toward the two infected. I had no idea what I was going to do when I reached them. I just knew I had to stop them from getting to Kara.

The first one was a woman. She was growling wildly when she saw me running at her. I quickly stepped aside as she lunged at me. Then I swung the machete at the back of her neck. I was surprised at my accuracy: I actually hit what I was aiming for. The woman's head was on the ground even before her body came to rest a few yards behind me.

The next one was a short Asian guy. He paused before approaching me. I swung the machete at his head at a downward angle. When I spun around for a second strike, I realized that I didn't have to. I had split his head in half. He went down on his knees and then dropped to the ground.

When I reached Kara, I could tell through her teary eyes that her injury was serious. I couldn't bear the thought of leaving her behind. "Let's go," I said gently as I reached out a hand for her.

"I can't get up!" she cried. "I think I broke my ankle!"

That was not what I wanted to hear! Such an injury would be a death sentence for her now. More infected would be arriving soon. I couldn't stay any longer. "Can you still move your ankle?" I asked.

"Yes, but it hurts when I do it."

"Then it's not a break. It's just a sprain," I assured her. "Just try to get up. We have to leave right now."

I tried to be positive and encouraging, trying to ease her despair. But her situation wasn't any better. She still couldn't walk, let alone run. If more infected arrived, I would have no choice but to leave her and save myself.

As difficult as it was for me to bear that thought, it was actually minor compared to another thought that was plaguing me: *I don't know if I'll have the strength or the courage to kill her. But I can't leave her to a horrendous and agonizing death!*

A loud growl quickly alerted me to a brown garage twenty yards away. A man was coming at us. He looked partially eaten. His blank, emotionless expression reminded me of Freddie.

"Shit! They're coming, Kara! Try to get up while I kill this guy."

I ran toward him and quickly took his head off with the machete. When I turned around, I saw four more infected closing in on Kara. Three of them were closing in fast while one of them was lagging behind. Kara was still focusing on trying to get to her feet. She hadn't seen them yet. That was a good thing, because if she screamed again, we'd be in more trouble.

Without warning her, I ran to the infected. I had no idea what happened after that. Everything was a blur. It was like I blacked out. When I came to, the mangled bodies on the ground left me speechless. I'd completely dismembered and chopped all four attackers to pieces.

Kara was up on her feet now. The carnage around her didn't seem to faze her anymore. I was relieved to see that. "Can you walk?" I asked as I approached her.

She slowly took a step with her injured foot and immediately groaned. "It hurts a lot when I put weight on it," she replied.

Noticing that there were no more infected coming our way, I began to relax. The only concern I had at that moment was how I was going to bring her along. I went over to a small tree nearby and cut off a branch that had its ends split into a fork. I returned with it and began clearing off the rough edges.

"What are you doing?" she asked.

"I'm making a crutch for you," I replied. "We're too far away from the grocery store. We have to keep going. We'll find another place to stay so you can rest your ankle. I'll carry the bat with me."

CHAPTER 12

With Kara's injury hindering us, the only thing I could do was to look for a suitable place for us to stay for the night. As I continued watching Kara wincing in pain every time she put weight on her ankle, I was getting increasingly desperate. The thought of self-preservation was still on my mind. If we were spotted and she couldn't run, then what was I going to do? I didn't know if I'd have the strength to leave her. But it was just a matter of time before that happened. And I was dreading it.

After two more blocks a large white duplex caught my eye. Somehow I knew it was going to be our sanctuary. It was exactly what I was looking for. The upper unit would provide us with the security we needed for a few days.

With Kara safely concealed between the detached garage and the trash bins, I started toward the house. The front yard stretched for about twenty-five yards from the house to the street. There was a large balcony at the front of the house. I felt slightly relieved when I noticed that there were no stairs leading up to the balcony. A door was below the balcony, but I could only assume that that door was for the lower unit.

After I was satisfied that there was only one entrance to the upper unit, I went to the back of the house. The rear door was ajar. The damage to the locks was consistent with someone kicking it in. A dark hallway led to two separate doors at the end. Unfortunately, there wasn't a number or a letter to indicate which door led to which unit.

After I'd cleared the hallway, I went back to get Kara. I didn't want her to be out there too long. The hallway would keep us safe for now. Ideally, I wanted to be in the upper unit. But with Kara's injury, I no longer cared which unit we were going to be in. I just wanted a place to stay for the night.

I began focusing my attention on the door that was easier to open—the door without a deadbolt on it. It was a sturdy door. But with only a knob lock, it could be opened with a small knife or a credit card. I wondered why the residents didn't put in a deadbolt. Maybe they thought the deadbolt on the main door would be sufficient.

I reached for my wallet and took out my one and only cash card. Sighing deeply, I stared at it for a moment. If I damaged it, I would have no way of getting cash. Then I quickly shook off the thought. I didn't know why thoughts like that occurred to me. I was definitely getting old. *Who needs money at this point?* I asked myself, shaking my head.

"What are you doing?" Kara asked after seeing me attempting to slide the cash card into the doorjamb.

"I'm trying to open the door."

"You need a key, not a credit card."

I chuckled. "Well, I used to be a burglar before I became a cop," I joked.

Sliding the card between the latch and strike plate, I felt a resistance. But when I pushed it through, I heard a pop. The door opened slightly.

"Wow!" she said in wonder, as if she'd never seen anything like it on TV before.

A staircase was beyond the door. I was thrilled that it led to the upper level. But my elation lasted for only a few seconds. I still had to go up there and contend with whoever was still inside.

I gave Kara the shotgun. "Stay here and don't come up until I come back for you," I said.

There was another door at the upper level. It also had a knob lock, which I opened with the same method. The door led into to a dining room. The kitchen was at the other side, opposite the door. The living room was to the far right.

Although the stillness inside was encouraging, I was reluctant to enter. I had no idea what was waiting in there. So I decided to announce myself first. I was thinking that maybe if someone was hiding in there, they'd know that I was human. And if some infected were in there, they would come over to me.

"Hello," I said quietly. "Is anyone in here?"

There was no response, and no movements anywhere. Still, I was reluctant to enter. I decided to announce myself again, but louder this time. "Hello? Is anyone in here? I'm not here to hurt you! Please show yourself!"

After a period of silence, I was finally satisfied. But as I took a few steps into the dining room, a voice suddenly shouted, "Get the fuck out of here!"

Instantly I jumped into a defensive posture. "Who's in here?" I said as I quickly scanned the room.

"Get the fuck out of here!" the voice yelled again.

Now I knew where it was coming from. "I know you're behind that counter!" I said, looking toward the kitchen. "Show yourself!"

A man slowly stood up. He had a large butcher knife in his right hand. He was clearly agitated, and I could understand why. I'd just invaded his home. "Get the fuck out of my house!" he shouted.

I lowered my machete and let it rest at my side. "Look, buddy," I said calmly. "I'm not here to hurt you. I was just looking for a place to stay for the night."

"You came to the wrong place, motherfucker! This is your last warning! Get the fuck out or I'll kill you!"

"Take it easy, buddy. You don't want to do that. If you come at me with that knife, I will have to defend myself. I was just looking for a place to stay. If you let me stay here tonight, I promise you I'll leave in the morning."

As I continued staring at him, I realized who he was. He had cut off his dreads and shaved his head. But that huge distinctive scar on his right cheek, and that weird cockeyed glare, gave him away. It was Cordell Jones, a career criminal. His handiwork included drugs, burglaries, assaults, and rapes. He had violated his parole two months back. We had been looking for him for weeks.

"Cordell," I said. "You're Cordell Jones, aren't you?"

His eyes widened. "I ain't going back!" he spat furiously. "You ain't taking me back! Drop your weapons or I'll kill you!"

Now that he'd confirmed who he was, it was time for me to be a cop again. Lifting the machete, I said to him in a sarcastic manner, "Do you actually think that you're going to get a chance to kill me? You'll be dead before you come close enough to stab me. Now, put your small knife down or I'll chop you up with this sword."

That should have been enough to encourage him to give up. But he was still being defiant. He was going to need a lot more encouragement than that. I didn't know what he was thinking. I also didn't know how good he was with a knife, but I wasn't willing to find out. So I put the machete away and instead withdrew my pistol.

Aiming the gun at him, I sternly said, "I also have a gun. Now drop the knife or I'll shoot you right between the eyes!"

I tried to sound as if I was an expert shooter. In truth, I wasn't good at all with that gun. I couldn't hit anything beyond ten yards. If he had known that, I would have been a dead man right there and then.

Cordell finally got the message and slowly placed the knife on the countertop.

"Now put your hands on your head and walk slowly over to me!" I ordered. "You better be wise about it, or I'll blow your head off!" I warned.

I had no intention of shooting him. But knowing how dangerous he was, I would not hesitate if he tried to disarm me. After he got within a few feet of me, I ordered him to get down on his knees and put his hands behind his back. My plan was to handcuff him and secure him for the night. Then I'd let him go in the morning.

"Man, fuck you! I ain't done nothing wrong!" he said defiantly.

Obviously he was trying to stall. He probably had something planned for me. But I was not going to play into his game. "Get down on your fucking knees and put your hands behind your fucking back!" I said forcibly. "I ain't playing your game, motherfucker! I'll put a cap in your ass right now!"

Finally he complied. But even as I handcuffed him, he continued being an asshole. "Is there anyone else in here with you?" I inquired after cuffing him.

"No... I'm it, dawg."

"Don't be lying to me! If someone else is in here setting up an ambush, I'm going to blow your fucking brains out first! Then I'll find your accomplice and blows their fucking brains out too!"

"OK, dude. There is someone else in here, but she ain't gonna do nothing."

"Where is she?" I asked, looking toward the living room.

"Bitch is sleeping in the bedroom," he said it with a calmness that made me feel uneasy. Obviously he knew something I didn't.

I quickly stood him up and shielded myself behind him. "Call her out here!" I ordered.

He let out a slight chuckle. "Like I told you, dawg," he said with a smirk. "Bitch is sleeping. She ain't gonna hear me."

"Don't be playing with me, Cordell! Call her out now!"

"Man, I *told* you! She's *sleeping*. She ain't gonna hear me!"

I pushed him into the living room. There were two doors to the right. The first door opened to the bathroom. After clearing it, I pushed Cordell to the second door. Then I placed him directly in front of it. His calm demeanor baffled me. He seemed unfazed by whatever was beyond that door.

With a swift kick of my foot, the door swung open. Hiding behind Cordell, I braced for someone to charge at us with a weapon. But none of that happened. The room was eerily silent and still. Through the darkness, I could see a bed at the southwest corner. There was definitely something or someone in it. But I couldn't make out what it was from where I stood.

I pushed Cordell into the bedroom, knocking down a small lamp on the desk. The loud crash would surely wake whoever was sleeping in the bed. But it didn't. There was absolutely no sound or movement from the bed. *How can this person still be sleeping with all this noise?* I asked myself.

I walked over to the window and opened the curtains. Sunlight poured into the room. I was stunned by what I saw! A nude woman was lying in the bed. Her arms and legs were spread out and tied to the bedposts with ropes. I looked closer. The cause of death was obvious from the handprint deeply embedded across her throat.

I had to avert my eyes for a moment after noticing her injuries. There were countless bite marks and cigarette burns scattered on her body. Her inner thighs were badly bruised, as if she had been grabbed there repeatedly. A milky substance oozed from between her thighs.

I placed a hand on her shoulder. She was still a little warm. I couldn't be sure about the time of death due to the warm temperature inside the room, but I guessed she had been dead for an hour or two.

As I continued examining her injuries, the thought of how she had suffered began to overwhelm me. My body started shaking with a growing rage. Then my mind began focusing on only one thought: vengeance. It was going to be payback time for what this asshole had done to her!

I stepped toward Cordell and punched him in the face, sending him to the ground. I winced in pain. *Shit! Did I break my hand?* I thought, panicking. Luckily the stinging subsided and I was able to move my fingers. I was very lucky. *I need to be more careful,* I thought, *and not let my emotions take over like that.*

Cordell moaned as he regained his consciousness. I went up to him and placed the pistol to his head. "Get up motherfucker!" I shouted directly into his ears. "Get on your fucking knees!"

"Don't shoot me!" he pleaded. "She was already dead when I got here!"

I took a few deep breaths to calm myself down. Although I knew in my heart that he'd killed her, my mind was telling me otherwise. A thief will always steal. A rapist will always rape. He was both a burglar and a rapist. But he wasn't known to be a murderer. What if I was wrong? What if he was telling the truth? What if someone else had killed her? Yes, he had broken into the place. Yes, he had raped her. But what if he raped her after she was already dead? My stomach turned. He would be a sick motherfucker if he'd done that. But I didn't want to kill him right away. I had to know what he had done. I had to be sure before I shot him.

I walked over to the nightstand and noticed an envelope on it. I picked it up and looked at the name. "So who is she, Cordell?" I calmly asked.

"She was my girlfriend," he quickly replied.

I walked back to him with the envelope in my hand. "So what did you do to her?"

"Man, when I got here, she went crazy. She tried to kill me, but I killed her first."

"You told me that she was already dead when you got here. Why did you just change your story?"

Cordell went silent for a moment. "I'm telling the truth," he said. "She was my girlfriend. She was dead when I got here."

"Why did you kill her?"

"I didn't kill her! She was already dead!"

"You told me she went crazy and you killed her."

Cordell was silent. Perhaps his small brain was getting overwhelmed. "If she was your girlfriend, then what was her name?" I asked.

He hesitated for a moment. "Umm...Lisa," he replied.

"Are you *sure* about that?" I asked. I knew I had him.

"Yeah," he replied, nervously.

"It says here that her name was Anne," I said, showing him the name on the envelope. "She was not your girlfriend, motherfucker! You and I both know that. She's way too pretty and classy to be dating a fucking loser like you!"

He took a deep breath and slowly let it out. "All right man, you got me," he said. "I was trying to find a place to stay, so I broke into this place. But she was already dead when I got here. It's the truth!"

"How long ago was that?"

"I don't know. I was here like maybe this morning."

As soon as he said that, I knew he had killed her. He had been in the house all day, and her body was still warm. "You're a shitty liar, Cordell," I said. "Now I *really* don't believe you. You came here with the intention of finding a place to stay. That much is true. But when you saw her, alone and scared, you couldn't help yourself. You tortured her, you raped her, and then you killed her!"

"Dude!" he quickly responded. "That's *wrong*!"

I held my pistol against the side of his head. "You sick motherfucker! Do you think that I'm going to believe that crap you told me? Not only are you a rapist, now you're a murderer too!"

"OK! Don't shoot, dawg! I swear! She was going to attack me!"

"That's *bullshit*! She wasn't going to attack you. She hadn't been infected. You killed her, you sick fuck! You tortured her, you raped her, and you killed her!"

I almost pulled the trigger. But I just couldn't do it. I was still a cop. No matter how much I tried not to be, I was still a cop. *Yes, Cordell needs to die*, I told myself. *But I can't execute him like this. He deserves a fair trial.*

I brought him back to the living room and made him sit on the floor. Still enraged, I went to the couch and sat down. I wanted to make him pay for what he had done to that woman. But how was I going to do that? If the city hadn't been in such a mess, he would be spending the rest of his life in prison.

"Man, I didn't do nothing to her!" he said, still denying everything.

"You need to man up, motherfucker," I said. "You know I can't take you to jail right now. Be a man and own up to what you did. I bet you're proud of what you did, aren't you?"

Suddenly, a light switch seemed to turn on in his brain. He knew that I couldn't shoot him. I'd already tried, and I couldn't do it. And he now knew that I couldn't take him to jail. So he confessed, revealing in great detail what he had done to the woman for the past two days.

I had asked for it, and now I couldn't handle it! The asshole laughed and smirked as he described the pain he had inflicted. He had repeatedly raped her, he said, and choked her countless time before he finally decided to strangle her.

I wanted to kick him in the face. But I didn't want to waste my energy. Instead I looked away and tried to focus my anger on something else.

Cordell could see he was torturing me. He was enjoying it and getting bolder. But the asshole had no clue how much he was at my mercy. And he had no clue that I was doing my best not to become a monster like him.

"Shut the fuck up!" I yelled.

"Am I getting to you, dawg?" he said, flashing a sick, sadistic smile at me. "You wanted the truth. Now you can't take it."

I could slap him right now, I thought. *But that would only stroke his ego even more.* I turned away and tried to concentrate on something else. "This whole city is going down, dawg," he said. "I can do anything I want. Who's going to stop me?"

"I just stopped you, motherfucker," I said, glancing back at him.

He laughed. "So, you gonna take me to jail? Come on, take me to jail, then."

I turned away again and tried to ignore him. I thought about handcuffing him to the balcony and leaving him out there for the night. At least then I wouldn't have to deal with him. But then he said something that made my blood boil so intensely that I couldn't take it anymore.

"There are three more just like this one," he said laughingly. "I did three more bitches like I did this one."

I couldn't bear to listen as he bragged about what he had done to the three other women. At that point ethics and morality had no meaning for me. The guy was a sick, sadistic killer and he deserved no mercy from me! *I don't care if I go to hell for what I am about to do*, I told myself. *He is going to pay!*

I rose from the couch and kicked him repeatedly in the head, then dragged his unconscious body out onto the balcony. I slapped him a few times to wake him up, lifted him to his feet, and stood him against the edge.

"Hey! What are you doing?" he said, panicking.

"Like you've said, motherfucker," I replied. "'I can do anything I want. Who's going to stop me?'"

With that, I raised my pistol in the air and fired off three shots. Moments later a mob appeared. As the infected began growling loudly from below the balcony, Cordell finally understood that he had gone too far. Desperate, he pleaded for his life.

"Did those women beg for their lives like you're doing right now?" I asked.

"Dude, please! Don't do this to me!"

Grabbing his head, I forcibly turned his face to look down at the growling mob. "Look at them, motherfucker! The judge, jury, and executioner are all down there. You will pay for what you've done! You will be judged today!"

I pushed him off the balcony. Seconds later, his blood-curling screams were evidence that he had been denied a merciful death. *What a fitting end for you, asshole*, I sneered to myself. *You denied those women their lives. Now I just denied you yours.*

I slowly walked back to the living room and sat on the couch for a while. I wasn't satisfied or proud of my actions. I knew I'd done a horrific thing to another human being, something that would haunt me for the rest of my life. Sadly, I knew that I would have to do many horrific things to many people if that kind of chaos continued to run amuck inside the city.

Even with Cordell gone, there was still a deep feeling of despair inside me. My heart was unsettled and was begging to be released from its sorrows. So I went back to the bedroom.

As I gazed at the dead woman, I couldn't help but think about her last moments. She must have been terrified, desperately begging for her life, to no avail. I felt an overwhelming urge to say something to her. Maybe I could say something so that her soul could be at peace. And maybe my soul could be liberated also.

After taking a deep breath, I said aloud, "I'm sorry that this happened to you. I want you to know that I've killed the person who did this to you. I've sent him to hell. You can be at peace now."

I gently wrapped the woman's body in the bedsheets and carried her out to the balcony. I was hesitant to toss her down there to be devoured. But I didn't want her body to decompose out there on the balcony either; that would be unbearable for me and Kara. We needed to stay put for a while.

After a brief moment of silence, I gently rolled her over the edge.

CHAPTER 13

A week had passed since Kara and I left the little grocery store. We were still inside the upper unit of the duplex, and I was getting increasingly concerned about our situation. We were getting very low on food, and there were still no signs of help coming. And we were nowhere near West Team.

Kara had begun walking without the use of her crutch, but her ankle was still bothering her. As much as I wanted to stay there for a few more days to allow her ankle to heal a bit more before we headed off to West Team, I just couldn't wait any longer. If we didn't leave that day, our situation would be dire.

As I thought about the previous few weeks, I was still in disbelief. No matter how much I tried to make sense of it, I still couldn't. I felt like I was trapped in a hellish nightmare that I couldn't wake up from. Every night I went to sleep hoping to wake up in my own comfortable bed, with the smell of my wife's cooking seeping through the cracks of the bedroom door, filling the room with a sweet aroma. But I woke up to nothing of the kind. I woke up to another day of death and despair.

I often wondered how long it would be before I finally lost my mind and put an end to my misery. If death was the only way out of it, then I'd have to accept death. What if...?

"What are you doing?" Kara interrupted my train of thought as she came into the living room and sat next to me.

"Nothing," I quickly replied, closing my journal and keeping it from her prying eyes.

"You keep a journal?" she asked, raising a brow.

"Yes," I replied nonchalantly as I placed it back in my backpack.

"Hmm... interesting," she said, smiling. "So, why do you keep one?"

"I've had one ever since my first year on the job. Almost every night after work, I sit and write down everything that I saw that day. There were days when I would be too busy, too tired, or just simply forgot to write, but then I would try to catch up on it. In a way, I think that keeping a journal has helped me keep my sanity while trying to do my insane job. I also enjoy looking back and flipping through the pages years later, because it reminds me of certain moments in my life."

She smiled and nodded. "I thought about starting one now," she said, "but I would be too afraid to look at it years down the road."

I chuckled at the way she said it. I knew she wasn't trying to be funny, but it cheered me up a little. Flashing a faint smile at her, I pondered what to say next. I didn't want to dampen her spirits by telling her that we had to leave. But our situation was getting critical.

"How's your ankle?" I inquired. "Are you ready to go back out there?"

She let out a soft sigh. "My ankle is getting better now," she quietly replied. Then she glanced away and added, "But I'll never be ready to go back out there."

I couldn't blame her. Considering what we had gone through, how could anyone honestly say that they were not afraid? I was just as terrified as she was, but I was better at hiding it.

I gave her a quiet, simple nod. "We have to leave today," I said gently. "We're almost out of food. We have to make it to West Team with the little food we have left."

She quietly responded with a simple nod of her own.

"Could you do me a huge favor?" I added.

"What is it?"

"We're going to encounter a lot of gruesome sights out there. For your safety as well as mine, you need to be strong. Please try not to scream."

"I'll try my best," she said. Then she looked away and quietly added, "But sometimes, I just can't control myself. Screaming is the only way to release my anxiety."

"I know," I said. "I'll do my best to protect you."

I went out to the balcony and scanned for a route to West Team. The deserted streets were a welcoming sight. But it didn't deter my despair as I gazed down below the balcony. What was once Cordell Jones were now just bits and pieces. A few feet away was a ripped-up, bloody bedsheet. The woman Cordell murdered had also been reduced to bits and pieces. These were solemn reminders of what was to come.

As I looked some more, I realized that we were just on the outskirts of the Charlestown neighborhood. The house that we were in was three blocks north of University Boulevard. Charles Street was a block to the west. Beyond Charles Street was Charlestown.

I sighed deeply as I scanned the Charlestown area. Although I was familiar with most of the streets and alleys, I couldn't come up with a safe route through the neighborhood. Charlestown was the most populated neighborhood in the Western Sector, and there was no way we could get through that area without being seen. And we couldn't outrun the infected, especially with Kara's ankle still bothering her.

As I scanned University Boulevard for a while, I realized that the freeway was a few blocks south of it. The freeway embankment was at least fifteen to twenty feet high. If we could make it down to the freeway, it would greatly reduce our chances of being seen. We'd have an easier, faster, and safer route to West Team.

Although I was sure that the freeway route was the best option, I couldn't stop my surging anxiety as I tried to figure out how we were going to make it over there. We'd have to cross University Boulevard. There was a strip mall south of University that we'd have to get by. Then, we would still have to go through a park and several apartment complexes to get to the freeway.

When I went back inside I noticed Kara had already packed up our backpacks. I sat with her on the couch and went through the plan with her. I left out the part about the strip mall, park, and apartment complexes because I thought it would be too overwhelming for her.

"If something happens to me, then I want you to continue to the freeway," I said. "If you continue going west on the freeway, you'll eventually get to the Midway Avenue Bridge. West Team is on Midway Avenue, about a block north of the freeway. Someone will be inside, and you will be safe."

As I inspected my weapons, my body, mind, and spirit were overwhelmed with the thought of death. I took a deep breath as I thought about what I was about to do. I would be bringing death to a lot of people. *Today might be the day of my death*, I thought. *But maybe in death, I can wake up from this nightmare.*

CHAPTER 14

K ara and I made it to the old, rundown Miller house on Fillmore Avenue, midway between Tillman and Prince Streets. As I gazed at the bullet holes inside the distressed wood-panel walls, vivid memories of the house came back to me. It had been around the same time last summer when Old Man Miller finally lost his mind and went outside with a rifle. I was the first officer on the scene, and he shot several rounds at my squad car. Miller was eventually shot and killed by a SWAT team.

I don't know why we ended up at that house. Maybe death was reminding me of the day I had cheated it? Or maybe death was telling me that that this day was going to be my last?

The narrow alleyway at the side of the house provided a path to University Boulevard. Kara and I took cover behind a large white Cadillac at the end of the alleyway, on the north side of University Boulevard. A horde of infected was at the intersection of University and Charles Street, gathering in front of the University Meat Market at the northeast corner. *With so many of them over there, someone must be inside that store,* I reasoned. Although the thought of someone being trapped inside was depressing, I was relieved that the horde's attention was drawn elsewhere.

As I shifted my attention to the strip mall across the street, an idea came to me when I saw the Dragon Oriental Supermarket at the east end of the mall. The owner, Charlie Lor, was a childhood friend of mine. I'd done some off-duty security for him inside the store a while back. I still remembered the code to the service door at the loading docks. If I could get that door to open, then we could go inside the store and stock up on some food before we moved on.

"We're going over there," I whispered, directing Kara to the store.

As I slowly crept over to a smashed-up green SUV, I felt a quick tug on my shirt. I turned around and saw Kara covering her mouth with one hand and pointing to her injured ankle with the other. A hand had reached out from underneath the vehicle and grabbed onto her ankle. As I crouched down to look, I ended up staring directly at the mangled face of an infected. Although half of his lower jaw was missing and the bottom half of his body was crushed and trapped underneath the tire, he was still alive. He was holding on to Kara's ankle and trying to pull her toward him.

I reached my leg over and kicked him several times in the face. But because of the angle I was at, I couldn't generate enough power. The effect was minimal, and he wouldn't release his hold on Kara. I knew it was pointless to do that again, so I took out the machete and chopped off his hand. I was amazed at the guy's pain tolerance. I'd just chopped off his hand, and there wasn't a moan or a scream—even his facial expression didn't change. *Maybe the monsters can't feel any pain at all?* I wondered. *Is that why they can sustain so much damage to their bodies?*

"Come on, let's go," I said quietly as I pried the hand away from her ankle.

We crossed the street and were soon running across the parking lot toward the supermarket. Upon reaching the front doors, I tugged on them and realized they were locked. I was relieved, however, because that probably meant no one had been able to get inside. Now we could enter the store through the service door and we would be safe inside.

"Come on, follow me!" I said as I led Kara eastward toward the loading docks.

As we turned the corner, I paused as I noticed the new additions to the loading docks. Two huge concrete walls—one on the north and the other on south—had partially enclosed the lot. The length of the walls began from the building and stretched all the way out to the service road at the end of the parking lot. They were certainly a welcoming sight. But what worried me was that one of the two huge chain-link gates was missing from the north wall.

I knew that if we entered the loading docks and I couldn't get the service door to open, we would be trapped inside. But we desperately needed food. I didn't know how long it would take us to get to West Team. I didn't want us to be running out of food and then have to be searching for it. This was our chance; we had to try.

After entering the lot, we ran up the metal staircase to the service door. The metal platform that we were standing on was a foot higher than the north wall, and we could easily be seen up there. I had to get the door open before someone spotted us.

Frantic, I entered the code on the electronic keypad above the door handle. Then I held my breath as I waited for the comforting beep from the keypad to assure me that the door was unlocked. But to my dismay, I didn't hear it. The door was still locked.

I paused for a few seconds and re-entered the code. Again, no comforting beep. I knew I hadn't forgotten the code. The only conclusion was that maybe Charlie had changed it.

I was thinking about giving it one more try and then leaving if it didn't work. But as I re-entered the code, Kara tapped insistently on my shoulder. I turned to see what she wanted. "They're coming!" she said, pointing to the parking lot.

A horde of infected was already inside the parking lot and rapidly approaching the wall. I was amazed at the speed of their approach. We had only been up there for a minute at most, and they got there fast. The crowd stopped at the wall and gazed up at us. The wall was preventing them from getting to us. They seemed to be at a loss, unable to figure out how to reach us.

I knew then it was too late to make a run for it—they would follow us and catch up to us at the gate. Besides, we would not be able to outrun them, especially with Kara's bad ankle. We had to stay where we were and keep them focused on us so they didn't wander off to the end of the wall.

As more infected continue arriving, I was getting increasingly desperate. *We're trapped and helpless up here*, I thought. *It's only a matter of time before they reach the end of the wall and figure out how to get to us.*

The only thing I could do was to try the code again and hope that the door would unlock somehow. But after a few more failed attempts, I was ready to accept my fate. *This is probably where it's going to end*, I told myself.

Kara was still looking to me for answers. But I only had one for her. It was not going to be what she wanted to hear. But it was honest. With a faint smile, I quietly said to her, "This is it, sweetie. This is where we'll be making our last stand."

I took out the box of shells and placed it down on the platform. Then, I took out two bullets from my magazine and handed them over to Kara. "Hold on to these and stay behind me," I said. "I'm going to kill as many of them as I can." Reaching a hand up to cup her cheek, I let out a deep, agonizing sigh before telling her what I was going to do after that. "When I run out of bullets, I'm going to use those last two on us. We'll be dead before they reach us."

With Kara standing at the door, I went to the edge of the platform and sat there quietly. I was facing the gates. The box of shells was next to me on the platform. Taking several deep breaths, I raised my shotgun onto my shoulder. Tears began streaming down my face as I thought about my wife and children. I would never get to see them again. I was going to miss them so much. I felt even sadder as I thought about the young woman behind me. In a short while, her life would end. And I was the one who was going to end it.

The first group of infected finally appeared at the gate and started running our way. I took a deep breath and steadied myself as I waited for them to come into range. I had to conserve my ammunition. I had to wait for them to group together so I could take them down with as few shots as possible.

The first two blasts sent all of them tumbling to the ground. They were mangled by the rounds, but they were still alive and continued to crawl toward me.

Then the second group appeared, and I opened fired. Again, I managed to mangle them and knock them to the ground. Although they were still alive, they were helping me out. Their fallen bodies were hindering the ones behind them, slowing down their progression enough for me to breathe and collect myself.

After my shotgun went empty, I didn't have time to reload. The infected were approaching too quickly. I had to perform an emergency reload. Grabbing a shell from the box, I placed it into the empty chamber and fired it off. I repeated this process over and over again until I finally had time to reload.

The infected were relentless, and I was getting desperate. I was running out of ammo, and they just kept coming. It seemed that for every group that I shot down, another group simply replaced them. And to make matters worse, with each thundering sound of the gunshots, more of them started appearing from every direction.

The box of shells was emptied, and I'd finally shot the last round inside my shotgun. It was useless to me now, so I tossed it down the stairs. With a little bit of time to regroup, I stood on the platform and gazed down at the lot. Piles of dead and dying bodies littered the ground. Their blood had turned the darkened asphalt into a pool of red. The sight would be enough to deter any rational-thinking person from approaching. But it didn't matter to the infected. I couldn't comprehend why they were still coming. Why would they give up their lives in such a senseless manner? Did they want to die? Maybe they wanted to get out of this nightmare, too?

I pulled out my pistol and sighed deeply as I looked at it. I couldn't shoot worth a shit with that gun. But now, I had to make every shot count. I just hoped I didn't miss too often.

As I began shooting, I became more confident. I was amazed at my accuracy. Every shot went right through their heads, stopping them almost immediately. I don't know what was helping me be so accurate. Maybe it was fear and desperation that greatly improved my aim.

After I emptied my first magazine, I took it out and gave it to Kara. "Load it with the two bullets I gave you," I said.

I inserted another full magazine into my gun and continued shooting. As I watched heads exploding before my eyes, everything was becoming so pointless. *If I was going to die anyway, then why continue on with this massacre?* I thought, *I should put an end to all of this right now by shooting myself.* But my extreme desire to live kept me fighting. I was going to keep fighting for the life I still had left.

After the slide on my gun locked back, I knew I'd shot the last round in the third magazine. I'd done all I could. There were still a lot of the infected left. But it was time to put an end to it all. The time had come for our merciful deaths!

Letting out a deep, painful sigh, I turned to Kara. With a desolate expression, I quietly asked her for the magazine with the two bullets that I'd given to her. She handed the magazine over. After I inserted it into the gun and racked the slide forward, the gun was loaded again.

Kara's teary eyes were unbearable to look at. Of course she didn't want to die. Obviously I didn't want to kill her either. I gave her a warm embrace—just like the one I had given my wife before leaving her weeks earlier. "It has been an honor to know you, Kara," I said softly.

I told her to close her eyes as I placed the gun at the back of her head. Her body was trembling as she anticipated the impact. "You won't feel a thing," I gently assured her.

My finger felt numb, and I couldn't squeeze the trigger. My mind was telling me to squeeze it. But I was still reluctant. I was going to kill someone I had come to know, love, and respect. I was going to kill a person who truly didn't deserve to die.

I was still struggling when the service door suddenly swung open. A hand reached out to Kara, grabbing her and pulling her inside. "What the fuck!" I shouted.

I quickly ran inside and grabbed the person who was holding on to Kara. I threw him against the wall and placed my gun to his head. I was just about to shoot him when I heard him speak. "Hey, don't shoot! I'm here to help!"

I instantly paused and lowered the gun after recognizing the familiar voice. As my eyes adjusted to the darkness, I recognized the face I was pointing my gun at: It was Kevin! He quickly bolted to the door. "Hurry, help me secure this door!" he shouted.

Kara and I ran over assist him. The infected were just outside, pounding and pushing on it. I anchored my back against the door and kept pushing with every ounce of energy I had left. We continued pushing until I heard a loud click from the latches. The door was finally locked again.

After taking off my backpack, I immediately dropped to the floor. The infected were still pounding vigorously on the door, but I didn't care. I was just so happy to be alive! I continued lying there, trying to slow my heart rate down with deep, even breaths.

After I felt my strength returning, I sat up and leaned my back against the cold concrete wall. My shoulder was in tremendous pain. My entire body felt like I'd just gone through a full kickboxing match. But I had never felt so good. *The pain is good!* I told myself. *It reminds me that I am still alive.* It wasn't my fate to die out there.

Kara came over and sat down beside me. The look on her face said it all: She was grateful. But I wasn't sure why or what she was grateful for. Was she grateful that I had saved her life? Or maybe she was grateful that I didn't kill her? I was grateful, too—grateful that she was still alive. And I was even more grateful that I didn't kill her!

Kevin came back a few minutes later with two cans of pop in his hands and handed them over to us. I happily accepted my can and immediately gulped it down. The tingling sensation from the carbonation was soothing and refreshing as it went down my dry throat.

I took a deep breath and continued gazing at Kevin as if I was gazing at my son. I couldn't be happier to see him again. I would be forever indebted to him for saving my life. "Who else is in here with you, Kevin?" I asked, glancing down the dark warehouse.

"Just me and Tommy," he replied.

"Where is Tommy?"

"He's out and about inside the store, trying to make it safe."

"Why didn't you open the door earlier?"

"I tried to. But the lock was an electronic lock. When the power went out, it didn't work anymore. I was frantically running around, trying to find something to pry open the door. I'm just glad that I got it to open in time."

"I'm glad, too," I said, glancing at Kara. "I was just about to shoot both of us out there."

After a brief silence, I asked about the protest. "What the hell happened at the hospital, Kevin?"

He took a deep breath and slowly let it out. "When Tommy and I got there, Commander Bradley wanted everyone to be in full riot gear. Then we just hung around and monitored the crowd from the park. At first, the crowds were just shouting at each other. But then, another crowd came out of the hospital and began attacking them. We dispersed tear gas into the crowd to stop the fight. But it didn't work. Then we were ordered to move in. But when we got to the hospital, the crowd turned on us. We didn't have our guns with us so we were overwhelmed."

"Why didn't you have your guns?" I inquired, curious.

"Bradley ordered everyone to leave their firearms inside the trunk of their squad cars prior to us gearing up. We were grossly outnumbered. Our baton strikes didn't do anything to stop the crowd from attacking us. When I saw an officer being ripped apart by several people, I took off running. Everyone was scattering everywhere. Tommy and I ran from the scene and just kept running until we got to this place. This is Tommy's uncle's store. Tommy knew the code to the service door."

I was disgusted by Bradley's despicable action. That asshole had violated policy for his own personal agenda. He had been kissing ass for years thinking that he was going to be the next chief of police. He knew he couldn't afford to get any citizens hurt. He had doomed every officer that day by ordering them to leave their firearms behind!

I became quiet for a moment. The thought of so many officers being killed because of one man's selfish act was agonizing. I wished I had been there with them. I could have done something about it. I could have killed Bradley!

"Did Bradley die, too?" I asked Kevin. I would feel so much better if he did die.

"I don't know," he replied, "but I assume so."

That's not what I wanted to hear. *Hopefully he'll turn into one of those monsters*, I told myself. *If I see him again, I'll chop him to pieces.*

"Do you guys still have your guns with you?" I asked.

"No, we left our guns inside our squad car, which is still at the park as far as I know."

Tommy suddenly appeared. "Hello, sir," he said. "How are you feeling?"

I smiled at him. "I feel like hell, Tommy," I replied. "I believe we're all in hell right now."

CHAPTER 15

I woke up to a dimly lit room. The two small battery-operated lamps at Charlie's desk provided enough light for me to see inside his office. The couch I sat in reeked of booze and some sort of bodily fluids, though I didn't want to know which ones. An old picture of me, Charlie, and our soccer teammates was displayed above me on the wall. I laughed at the bad mullet haircuts we all sported at the time. Those were the good old times. How I wanted to go back to those days again—driving my buddies around in my father's old station wagon. I wasn't ashamed to be driving a station wagon then; I was just grateful to have a car.

Kara was still sleeping on the other couch. Her face was planted right on one of the stain-covered cushions. I grimaced. I knew Charlie too well. This office had been his little love shack during after hours.

Kara's blanket was on the floor, and she was shivering. I smiled warmly as I placed my blanket over her. I was so grateful I had hesitated to shoot her. Although she was a hindrance to me, I was thankful for her company. In a way, she was my sanity. She had allowed me to get as far as I had without going insane.

Kevin and Tommy came into the office thirty minutes later, bringing a huge plate of food that they'd cooked inside the warehouse. It was quite a selection!

"How are you this morning, sir?" Kevin asked.

"I haven't slept that well in a long time, Kevin," I replied. "I almost forgot where I was."

"Where did you find the babe?" Tommy inserted himself, gazing at Kara.

"She was at the protest. She ran into me a few days ago when I was at Thao's market on University."

"And don't even think about it, Tommy," I added jokingly after noticing his perked-up eyes as he stared inquisitively at Kara. "She's like a daughter to me. And you know how I am about my daughter."

Considering that Kara and I had eaten nothing but beef jerky, dried squid, and crackers for the past week, this meal was an absolute feast! I was so grateful to Kevin and Tommy. The food was abundant and tantalizing to the eyes, including lobster tails roasted over a propane stove and some exotic Asian foods that I normally wouldn't eat.

"So, what do you think we should do, sir?" Kevin asked, nibbling on a cracker.

"Well, before Kara and I came here, we were planning to go to West Team. I'm not sure what to do after that. But we'll find out when we get there."

"Do you really think anyone made it back there?" Tommy asked.

"I don't know," I shrugged. "But I was hoping to find survivors."

"Why do we need to go over there now when we're safe right here?" Kara asked. "And we have plenty of food in this place."

"Well, it's still a police station," I replied. "And if we're over there, we'll be in contact with the government. Maybe there are evacuation protocols being implemented already. We have to get out of this city."

"Is the government sending help?" Kevin asked.

I let out a deep sigh. "I'm not sure," I replied. "But from what I saw on TV a few days ago, I'm not sure what to make of it. I'm really concerned about it."

"What did you see on TV?" Tommy quickly asked.

"The military already has this entire city under quarantine. They'll shoot anyone who tries to get out. I'm not sure what they're planning to do next, but my gut feeling tells me it's not going to be good. That's why I wanted to go to West Team for answers. If I can't get answers there, then I'm heading to the border to look for a way out."

"How are we going to make it to West Team?" Tommy asked. "We don't have any weapons. And there are thousands of those crazy people out there!"

"Tommy, let me tell you something about your uncle," I said. "He and I grew up together. Back when we were young, he was always into something dirty. Even now, he is still doing the same thing. Your uncle couldn't have made his fortune from this store alone. He made the bulk of his money by smuggling opium into this country, and selling guns to the Hmong rebels in Laos."

Tommy didn't seem surprised by what I'd told him. Maybe he did know something about Charlie. "I have to admit I knew my uncle was dirty—like doing shady business deals," he confessed. "But I never thought it was that bad. I thought he'd gone legit now."

"Well, he slowed down quite a bit," I said, "but he never completely stopped."

"So, do you think he still has guns in here?" Kevin asked.

"I'm pretty sure he still has a couple of guns stashed away somewhere inside this store."

"Do you know where?" Tommy asked.

"I saw where he stashed them once, but I'm not sure if they're still in the same place now." Seeing the curious but somewhat disappointed expressions on their faces, I had to confess. "Listen guys," I said. "The reason why I turned a blind eye was because I still believed in Charlie's cause. He wanted to help arm the Hmong rebels who were still being exterminated by the Communist Laotian government. If you had been children of the war, you'd understand why I did what I did."

After the meal, we took a few lamps and I led them to an old broken-down refrigerator at the southeast corner of the warehouse. It took all four of us to push the refrigerator off of a dirty carpet that was nailed to the floor. Using a small knife, I cut off the ends of the carpet and pulled it away. Underneath were several wooden boards, all laying parallel to each other, covering a huge rectangular hole in the concrete floor. Using a crowbar, I removed the boards to reveal a wooden crate inside the hole. The crate was very heavy, and it took all four of us to get it out. Prying off the padlock, I was mesmerized by the array of weaponry inside.

There must have been dozens of AR-15s, carbines, and pistols lying on top of a blue tarp. Underneath the tarp was a vast array of ammunition. I was grinning from ear to ear when I saw the boxes of shotgun shells. Maybe my shotgun was no longer out of commission. The hard part would be to go back out there and retrieve it. I thought about using an AR-15 instead. But from what I'd seen of what the shotgun could do, I didn't want to use any other weapon.

I went back to the office and sat on the couch for a while. It felt serene in there. The chaos outside seemed to be a million miles away. And for the first time since Kara and I were inside the little grocery store, I didn't have to worry about food. I really didn't want to leave all of this behind.

Soon the others joined me in the office. The silence and the gloomy expressions on their faces were evidence that they, too, didn't want to leave this place of comfort. "So, how are we going to get to West Team?" Kevin finally said, breaking the silence.

"We have to get to the freeway," I replied. "Then we'll just go west from there."

"But do you know what we're up against?" Tommy asked, his eyes wide. "All I saw was a lot of crazy people."

"I really don't know what they are," I replied. "I'm really not sure if they're human anymore. They were infected by some kind of virus. I don't think they possess any human thoughts or rationalization. From my encounters with them, I noticed two types: the *slow movers* and the *fast movers*. The slow ones are like zombies. You know, what you see in the movies. Anyways, they are easy to outrun and easy to kill. The fast ones are the ones that were bitten and then they turned. I'm not sure if they still have the ability to think, but they seem to be smarter. They're the ones that you'll have to be really concerned about. They come at you with tremendous speed and power. And they are hard to kill."

"How do we kill them?" Kevin asked. "I've never killed any of them before."

"Just like what you see in the movies. You have to shoot them in the head or completely sever their head from their body."

"So how many of them have you killed?" Tommy asked curiously.

"I've killed enough to haunt me for a very long time."

"How did all of this happen?" Kara asked. "Who infected them?"

"I think Robbie was the carrier of the virus," I said, thinking back to what the medic captain said about Robbie.

"Crazy Robbie did this?" Tommy quickly asked.

"Yes, he bit a bunch of people and they all ended up at the hospital."

"My God," Kara said. "So that explains the crowd coming from the hospital."

"Yes," I replied. "If one of them bites you, you will turn into one of them."

"How do you know all of this?" Kevin asked. "How do you know that Robbie really did this?"

"I was sent to the Pine Street Bridge to check on Robbie. When I got there, he tried to attack me. I subdued him. Medics later transported him to the hospital. He also bit Swede, the medic, when he arrived. I didn't know until later that Robbie also attacked Freddie and partially ate him. When I returned to the bridge, Freddie tried to attack me. I shot him several times, but he didn't die. Then I shot him in the head and killed him. When I was at the grocery store, I saw Swede. He had turned into one of them. He tried to attack me. I killed him by chopping off his head."

I really wanted to leave the next day. But I knew that Kara was still not ready for the long trek. Her ankle was still bothering her tremendously when she walked. So the vigorous pace of running, along with the long hike to West Team, would be way too much for her. She would hinder us greatly. We needed to stay where we were for a few more days to allow her ankle to fully heal before moving on.

I brought it up to the guys and they embraced the suggestion. I, too, embraced it. I would be more than content to stay where we were for the duration if there was a possibility that help was coming. But my intuition could not be ignored. And my deep-rooted need to be with my family was also fueling my desire to leave.

CHAPTER 16

Squeaking noises quickly alerted me to movements outside the office. My eyes opened to a dark room. The lamps were not in their usual places at the desk. Kara was not on her couch either. *It's got to be Kevin and Tommy out there,* I thought.

As I looked outside the small window above me, I let out a deep, despairing sigh. The sun was shining brightly through the small windows of the huge overhead garage door. I could see silhouettes of people in the warehouse, pushing a table to the spot where the light touched the ground. They were getting ready for breakfast. It would be our final breakfast inside our refuge.

Kevin, Tommy, and Kara were sitting at the table, chatting away and chuckling as if they were at a restaurant. I smiled pleasantly as I approached and settled myself in a chair in front of an empty plate. The array of dishes on the table diverted my attention from their lively conversation.

The mood became somber as we ate breakfast. It was the fifth time we had eaten breakfast together. The first four times were spirited and upbeat. Our conversations were lively, energetic, and jubilant. But this morning wasn't the same. Everyone was eating quietly. I guess the food said it all. We might not eat like this again for a very long time, if ever. It was definitely going to be very hard to leave it all behind.

I was still agonizing about my decision to leave, but I decided to put it out there and see how they would to respond. "Look, guys," I said. "What I said a few days ago was just speculation. I really don't know what the government is planning to do. There's still a chance that help is coming. I'm not sure we will ever find a place as safe as this. If you guys want to stay here until help arrives, then I'm OK with it. But as for me, I'm still sticking to my decision. I'm leaving today. If any of you want to stay here, I'll understand. I will respect your decision."

They glanced at each other for a moment. Then Kara quietly replied, "I'm going with you."

Tommy and Kevin gazed at each other for a few more seconds. Then Kevin glanced over at me. "We are going too, sir."

After breakfast, I went into the shopping aisles and found a couple of cigarette lighters, three flashlights, a small box of hand wipes, and an antiseptic spray. I also found two hatchets that could be used as melee weapons. I was primarily looking for bug spray. I knew that if things didn't turn out as I expected at West Team, then I would have to go to the border. And I didn't want to be eaten by the bugs while inside the woods. But to my dismay, I couldn't find any bug spray.

Kara came back to the office with a shopping cart full of food. "You did good, kiddo," I said after seeing the small packages that could easily fit into all of our backpacks.

Kevin and Tommy came back with their AR-15s and two huge bags of ammunition. "This is for you, sir," Kevin said, handing a plastic bag over to me.

I peeked inside and saw six boxes of shotgun shells and three boxes of bullets for my pistol. "Thank you, kid."

After everyone was packed up and ready to go, I went to the service door and slowly cracked it open. The infected seemed to have moved on. The piles of corpses were still there, littering the ground, decomposing in the hot, humid weather.

The stench overwhelmed us as soon as we stepped out onto the platform. "Breathe through your mouth and not through your nose," I advised them.

My shotgun was hanging on the railing at the bottom. It still seemed in good condition. I was grateful that the sling had become caught on the railing and the shotgun hadn't fallen to the ground.

As we maneuvered around the bloated corpses, the nauseating stench was unbearable. I choked every time I took in a breath. The guys were also struggling for air and couldn't stay focused. I knew if they vomited, then they'd get hungry again. But there was really nothing I could do to prevent that except keep encouraging them to move faster.

After we finally made it out of the lot, we went south for three blocks. A small shack behind the blue house at the north end of the park provided us with cover. From where we were at, Bellows Park was just a few yards away. About the size of two city blocks, the park was basically an open, grassy field with some trees and a few picnic tables scattered here and there.

The small pavilion at the south end of the park was our next objective. It was about twenty-five yards north of Bellows Avenue. The dreaded apartment complexes were just south of that street.

"We have to get to the pavilion," I said to them. "We have to make a run for it. We'll hide in the bushes at the rear once we get there."

About one hundred yards remained between us and the pavilion. I was doing fine for the first twenty-five yards. But I soon found myself lagging farther and farther behind everyone. My breathing was labored, and my heart kept beating faster and faster. My body felt heavier and heavier with each step. But the fear of being left behind kept me moving. *Just a few more yards*, I kept saying to myself. *It's only a few more yards.*

I finally made it to the pavilion and went straight to the rear. Still dizzy and disoriented, I stumbled over to the bushes and fell down with a crash. Kevin and Tommy noticed my pitiful condition. They guarded the sides and waited for me to recuperate.

"Sir, you better come and take a look," Kevin said, after seeing that I was able to sit up.

I slowly crawled over to him. A large crowd was gathering in front of an apartment building about twenty yards from the path to the freeway. "What are we going to do now?" Kevin asked, looking a little defeated.

I sighed as I tried to come up with an option. The apartment complexes were about five city blocks in length and two blocks in width. The freeway was two blocks away if we took the path. But, it was going to be a bloodbath!

"Well, what should we do?" Kevin asked again.

"We have to take the path," I replied. "We have no other choice but to fight our way to the freeway."

After loading my shotgun, I could tell by the expression on the guys' faces that they didn't think this was a good idea. I gave them a slight nod of acknowledgement. "Just keep running as fast as you can," I said. "When we get to the fence above the freeway, we'll make our defense over there."

We were just about to head out when the sound of gunshots rang out from one of the complexes. Looking out from the pavilion, I saw that the crowd was heading toward an apartment building at the end of the block, leaving the path unguarded for the time being.

"This is our chance," I said to them. "Let's go!"

We made it past the first of three apartment buildings without any issues. The next two were a breeze. The small, open field was the only thing left between the freeway and us. The six-foot chain-link fence above the embankment was getting bigger and bigger as we got closer and closer.

Reaching the fence was like finishing a long, grueling race. But, the victorious moment was short-lived as Kara kept tapping me on the shoulder. She was frantically pointing behind her. Then I saw two people heading our way, quickly closing in on us. Kevin already had his rifle aimed at them. "No!" I said, reaching over to stop him. "The noise will bring more of them over here."

Taking the machete, I started toward the two infected. As the first one quickly approached, I lunged forward and took off his head. As I spun around to strike at the other, I felt a hard impact that knocked the wind out of me. Then I realized that I'd been tackled. I was fighting for my life with the infected on top of me! I was holding on to his head to avoid being bitten. But he was so strong! His mouth was getting closer and closer to my neck. I didn't know how long I could hold him off. Then suddenly, he stopped moving. His eyes slowly closed and his body went limp. After pushing him off me, I saw Kevin standing over me holding his bloody hatchet.

"Let's go, sir," he said, extending his hand to me.

We stayed close to the embankment as we headed west along the freeway. The pace was slow and methodical. But the distance we were making was encouraging. I felt a certain serenity, like I'd entered a different world. The death and destruction above us seemed to be far away. The stillness of the vast empty highway was comforting and assuring. My spirit was uplifted. My mind began to relax, and my anxiety slowly dissipated.

Two hours into the walk, however, my body was failing. The cruel midday sun relentlessly blasted its ninety-degree rays, draining every ounce of energy from my body. I felt like I was on a death march.

After thirty more agonizing minutes, we finally reached the Solomon Avenue Bridge. I was completely spent. I couldn't go any further without a rest. Kara also was about to pass out. I was surprised that Kevin and Tommy, being the workout freaks that they were, were also feeling the same effects.

The four of us settled underneath the bridge. The shade and the cool, gentle breeze were hypnotically soothing. Slowly, my eyes began to close. "Go ahead, sir," Kevin said after noticing that I was nodding. "Take a nap. We'll keep watch."

"Thank you, kid," I said. Then I took my backpack off and placed it underneath my head.

I felt a gentle tug on my arm and I opened my eyes. Kara was sitting next to me, smiling warmly. "How long was I out?" I asked.

"About two hours."

I sat up and noticed that both Kevin and Tommy were sleeping, too. "I thought that they were supposed to keep watch."

She chuckled. "Well, I fell asleep shortly after you did," she replied. "I woke up an hour later. I saw that they were very tired, so to be fair, I told them that I would keep watch."

I glanced at my watch: it was almost five o'clock. We still had a little ways to go. Although I wanted Kevin and Tommy to get their share of sleep, we needed to get to West Team before nightfall.

After another hour of walking, the Orbit Parkway Bridge was coming into view. But I also saw something up ahead that was beginning to concern me. The entire westbound side of the freeway was crowded with endless rows of vehicles, all tightly compacted together. A few abandoned vehicles were scattered here and there on the eastbound side. I wasn't sure what had happened. But then I realized that we were a few miles from the border of the city of Hiawatha. The lines of vehicles must have stretched at least that far. I guessed all those people had been trying to leave the city, but with the bridge being closed off, they were forced to abandon their vehicles and seek shelter elsewhere.

Our pace was considerably slower now with the vehicles cramming the street. There was no telling what or who could suddenly pop out of those vehicles. We had less than a mile to go. But being on constant high alert, and with my blood pressure shooting through the roof, I knew it would be the most grueling mile I would ever have to walk.

It wasn't until two hours later that my anxiety finally came down to a manageable level. The sight of the Midway Avenue Bridge was like a beacon of hope. My eyes perked up, and my pace quickened. I felt like I was coming home. West Team was on Midway Avenue, just a block north of the freeway. I was really going to go home now!

As tired as I was, the ascent up the twenty-foot embankment was a breeze. The small wooded area between Midway Avenue and Sills Street provided perfect cover as I plotted a route. One hundred yards was the distance to our salvation. Casper Road was just in front of us. Going across that street and getting to the old Vincent and Karl buildings was the first priority. The narrow alleyway between the buildings would provide us with the cover we needed to get to the rear. West Team was fifty yards beyond those buildings.

Our sprint across the street to the buildings didn't take more than a minute, and the effect on me was minimal. Following the alleyway to the rear, I quickly stopped when I noticed a commotion at the police parking lot. A crowd stood in the lot. There was a huge gathering at the front of the building spilling out onto Midway Avenue.

"There's got to be people inside. That's why there are so many of them out there," I said to Kevin, Tommy, and Kara.

There was no doubt in my mind that there were survivors inside West Team. The only question was, how were we going to get in there? There were too many infected. We couldn't defeat them all.

The sun was steadily sloping toward the horizon. I still couldn't come up with a definite plan. Getting into West Team would be ideal, considering the time. But it would be suicidal. Going back to the freeway seemed to be the only option, but I really didn't know what else to do once we got back down there.

As I continued staring at the crowd, I realized that the infected at the front didn't seem to make any effort to go to the rear. The trees and bushes that ran along the south side of the building were blocking their view of the rear. The chain-link fence, which partially enclosed the lot, would also be beneficial to us. It could hinder the crowd at the front just long enough for us to fight our way through the crowd at the rear.

"We have to fight our way through that crowd to get to the rear entrance," I said to them, pointing toward the parking lot. "I know it's not going to be easy, but we have no other choice. It's going to get dark soon. I don't want to be out here when I can't see."

"If we make it over there, how do you know if the door is still working?" Kevin asked.

"Just look at the light," I said, pointing to the small blue light above the rear door. "That light is on. This building has an emergency generator inside the garage. I still have my keycard with me."

"Are you positive the door will open?" Tommy asked.

"No," I replied, "but let's just hope so."

CHAPTER 17

The crowd began moving toward us as we entered the parking lot. Seeing how they had grouped together, I was tempted to use the shotgun to blast them out of the way. But good sense prevailed, and I took out the machete instead.

After seeing their slow, awkward movements, I was greatly relieved that they were all slow movers. Although we were vastly outnumbered, we could win this fight. "Use your melee weapons first," I said to them. "Our guns are too risky—the noise could bring the rest of them over to us. If we become overwhelmed, then we will use our guns and unload everything."

Hacking our way through the crowd, I was surprised at how easily we mowed them down. I felt like I was fighting a bunch of elderly people. They offered very little resistance and made no effort to defend themselves. The best part was that they didn't even make a sound.

We finally made it to the rear door, and I quickly placed my keycard over the reader. The beep from the reader was a wonderful and soothing sound to my ears. The door unlocked. We were finally home!

But a pungent odor of decomposition greeted us inside the hallway. I instantly went on high alert. I had no idea what had happened, but I feared something dreadful was lurking somewhere further on.

The card reader to the door of the second floor had been ripped off, so our only option was to go into the garage and use the access door on the other side. But the reeking odor seemed to be more potent from beyond the door to the garage. Something was waiting for us in there. I was reluctant to open the door. *But three of us have guns*, I reminded myself. *We can contend with whoever is in there.*

As soon as I opened the door, the stench immediately rushed into the hallway, overpowering and suffocating us. It seemed as if it had been stewing in there for days or weeks, just waiting for a chance to be let out.

The paddy wagon was parked in the middle of the garage with its rear doors left wide open. With the evening sun still coming in the windows above the north walls, I was able to piece together what had happened. I looked at the bullet holes on the wagon, the hundreds of casings on the floor, and the huge pool of blood below the doors. There had definitely been a huge gunfight there.

Although there were no bodies inside or around the wagon, the stench was still extremely potent. As I wondered what had happened to the bodies, I noticed a trail of dry blood leading away from the wagon to the darkest area of the garage. With my flashlight leading the way, I finally found the answer to my question: there, at the southeast corner, lay around fifteen corpses. They were still in their police uniforms. But their faces were so badly decomposed that I couldn't tell who they were. I just knew that they were people I had once known and worked with. Judging from how the bodies were positioned next to each other, someone had placed them there. And that someone was probably lurking nearby.

The keypad to the access door that led to the other side was still operational. The door opened to a dark stairway. Upon reaching the second floor, a familiar hallway greeted us. As I gazed down the quiet, gloomy corridor, a touch of sadness came to me. This hallway was so familiar, yet so strange to me now. Everything seemed to be in its correct place. Even Bobby's "timeout chair," where he was forced to take a break by the sergeants for talking too much during roll call, was still at the end of the hallway, next to the roll call room. But gone were the liveliness and the frantic pace of police work.

The administrative offices were directly to our right. We needed to clear those rooms before proceeding. We had just made it over to the detective cubicles when the terrifying sound of a shotgun being racked stopped us dead in our tracks. Slowly, I turned around. Bobby was in the doorway aiming a shotgun at us!

I was definitely surprised to see Bobby. I was even more surprised that he had snuck up on us like that. Never in a million years did I think I'd get ambushed by Bobby. I mean, during my shift I could hear him clumsily walking down the hallway from inside the locker room.

"Bobby," I said calmly. "It's me, Hua."

"How do I know you're not a zombie?" he quickly responded.

I could hear giggling from both Kevin and Tommy. I tried not to laugh myself. "Bobby, you idiot," I said. "Would a zombie talk back to you? Put the gun down before you accidentally shoot us."

Upon hearing us laughing, Bobby lowered his shotgun and quickly came over to us. He was so happy to see us that he grabbed each of us, including Kara, for a huge hug. He was holding me so tightly that I feared my ribs were about to break. "OK! Take it easy, you big ape!" I said, pushing him away. "You're going to crack my ribs with those gorilla arms of yours."

"I'm so happy to see you guys," he said.

"I'm glad to see you too, Tubby," I said. "How many of you are still here?"

"Me, Jack, Liam, and Mo," he replied. "Well, Teng and the new sergeant are here also. But they were attacked by the zombies earlier."

"How long ago was that?" I quickly inquired.

"About an hour ago," he replied, "maybe longer than that."

"Where are they?"

"We put them inside the Quiet Room. Mo and Jack are over there."

The Quiet Room was located down the hallway across from the women's locker room. It was equipped with two sofas that could be turned into beds. It also had a flat-screen TV mounted onto the wall. The purpose for the room was to serve as sleeping quarters for officers who lived too far away from the city and had to go to court the following morning. Bobby used to take full advantage of the room until the commander found out that he was sleeping in there every night. He was ordered to stay away from the room indefinitely.

As I walked down the long hallway toward the room, I had a sinking feeling. Teng and Paul, the new sergeant, would have to be killed. It would only be a matter of time before they turned. If they hadn't already.

Mo was coming out of the break room with a bucket of ice in each hand. "Hua!" he shouted. "Man, am I glad to see you!"

"I'm glad to see you too, buddy," I said. "How are Teng and Paul doing?"

He shook his head. "They're not doing well," he replied, sadly. "I think they're getting worse."

"How long ago were they injured?"

"I'm not sure. Maybe two hours."

Teng and Paul were lying in the sofas when I entered the room. Their faces were pale and drenched with sweat. They were trembling even though they were covered with several blankets. As I touched Paul's forehead, I was bewildered. His forehead was very cold even though he was sweating profusely. I checked one of his eyes and could see that the blood vessels were swollen to the point that it seemed they would burst.

I was still with Paul when Teng suddenly began shaking violently.

Thick white foam was oozing out of his mouth, and blood was leaking out of the corners of his eyes. He was about to turn! I quickly got up and went to the doorway.

Mo ran into the room and went over to Teng. "Mo! Get away from him!" I said as I withdrew my pistol.

"He needs my help!"

"He is turning into one of those monsters! Get away from him now!"

"He's my fucking partner! I ain't leaving him!" he said defiantly.

As we continued shouting at each other, Teng suddenly stopped shaking. Then he began gasping for air. After a short while, he finally stopped breathing. Mo let out a loud cry as he held Teng.

I knew what was going to happen next. So I ordered Mo to get away from Teng. But he wasn't listening. "He's dead!" Mo shouted.

"He's not dead!" I shouted back. "Get away from him!"

As I tried desperately to get my message across to Mo, he suddenly let out a loud, high-pitched scream. Then he quickly backed away from Teng. While doing that, he tripped over his own feet. He was now flat on his back and couldn't pull himself up. Teng had his eyes fixed on Mo as he sat up.

I quickly went up to Teng and placed my gun at the back of his head. With a squeeze on the trigger, he fell foreward.

"What the fuck is going on in here?" Jack shouted as he entered the room.

I was just about to explain when Paul began to shake. I went up to Paul and placed my gun at his forehead. "Whoa!" Jack shouted as he rushed in and pushed me away from Paul. "You can't shoot him! He's one of us! He's the sergeant, for fuck's sake!"

"He's not one of us anymore!" I shouted back. "I have to shoot him before he turns! Now, get the fuck out of my way, Jack!"

I pushed past Jack and went up to Paul. As I aimed my gun at his forehead, he slowly opened his eyes to look at me. I hesitated for a moment. Although I had held a deep-rooted grudge against him for being a power-hungry, back-stabbing piece of shit, I'd never really hated him. He was still a friend. "I'm so sorry, buddy," I said. "I'm sorry for all these years of being an asshole to you." I squeezed the trigger and his eyes rolled back into his head.

"*Man, this is fucked up!*" Jack shouted as he aggressively moved in on me. "What makes you think you have the right to kill him?"

"Hey! Take it easy, Jack!" Mo said as he stepped in between us. "Hua was right! Teng was shaking just like that before he turned. He was just about to attack me and Hua shot him."

Jack was still angry when he left the room. I could understand his frustration. Hell, I was frustrated too. This whole ordeal was steadily chipping away at my morale and my sanity. And I still couldn't make sense of it.

Bobby and I took Paul's and Teng's bodies into the garage and laid them next to the bodies of the other officers. Bobby told me it was Jack's idea to do that. Jack believed that when help arrived, the officers would get a full and proper officer's burial. That wouldn't have occurred to me. It was a kind and thoughtful idea.

Everyone was inside the break room when we came back up. The conversations were upbeat. We talked as if we hadn't seen each other in ages. Even Liam got into the mix. He was actually joking and laughing with us—a side of him that I rarely saw. Jack wasn't angry with me anymore. He seemed to accept what I'd done. I, on the other hand, was still trying to come to terms with the fact that I'd just killed two of my friends.

Everyone seemed to have a story to tell. As I continued listening, I was glad to know that Bobby was still living up to his nickname as "Crash." He told us that on the day when all of this started, he crashed his squad car while en route to the hospital. He was four blocks away from West Team. Since he couldn't get anyone to come pick him up, he decided to walk back to West Team and wait for another ride.

Jack said that he and Liam were at the park. They were put in charge of the paddy wagon. They stayed back while the others advanced toward the hostile crowd. When everyone was getting attacked, they took the injured officers into the paddy wagon. They were planning to drive the officers to another hospital, but they were informed that all of the hospitals inside the city were on a lockdown. They tried to go over to Hiawatha, but the streets were congested with vehicles. So they decided to go to West Team. While inside the garage, some of the wounded officers began attacking the others. Jack and Liam tried to stop the fight, but they also ended up being attacked. Then Paul came into the garage with an AR-15 and began unloading on everyone. After Jack and Liam finally wrestled the gun away from Paul, all of the officers were dead. They took Paul into the Quiet Room and locked him inside.

Jack also said that they hadn't eaten anything for days. So earlier this afternoon, he, Liam, Bobby, Mo, and Teng planned to go scavenge for food. They didn't trust Paul being left by himself, so they made him come along. They were a few blocks away from West Team when they ran into a mob. They all managed to make it back, but Teng and Paul had been seriously injured. They put them in the Quiet Room and tried to tend to their injuries.

"Did you guys find any food?" I asked.

"No," Bobby replied. "Every store and restaurant had been ransacked. We couldn't find anything."

"Well, we have some food with us," I said. "If we carefully ration it, we might have enough food to sustain us for two or maybe even three weeks. But eventually, we'll have to leave this place or we'll starve."

"Well, we only need a few days' worth of food," Jack said.

"Really? Why is that?" I asked, glancing at Jack.

"The military is coming to rescue us," he replied confidently. "I got a message from one of my military buddies. He told me the military was sending help and for us to stay where we are."

"How long ago was that?" I inquired.

"Maybe a week ago," he replied. "That's the only message I got before the communications got disrupted again."

After noticing that I was a little skeptical, Jack tried to reassure me again. "Listen, this buddy is a very good friend of mine. I've known him for over twenty years. He's not going to lie to me. The military is going to come for us. It might take them a while to get here because they're probably too busy extracting people from other parts of the city. But eventually, they'll reach us."

I was elated to hear that, and completely content to stay where we were and wait it out. My decision to come to West Team was definitely the right decision. The horrific nightmare was almost over!

CHAPTER 18

As I stood by the coffee machine and waited anxiously for it to finish brewing, I couldn't help but marvel at the beauty outside the windows. The morning sun was just above the horizon, emitting its golden rays of light across the vast, endless sky. A few puffs of clouds were scattered here and there. The scene couldn't be any more beautiful.

I tried not to look down at the streets. My eyes could no longer bear the poison, and my heart could no longer stand the despair. Hell on earth best described where I was.

It had been almost two weeks since we'd arrived at West Team. Every new day was exactly like the previous day. I would get up and be optimistic that help was coming. But by the end of the day, I was left with the same despairing result. I shouldn't have been too disappointed. I had known for a while that the only way out of the city was to look for a way out. But still, I was reluctant to leave. I guess I was still holding on to the hope that help would soon arrive. And I might miss out on it if I left.

My desire to leave was getting stronger with each passing day. But each time I pondered where to go next, I was always at a loss. The rivers that surrounded Riverdale and made it unique were now our keepers. Every possible route I came up with would only lead to the rivers. Getting across them would be nearly impossible. The currents were too strong. And the patrol boats would shoot me on sight. *I'm doomed if I stay here*, I despaired, *and doomed if I leave.*

Jack had assured me many times that his friend would never lie to him. I was very optimistic in the beginning, but now I found it difficult to stay the course. We had put our fate in one man's words, trusting that he'd be right. That was something I could no longer do. I had to go with my intuition. I had to put my fate in my own hands now.

After thinking about it for a while, I finally came up with a possibility. I remembered a moment back in time when I was a teenager.

A couple of my friends and I went to South Park, a scenic area located in the Crosby Park neighborhood, to explore the caves along the cliffs. While maneuvering through the labyrinth of passageways, we entered a small, cramped corridor and followed it. As we went farther, the corridor seemed to be dropping deeper. It also continued on with no end in sight. After a while, I had become concerned that we might not have enough battery power left in our flashlights to make it back. I wanted to go back, but my friends wanted to continue on to see where it would lead. When we finally emerged, I realized that we were at the caves at the Coral Cliffs in Antiman City, which was south of Riverdale. The corridor had actually taken us *underneath* the Mississippi River, underneath Solomon Park, and extended all the way to the Coral Cliffs.

I knew that the three bridges across the Mississippi River to Antiman City were blocked off by the military. I also knew that the military was patrolling the river to ensure that no one made it to the other side. But I was confident that the military didn't know about the caves. *If I make it to South Park*, I thought, *then I can leave the city through the caves.*

Although it had been thirty years since I'd been inside the caves, I was positive that I could still find the exact corridor. I just hoped that the caves weren't sealed off by the city. Because then the journey would only lead to my demise.

I had only one thing on my mind as I waited for everyone to come into the break room for our first and only meal of the day: to tell them that I was planning to leave West Team that day. I wanted to let them in on my plan to go to South Park and leave the city through the cave, but because of Jack's connection with his friend in the military, I had to be discreet. So, I told them that I wanted to leave West Team to look for a way out of the city.

"That's bullshit!" Jack snorted. "Help is coming!"

"It has been almost two weeks since I arrived here, Jack," I said. "Where is the help that was supposed to come?"

"Just have a little faith," he said. "They're coming!"

"Well, I'm still sticking to my decision," I said. "I know that it's going to be very dangerous out there. But I'm going to find a way out of this city. And if I don't make it, then at least I know I tried."

I paused for a moment to glance at everyone. "If any of you want to come with me, I would be grateful to have your company," I added.

I could tell by their expressions that no one wanted to go back out there. I didn't blame them. Everyone wanted to believe Jack and his friend. But at least I was thinking clearly enough to know that it might be a false sense of hope. It had been over a month now. Help was not coming!

After a while, Bobby spoke up. "Hua," he said. "I've known you for a long time, and I've loved you like a brother. But I'm not going to take my chances out there when there is a possibility that help is coming."

I nodded. I didn't need to look to Liam for his decision. He would never follow me. And he would never go anywhere without Jack.

"I'm sorry," Tommy said quietly.

I nodded again and then turned to Kevin. He sighed deeply. "I'm sorry, sir," he said faintly.

Mo quietly shook his head and turned away to avoid further eye contact with me.

Finally I turned to Kara. I could tell she was struggling between her fear and her loyalty to me. "It's OK, sweetie," I said, trying to reassure her that I was OK if she decided to remain. "You stay here with them. I don't want you to get hurt out there."

"No!" she quickly responded. "I want to go with you!"

I was taken aback by her response. *Does she know what she's saying?* I asked myself. I didn't want her mind to be clouded by her loyalty to me. "No, Kara," I said. "You stay here with them. I'm not going to be mad or disappointed in you. It's way too dangerous out there."

"You've kept me safe, and I've believed in you. My decision is to go with you," she said confidently.

After a somber breakfast, I went to my locker to gather up some of my personal items to take with me. While rummaging through my locker, I found the boot knife that I used to carry with me during the first couple of years of my career. I knew that knife could come in handy, so I strapped it onto my right boot.

There were a lot of sentimental items that I had hoarded inside my locker over the years, but I failed to find one particular item that was very dear to me: the picture of my wife. It had been inside my locker for many years. But it was missing! Now all I had was memories of her. And with my forgetful mind, I knew her face would slowly fade.

Kevin came into the locker room and gave me all of the magazines from his duty belt. "Thanks, kid," I said as I shoved them inside my pockets. Then I placed a hand on his shoulder and whispered to him, "If you decide later that you want to come after me, then go to the freeway and follow it to River Road. Go down to the woods and follow the trail to South Park. There's a huge cave at the cliffs about two hundred yards from the marina. I will be there. I'm planning to leave the city through one of the caves."

I paused to look at him for a moment. "Please tell only Tommy about what I've said to you. Do not reveal this to anyone else, especially to Jack. If the military finds out about it, we will lose our only chance."

Kevin nodded silently.

Using a drill that was stored in the maintenance closet, I took Kara's baseball bat and drilled several holes through it. Then I drove several long metal spikes through the holes. After the spikes were tightly secured with shoelaces, I gave the bat to Kara.

We went in to the break room and packed all of our food into our backpacks. "Aren't you going to leave some for us?" Liam said angrily as he entered into the room.

"This is our food, Liam," I replied calmly. "We're going to need it."

"Fuck you! Leave one of those bags!" Liam shouted so loudly that Kara began to shake.

I stopped what I was doing and stood my ground. "*We came here with these bags!*" I shouted back at him. "We're going to leave with these bags! Don't you dare try to take them from us!"

The exchanges between Liam and me were so loud that everyone rushed into the room. "What the fuck is going on in here?" Jack shouted over us.

"They're leaving with all the food!" Liam said to Jack.

"The food inside these bags belongs to us," I said. "We're only taking what was ours!"

Jack gazed at me intently for a moment. Then he let out a sigh. "Are you sure you're going to need all that?" he asked in a somewhat threatening manner. But I wasn't worried that Liam and Jack would try to stop me. The rest of the guys would not allow it. They had more love and respect for me than they did for those two.

"Well, Jack," I replied. "You guys only need a few days' worth of food, right? Help is coming for you. Where we're going, we're going to need everything inside these bags."

Jack glanced away from me and turned to Liam. "Let them go," he said.

CHAPTER 19

Kara and I took the same route back to the freeway. Again, my plan was to walk west and get to the bridge at the border. If the bridge was blocked off, then we would head down to scenic River Road, which ran between the residential area and the vast woodland valley. From there, we would head down to the woods. There was a small nature trail down there that led to a bigger paved trail about three miles away. If we continued on that trail, we would eventually get to South Park.

As we continued along the freeway past the endless rows of abandoned vehicles, I was becoming increasingly paranoid and was on constant high alert. My blood pressure kept racing up and down at the slightest bit of noise. I felt as if someone or something was going to jump out at me at any time. The stress was becoming overwhelming.

I wished the guys were there with me for support. I almost regretted leaving. But there was really nothing back there for me. All we did day in and day out was to wake up and hope that help was on the way. In my heart, I truly believed that the government's real intention was to keep the police force content with a false sense of hope in order to avoid an all-out war at the border.

Three hours later we were only halfway to the border. At the rate we were going, I wasn't sure if we were going to make it there by nightfall. Kara was struggling to keep up. The heavy bag on her back and the bat she was carrying were taking a tremendous toll on her small body. I wanted to help her by carrying her bag for a while. But I was also feeling the effects from carrying my own bag and weapons.

The Vandenberg Bridge finally came into view. I was feeling more energetic and began to quicken my pace. We were very close to the border, and once we reached the bridge, we could rest there for a while.

We still had plenty of time to get to the border and look for a place to hide before nightfall.

We settled underneath the bridge and quickly shook off our burdensome bags. The shade and a constant breeze from the west brought a swift and welcoming relief from the scorching heat. Slowly, I began to surrender myself to the pleasantness. "Go ahead. Take a nap," I said to Kara after seeing that she couldn't keep her eyes open.

Kara was just about to lie down when a distant sound of gunshots rang out. The shots were coming from the west. They were sporadic at first, but became more rapid and constant. I knew then that the military was having a war at the border with someone or something.

I quickly rummaged through my bag for my binoculars. "Stay here," I said to Kara. "I'm going up to the bridge to find out what's going on."

Through the binoculars, I finally realized where all those people from the vehicles had gone. Obviously they had no other choice but to walk to the border. They were still trapped inside the city, though, and desperately wanted to get out.

There must have been hundreds, if not thousands, of people gathered at the freeway bridge entrance. On the bridge, about thirty yards in, stood a giant concrete wall—just like the ones I'd seen on TV. Several soldiers were standing at the top with their rifles aimed down at the crowd.

Looking back toward the crowd, I noticed that they were staying behind huge rows of concrete blocks at the front of the entrance. *Those must be there to stop the vehicles from getting through to the wall*, I reasoned. Then I noticed that the area between the wall and the blocks was littered with fallen bodies. I could only assume that anyone who was brave or desperate enough to venture past those blocks would be shot.

The military was serious about containment. But the dead bodies didn't seem to deter a small group of people from moving past the blocks and into the death zone. I knew what was going to happen, and I found myself pleading for those people to go back. But they kept going. Then several shots rang out simultaneously, and their fallen bodies just stretched the field of corpses out a little bit farther.

I felt sick to my stomach. I'd just witnessed an execution! Those people had no chance. They were unarmed and gunned down like animals. Those soldiers had no regard for human life. *If only I had a high-powered rifle*, I thought to myself, *I would even the score!*

My intuition and concerns were confirmed now. Clearly the government had no intention of bringing in help. Our lives were insignificant to them. The safety and well-being of the rest of the country was their only concern.

I wanted to go back to West Team and tell the guys, but it was too late. Kara and I would never make it back before dark. Plus, I would never be able to convince them without any proof. They had made their decision. All I could do was to hope that somehow Kevin and Tommy would come to their senses and persuade the rest to follow them to South Park.

I was still steaming when I came back to Kara. Noticing the intense, agitated expression on my face, she was hesitant to ask. "Help isn't coming," I quietly said to her.

"What about those guys at the police station?" she asked. "Should we go back and tell them?"

I sighed deeply. "I thought about it, but it's too late to go back now. We have to continue on."

"So, where are we going?"

I knew of a golf course about two miles to the south. The groundskeeper, Frank, was a friend of mine. He had wanted someone to patrol inside the golf course because people kept going in there to take the flags and ball washers from the field. He had given me a key to the garage at the southern end of the course a year earlier as an incentive for me to patrol there. His office was inside the garage, and he wanted me to go in there to watch some TV on slow nights. My squad car being inside the golf course would be enough to deter people from coming in. I still had the key to the garage with me.

"There's a golf course south of here," I replied. "I have a key to the garage. We can stay there for the night."

I paused for a moment as I thought about her safety. "If we are parted for some reason, then you find the golf course and head to the garage. I will try to make my way there."

CHAPTER 20

Kara and I walked along the top of the embankment on the south side of the freeway. The trees and fences along the embankment concealed us until we reached Rosemount Street. We had reached the Rosemount neighborhood.

As I gazed steadily at the deserted streets and the unattended yards, I couldn't stop the sorrow from engulfing my heart. This area had always been so lively. On days like this, the streets were usually bustling with people walking, jogging, and biking. Residents would be outside mowing their lawns, and children would be running around the water sprinklers. But now, the whole area was eerily empty and quiet. It was nearly impossible for me to accept.

Almost an hour later, as we approached Lauren Avenue, a loud scream quickly alerted me to the alley on the north side of the street. I couldn't pinpoint which house it was coming from, but it was one of the houses within the block.

I wanted to ignore it, just like I'd done many times before. But the desperate cries for help were testing my sense of humanity. Plus, the way Kara was looking at me, I knew I would never be forgiven if I gave in to my cowardliness and walked away. I was still wearing the uniform. I couldn't ignore the oath that came along with it any longer.

I took a deep breath and headed in the direction of the voices. I was still conflicted as I thought about the risks I was taking. But I knew that I wasn't doing it for Kara—I was doing it for me. I hated myself for ignoring all those cries before. I wanted to make it right this time.

Another scream directed me to a large yellow house. Beyond the detached garage, a couple of people were in the backyard. An elderly couple was on the ground, huddling together. Three people were slowly moving in on them. Obviously the people on the ground were the ones who needed help.

I ran to the first infected and took off his head with my machete. When I spun around, the next one was right in front of me, too close for a full swing. So I thrust the machete into his chest, pushing the blade all the way through to his back. He grabbed onto the blade and held on to it, making it hard for me to pull it out.

As I was in a tug-of-war with the infected for the machete, I felt a tight embrace from behind me. Then something began clamping down onto my left shoulder. I immediately released my hold on the machete, sending the infected in front of me tumbling down to the ground. I quickly broke away from the hold and I spun around. A pair of red, fiery eyes belonging to an elderly woman was staring back at me.

I knew I had been bitten. I was in complete shock and disbelief. My mind was reeling with the thought of my demise. *I will have to shoot myself before I turn*, I told myself. I almost cried when I thought about Kara. *She is not going to survive out here without me now!*

The woman began moving toward me. Her legs seemed very weak, and her slow, awkward walk was like those of a small child walking for the first time. With a push, I sent her down to the ground. She let out a grunt when she landed. Then she opened her mouth to hiss at me. Suddenly, all my despair and self-pity dissipated when I saw her pinkish gums: she was toothless! Her bite hadn't even broken through my shirt!

As I pondered what to do with the woman, I saw a blunt object come down onto her head. She lay motionless. Kara was still holding the baseball bat. The spikes on the bat had been driven deep into the woman's skull, killing her instantly.

I took the bat from Kara and headed toward the last infected. He was still on his back, trying to roll over, but the blade was hindering him. I swung the bat down onto his head, and he finally stopped moving.

I went back to Kara, who was still staring blankly at the dead woman. "You did the right thing," I said gently, trying to console her. "Don't think too much about it."

The elderly couple was still huddling together on the ground as I approached them. Without even looking at me, the man quickly shielded the woman with his body. "Please, leave us alone," he begged. "Please go away."

"I'm not going to hurt you," I said in a soft, comforting tone. "You're safe now."

Upon hearing my voice, they both looked up at me. With a warm smile, I reached out a hand to them. "Let's go back inside," I said. "More of them will be coming soon."

Their names were Bill and Patricia Toby. They were in their late seventies and seemed to be plagued with physical issues. Bill told me that the two elderly people that I killed were their next-door neighbors, Rob and Regina Mays. The four of them had been friends for over forty years.

Patricia told me she had seen Rob and Regina in the backyard earlier. Regina had been confined to a wheelchair for the last ten years. So Patricia was extremely surprised to see that Regina was up and walking on her own. Patricia went outside to talk to them. But as she approached them, she could see that they were not themselves anymore. When they tried to attack her, she ran from them, but she tripped on the uneven sidewalk and fell. Unable to get up, she called to Bill, who came out and tried to help her. But then the other person showed up. They were surrounded. They couldn't do anything except call for help.

We were still inside the kitchen when I noticed that the cupboards and shelves were completely emptied of anything edible. The glass covers on the cabinets revealed dishes, cups, and miscellaneous items, but nothing to eat. When I asked Bill about it, he told me that both he and Patricia had physical issues that kept them from driving. So they depended on the local supermarkets for deliveries. But the deliveries had stopped a long time ago. They were trying to get by with the little food they had left.

I couldn't get over the generosity displayed by these two wonderful people. I could tell that they were starving, yet they were gracious enough to want to share their last can of SpaghettiOs with us. "Thank you for your kindness," I said, "but that won't be necessary. Dinner is on us tonight."

I took out two packages of beef jerky and three cans of beef stew from Kara's backpack. Then I poured the stew into a large bowl and set it on the table. The stew was cold and oily, and the beef jerky was dry and hard. But the delightful expression on Bill and Patricia's faces said it all. I smiled warmly as I watched them quickly finish off their plates. I was very hungry, but I took only a few spoonfuls onto my plate and left the rest for them.

After the meal, we went to the living room. Although it was dark and the only illumination inside was from the small kerosene lamp on the coffee table, I still made an effort to check all of the curtains on the windows to make sure that they were tightly closed.

Feeling assured, I went back and sat on the couch next to Kara. The Tobys were sitting on the couch across from us. Although I was comfortable and relaxed, my backpack was still strapped tightly onto my back, and my weapons were beside me. I wasn't sure why I hadn't taken the burdensome bag off. I just had an uneasy feeling that something dreadful was about to happen. Not that the Tobys were going to attack us. But I feared something awful was about to occur, and I needed to stay ready.

Bill told me he was a retired engineer, and Patricia said she was a retired English professor. They had been married for over fifty years and had three children. Their oldest son was a doctor, living in California. Their daughter, an attorney, lived in Virginia, and their youngest son was an architect in Texas. They should be proud of themselves for raising such successful children, I told them, and for being such good role models.

What I found fascinating about the Tobys was that they were such a lively couple. Their conversations were profound, and they could chat about anything and everything. I was still intrigued and amazed as I continued listening. They had lived such wonderful and fulfilling lives. They had done things that I could only wish of doing.

"No regrets," Bill said. "We want to leave this world with no regrets."

I couldn't help but feel a little envious, because I did have regrets. I thought about my life, and a rush of sorrow filled my heart. I was always too busy for my family and never had enough time to be with them. With me working off-duty jobs most of the time, my wife was the one who actually raised our children. She never complained about it; she just accepted it. I just hoped she didn't have any regrets.

Two hours into the conversation, I was still mesmerized by the Tobys' life stories. It seemed as though they wanted to share everything with us. Maybe they both knew that this was going to be the end for them, and this was how they wanted to be remembered. I felt like I'd known them all my life. *Maybe someday, if I'm lucky enough to survive this ordeal*, I thought, *I will try to track down their children and tell them about my encounter with their amazing parents.*

I thought about the next day and how sad it would be to leave them behind. I wished I could take them with us. But due to their frailty, I knew they wouldn't make it. Their death was inevitable. I could only hope that when it came, it would be merciful. But in my heart, I knew that it was not going to be. They would either die slowly from starvation or agonizingly at the hands of the infected. Two cruel outcomes that I would never wish upon anyone.

Outside was serenely quiet. I was completely relaxed and was just about to take off my backpack when something suddenly came crashing through the large front window. It landed underneath the coffee table, knocking over the lamp. We all jumped out of our seats and immediately backed away.

With my machete raised, I slowly walked over to the table. Whatever was underneath it was still moving. I couldn't make out what it was due to the darkness. But then a low growl confirmed my suspicion. I immediately swung down at it, killing it.

I went over to the front window and looked out into the darkness. My fears were confirmed in the moonlight: A horde of infected were coming our way. I had no clue how they figured out where we were. But as I looked up at the large window, I sighed deeply. There were two small windows above it that I had failed to notice until now. The infected must have seen the dim light through the windows from outside.

"They are coming!" I said to Kara and the Tobys. "Go hide behind the staircase!"

The infected were almost at the house, and there was no time to run for it. All I could do now was to prepare for the onslaught. Quickly, I began moving things around, clearing the living room to make more space. I pushed one of the couches over to block the narrow hallway to the kitchen. Then I moved the other to block the front door.

As I glanced around to see where I should plant myself when the infected arrived, I realized that the large front window where the first one busted through was the obvious choice. The rear door was still secured. The windows in the kitchen were too small for them to squeeze through. The other window in the living room, opposite the staircase at the east wall, was high enough from outside that it would be difficult for them to reach it.

I went to the front window and stood beside it. Taking several deep breaths, I held the machete over my head, ready to chop at anything that poked through it. *I might not survive this fight*, I thought, *but I will make it the biggest fight of my life. The infected will get what's coming to them. All of us are going to die tonight!*

It didn't take long before the first head poked through the window. I struck down at it, taking it completely off. Soon after that, more heads began poking through. I quickly chopped them off as well.

With one decapitation after another, the floor beneath the window was beginning to pile up with heads. The bodies of the dead were stacking up outside the window as well, preventing the others from entering. There was a brief period of silence. I stood quietly, desperately hoping that they had given up, that maybe the bodies outside might have deterred them. But it wasn't so. A loud crash in the kitchen alerted me to a new set of problems.

The infected had broken through the rear door and were now inside the kitchen. But they had prevented themselves from getting through the narrow hallway by hastily pushing at each other, causing a jam inside. I quickly chopped down the ones that were able to squeeze through, which slowed down the ones behind even more.

Then, a loud thump alerted me to the front window again. Several infected had already squeezed through into the room. They hadn't seen Kara and the Tobys yet. I had to draw their attention to me. "*I'm over here!*" I shouted as I backed away to the wall opposite the staircase. "Come over here!"

I was up against the wall, swinging wildly at anything that came toward me. Then suddenly, I felt a strong tug from behind. I realized that my backpack had broken through the window. Someone had grabbed onto it from outside and was pulling me out. I tried to hold on to the edge, but a powerful jolt sent me straight through the window.

I didn't know who it was that pulled me out, but I was pretty sure I'd landed on that person. I quickly got to my feet and noticed that I had fallen on the biggest guy I'd ever seen. His arms were flailing about, but he couldn't get up. I wasn't going to take a chance and let him get back to his feet. He was just too big, and I was not going to win this fight. I needed to strike him down with the machete, but then I realized that I wasn't holding the machete anymore. *I must have dropped it when I went through the window*, I thought, panicking.

As I frantically scanned around, a glimmering reflection from the moonlight caught my eyes. The machete and the shotgun were on the ground, a few feet away. But the huge guy was blocking my way! I leaped over him, but a strong tug on my left ankle sent me tumbling down. The guy had grabbed onto my ankle and was pulling me toward him. His grip was so strong I couldn't break free. But he was having trouble pulling me closer because his bottom half wasn't moving. *I must have broken his back when I landed on him*, I thought.

With my other leg, I began kicking out at him. After several hard blows to his head, he finally released my ankle. I quickly stood up and began stomping on his head. My focus was solely on him now. *I have to stop him! I have to kill him!*

After realizing that I wasn't striking anything anymore, I stopped.

I was in total disbelief when I looked down at him. A pile of brains and bone fragments on the concrete floor were all that was left of his head.

Then a hand reached down, touching the top of my head. I quickly snapped out of it, looked up, and noticed that the other infected were jammed together at the window. No one could squeeze through yet. I ran for my weapons.

As I stood up, a feeling of defeatism echoed through me. I was surrounded on both sides of the alleyway. There was no way out! Now that my fate was finally revealed to me, I wasn't scared anymore—I was pissed off. If this was how I was going to die, then so be it!

Suddenly, an extreme rush of rage began to overpower me, sending a tremendous boost of energy through my body. A voice was shouting from deep within me, getting louder and louder. It was so loud that it exploded right through my mouth. "*Come on, you assholes!* You want to kill me? Come and do it! I'll kill *all* of you!"

As I braced myself for the final onslaught, I noticed that the infected, for whatever reason, looked baffled. They just stood there, staring at me as if I'd gone insane. I didn't know what to make of it. Could it be that they were actually thinking? Could it be that they actually feared for their lives? It was very strange, but whatever the reason was, they'd just given me time to think of a way out.

I put the machete away and picked up the shotgun. I knew I wasn't going to be able to kill them all. But I figured if I focused on one side of the alleyway and blasted through it, then I just might make it out. I had seven rounds to work with. I had to choose one side of the alley.

I quickly scanned both sides to see which way was easier for me, but it seemed the same both ways. Then I decided to go toward the front of the house. I would have an easier path to the golf course if I made it through there.

The first shot sent several of them to the ground. Two more shots and the crowd began to thin out a bit more. After three more shots, I had cleared a path for me to go through. The last shot blew away the remaining ones, and I was on my way out!

A few infected were chasing after me. But I was building distance between us. Then I suddenly stopped dead in my tracks when I heard screaming from the house. *Kara! I forgot about Kara and the Tobys!*

I quickly turned around and noticed that the infected were heading back to the house. I had to go back! I had to save them!

I ran back toward the house and was only a half a block away when I had to stop. Self-preservation finally prevailed when I saw that the house was completely surrounded. The screams had stopped. "It's too late," I whispered, staring.

Taking a deep, agonizing breath, I said my last words to Kara: "Good bye, Kara. I'm so sorry I failed you, sweetie."

CHAPTER 21

The full moon was luminous as it stood proudly in the sky. The dark patches of clouds opened up to reveal thousands of bright, twinkling stars against the dark grandeur of the blanket of night. Slowly, the earth began to reveal itself in silhouettes. The moon and the stars had become my companions now as they illuminated the ominous darkness, showing me the way to my salvation.

It had been such a long time since I'd stepped outside to bask in the sky's spectacular splendor. The darkness around me was comforting, and for once, I felt safe and unafraid.

Suddenly a breeze blew past me, and all of the exuberating feelings began to dissipate. The potent odor of decomposition reminded me that I was not alone. The creatures of the night either walked on shadowed feet or were hiding behind every silhouette of the trees and bushes around me.

As I continued on my walk, my mind began to soar up into the heavens. I found myself asking if there truly was a God. Even though I'd come to terms with my fate, I still couldn't understand what we, as human beings, had done wrong that had caused God to abandon us. *Was this the end of mankind?* I wondered.

My mind was still deeply pondering this question when an epiphany hit me. *Maybe we are the plague that was growing out of control,* I thought. Had God finally decided to destroy us? We deserved it, didn't we? Clearly, humans were the most destructive species on the planet. We had abused the planet and shaped it to our liking. We had completely upset the balance of nature. *If this is the apocalypse, then we only have ourselves to blame.*

I was so deeply engrossed in my thoughts that I didn't realize I had approached the garage inside the golf course. As I gazed at this place, a deep, agonizing pain filled my heart: *This was the place that I told Kara about. This was supposed to be our safe haven.* But I was there alone. The only thing I could do was to keep holding on to the tiny bit of hope that if she had somehow escaped the onslaught, she would remember to make her way to the garage. I knew the odds of her getting out of that house were extremely slim. But I would be waiting for her if she did.

The service door and the overhead garage door seemed to be untouched. After I'd unlocked the service door, a dark room awaited my presence. The silence and stillness inside was inviting, despite the nauseating odor of moldy grass and gasoline that still lingered. I took a deep, slow breath, welcoming it into my lungs. It was a pleasant replacement for the foul stench of death outside.

After covering the two small windows at the metal shop with some black trash bags, I lit a small kerosene lamp and brought it with me to the office. I lay on the sofa and stretched out my tired, aching body before letting my restless mind wander.

As I stared up at the ceiling, the popcorn texture reminded me of the stars in the night sky. I could almost reach up and touch them. I closed my eyes and imagined that I was lying in a beautiful meadow, underneath the moon and the stars. A cool summer breeze brushed up against my skin. I could feel the smile on my face. It was a smile of love, of life, and of gratitude.

A few minutes past midnight I was abruptly awoken by the sound of footsteps outside. Fearing an attack, I quickly grabbed the machete and ran to the service door. The metal door was sturdy, and the deadbolt lock was strong. I was quite confident that no one would be able to break it down without the assistance of a huge, blunt object of some type.

As I waited with the machete held tightly in my hand, I heard a soft knock on the door. Then a female voice called out, "Hua? Are you in here?"

I was stunned—it was the voice I had become so used to hearing. It was Kara! She was still alive! Quickly I opened the door and pulled her inside. She gave me a tight embrace and immediately broke into tears.

After holding her for a while in my arms, I gently pulled back. I couldn't believe it was her! "How did you get away?" I softly inquired.

She took several quick breaths before she sobbingly replied, "We were trying to go up the stairs. One of them spotted us, and Patricia screamed. Then the others immediately turned toward us. We tried to run upstairs. But Bill and Patricia were too slow, and they didn't make it. I ran into a bedroom and hid. When I heard pounding on the door, I went to the window. I noticed I was above the roof of the other house.

The gap between the two houses was just a few feet apart. I jumped onto the roof and ran to the other side. Then I jumped onto a small tree and climbed down."

She paused to wipe away her tears. "I ran from the house and just kept on running. After I couldn't run anymore, I realized that I was lost. I didn't know what else to do, so I hid behind a garage for a long time. Then I remembered what you told me. I didn't know where I was. I also couldn't tell which way was west. I kept walking, hoping that I was heading in the right direction. When I came to a huge grassy field, I knew that I'd reached the golf course. I continued until I found the garage, like you told me. I didn't know if you were here—I just kept hoping and praying that you were still alive. I don't know what I would've done if you weren't here."

"You did good, kiddo," I said, embracing her tightly. "I'm so happy that you made it here."

It was two o'clock in the morning, and I couldn't sleep. Kara was on the sofa, sleeping soundly. Although my body was succumbing to fatigue, my mind was still restless. Being inside the safety of the garage and far away from the chaotic streets should have given me some comfort. But it didn't. I was haunted and tormented by everything I'd done. The screams from all those people that I had ignored would forever be echoing inside my ears. The faces of all those people that I had killed would forever be staring back at me every time I closed my eyes. The only thing I could do now was to write it all down in my journal. *Maybe someday, someone will read it*, I thought. *Then they will understand what I've become.*

"What are you doing?" Kara whispered, approaching the desk.

Startled by her sudden appearance, I quickly closed my journal. "Nothing," I replied. "Why aren't you sleeping?"

"Are you still keeping that journal?"

"Yes."

"Why are you still doing that?"

"I don't know. Maybe someday someone will find it and tell our stories to the world. Maybe they will find my wife and give it to her. Maybe then, she'll know about my struggles. She'll know that she was never far from my heart. She'll know that I've loved her and will always love her."

CHAPTER 22

The sudden sound of gunshots quickly awakened me. I didn't remember falling asleep, but my head was lying on the desk. I sat up and looked around. The lamp was still next to me on the desk. The dim room was silent. Kara was still sleeping in the sofa. No one had gotten inside yet.

I looked through the large window behind me. The stillness inside the dark metal shop was reassuring. The sunlight was pouring in from the two small windows on the overhead garage door at the far end of the shop. It was morning again.

After a few minutes went by without hearing any more gunshots, I began to relax. I was hoping the shots were coming from somewhere far away. But then, a sudden hail of gunshots caused me to jump out of my chair. The sound was loud and seemed very close. A battle was coming our way!

Kara hopped off the couch and ran over to me. She cuddled her trembling body against mine like a scared child. "Stay here and keep the door locked," I whispered.

"Please don't go. I'm so scared."

"I'm not going outside," I assured her. "I'm just going to the other room to check on the door."

Taking my weapons, I went into the metal shop. The small windows along the north wall provided a full view of the grassy field outside. I could also see the service door to the far left. There was no one outside yet. Although I knew their arrival was imminent, I was still hoping they didn't come my way.

Suddenly, another hail of gunshots rang out and I quickly ducked away from the windows. Within seconds, I could hear frantic voices and thumping sounds of footsteps coming toward me. Moments later, the sounds were perilously close. Just as I feared: the battle had arrived! And we were right in the middle of it!

Peeking out the window again, I saw five guys at the service door, pounding on it and trying to kick it in. A horde of infected were heading toward them. I quickly ran and stood by the door with my machete raised and ready. If those guys succeeded in breaking down the door, then I would have to help them fight the infected.

The vigorous pounding was impossible to ignore. But I couldn't risk letting anyone inside. The door was the only way in and out of the place. I didn't want to be trapped in there.

Then the pounding stopped. The sounds of screaming and footsteps were moving away from the door. I quickly ran back to the windows. The guys were now running across the field, heading north, with the infected still chasing them. Relieved, I watched as the group moved farther and farther away. But I did feel bad for those five guys. They seemed to be in phenomenal shape, and I hoped they could stay ahead of the infected, who were relentlessly pursuing them.

To my dismay, a small group of infected appeared after everyone had left. They stopped short of going into the field. It seemed they had been attracted by the noise. But the others were too far away, and they'd lost sight of them. I held my breath as they sniffed the air. My heart nearly stopped when I noticed that they were heading toward the service door.

The scratching sounds at the door sent me into a panic mode. *Do they know we're in here?* I wondered. *Maybe they are intrigued by the smell of the others being here earlier?* I knew they were not going to leave anytime soon. And with them being out there, more were sure to follow. The only option now was to kill them. But to do that, I had to let them inside!

As I hesitated by the door, my body started to shake. I had neither the strength nor the courage to open the door. I wished I could use the shotgun—that would be a lot easier. But nothing I'd done so far had been easy!

Suddenly, more gunshots rang out from afar. I went back to the windows and looked outside. The group had stopped at the edge of the field, next to the woods. My heart sank for those poor guys. The infected had probably caught up to them. I just hoped they had a chance to shoot themselves before getting ripped apart and devoured.

Looking back toward the service door, I breathed a huge sigh of relief. The infected had left and were now heading in the direction of the gunfire. But it wouldn't be long before another group showed up. We had to leave or we won't get another chance!

I ran back to the office and began gathering up my things. "We have to leave, Kara!"

"You mean right now?"

"Yes! We have to go now or we'll be trapped in here!"

We made it to the clubhouse at the southwest corner of the field. The trees along the side of the building concealed us all the way to the rear. I took a deep breath and held it as I gazed at the huge open grass field. We would have to run across that damn field with no trees, no bushes—nothing to use as cover.

Although I dreaded it, I knew Kara and I might get separated again. I wanted her to continue to South Park without me if that happened. I didn't want her to be running around looking for me. I had to let her know what I was planning to do.

"Kara, listen to me very closely," I said. "River Road is beyond that field. If we get separated again, then you continue to the road. Once you get there, go down to the woods. There's a small trail down there. If you follow the trail and keep going south, you'll eventually get to South Park. Once you get there, go to the marina. I'll be waiting for you over there."

"What's going to happen to us?" she inquired, panicking. "You're talking as if you know something bad is going to happen."

"Nothing bad is going to happen," I assured her. "I'm just letting you know what I'm going to be doing. You go to South Park in case we get separated again. Got it?"

"What's at South Park?"

"The way out of this city."

The sprint across the vast, open field pushed my mental and physical endurance to its limits. Everything was a blur halfway into the run. I didn't remember getting down to the road or crossing it. All I could recall was that we were now hiding behind a large tree. And I was lying on the ground, panting and gasping for air.

Everything was still spinning around me. I had to close my eyes to avoid becoming too dizzy. My body was rapidly succumbing to exhaustion. "Are you all right?" Kara asked with a worried look.

"I'm just so tired," I mumbled. "Wake me up in ten minutes, Kara."

I felt a tug on my arm, and I slowly opened my eyes to Kara's smiling face. "How long was I out?" I asked.

"About two hours," she replied.

"What?" I slowly sat up. "Why didn't you wake me up?"

"I tried to," she explained, "but you were out cold."

"Damn, I've never had that happen to me before," I said softly.

I was concerned about my body shutting down like that. It was bewildering. But as I thought about it, I knew it was probably from the tremendous amount of stress and lack of sleep. *I have to be more careful from now on,* I said to myself. *If my body shuts down like that again, I could be in grave danger.*

The small dirt path that we were on took us into some of the most heavily wooded areas inside Kasey Park. I felt safe among the trees and thick vegetation. The chirping of the birds and the wonderful insect melodies were something that I hadn't heard for such a long time. And for the first time in what seemed like forever, I was able to breathe in fresh air without the stench of death coming along with it.

We walked from a forest filled with darkness out to a small field. The field was quiet, but the beauty was stunning. The small creek that ran down the middle of the field was a perfect addition to the picturesque scene. Blue and yellow dragonflies flew above the water like playful fairies. My spirit was uplifted as I basked in the sweet serenity.

After an hour or so, we made it to the paved trail. Our pace had quickened, and we were making more progress now. I was getting more optimistic about getting to Hidden Trails Park well before nightfall. My only concern now was to look for a place in or around the park for us to spend the night.

It didn't take long before Bobby's old van occurred to me. Bobby had been living out of his van for the past two years. He usually moved from park to park to avoid getting complaints from citizens. His last known location was at Hidden Trails Park. *His van should be in the woods down by the river,* I remembered. He also hid a spare key to his van behind the right front tire. His reason for doing that was that if there was a complaint about his van, one of his park ranger buddies could use the key and move the van elsewhere.

Although I had often made light of the fact that Bobby lived in his van, I did feel bad for him. *We all make mistakes at some point in our life,* I told myself. But Bobby's mistakes cost him everything.

Bobby was married for six years and had four kids with his wife. Two years back, Bobby had gone to a bachelor party and got shitfaced drunk. He took a dare and had sex with Lacy, the dwarf stripper at the party. His wife eventually found out about it. She might have been able to forgive him if he had cheated on her with someone else. But apparently having sex with a dwarf was just too much of an insult to her. She kicked him out of the house.

I used to think that Bobby would be able to save up a lot of money. He was living out of his van and had no expenses. But after finding out how much he was paying for child support, I knew he was going to be living out of his van way beyond his retirement.

Three hours later, we finally made it to the outskirts of Hidden Trails Park. I was pretty content with the idea of staying inside Bobby's van. But as we approached the area where the van was supposed to be, I was devastated: it wasn't there! Just then I remembered Bobby had told me the commander had found out about his van two months earlier. He was ordered to relocate. The last I heard he was staying somewhere at Meyers Park, inside the Central Sector.

Now I was getting desperate. It was late in the afternoon, and I couldn't think of another place to stay. We would have to keep going until something else came up.

Another mile down the trail, I finally came up with another idea. The towering, rocky cliffs of Wendy's Peak got me thinking: *There's a small cave inside those cliffs.* The cave was about fifty feet from the bottom of the cliffs. The steep incline would make it difficult for the infected, especially the slow movers, to climb up to it. Although I'd never been inside, I remembered being on patrol and standing at the bottom of the cliffs, yelling up to the drunks in there to move along.

The sun was creeping down toward the horizon as we climbed toward the cliffs. It seemed like perfect timing. As I gazed steadily up at the steep, rocky terrain several hundred feet above to the huge overlook at the top, I couldn't help thinking about the eerie history of the place. Wendy's Peak was named after a woman named Wendy Fine. She was murdered at the top of the cliff, and then her body was thrown off to make it look like a suicide. People said that every month when the moon is full, the ghost of Wendy Fine walks the trail. And anyone who encountered her would eventually jump off the cliff to join her.

I didn't know if that urban legend was true or not. But Wendy's Peak was infamous for its high number of suicides. As a Hmong person, I had grown up with the belief that the spirits were always among us—coexisting with us. Under normal circumstances I would never want to be out along the cliffs at night. *And tonight is a full moon!* I remembered, trembling slightly. *But then, there are worse things out here tonight than Wendy.*

CHAPTER 23

The small entrance to the cave could be easily concealed with tree branches and vegetation. The short, narrow passage was wide enough for only one person at a time to squeeze through. The rocky enclosure had enough room for maybe eight people. The strong smell of booze and urine still lingered. The damp dirt floor was littered with beer cans, bottles, newspapers, and other garbage.

Despite the odors and the garbage, I felt content and safe in the cave. The only thing that was bothering me was the pesky biting flies and mosquitos. I thought I could endure it at first. But after a while, it was getting irritating and uncomfortable. I had to do something or it would be driving me crazy throughout the night.

Although Kara strongly objected to the idea, I had to leave the cave. My plan was to make a small fire to keep the bugs away. I wanted to find a log that was light enough to carry back to the cave. And it would also have to be big enough to burn through the night.

I left the cave and headed down to the woods. The shotgun and my backpack were back at the cave. I was going to bring back some firewood, and there would be too much to carry if I brought everything with me.

A patch of deadfalls about thirty yards away caught my eyes—the dry wood would be ideal for a fire. A small, worn-down path seemed to lead to the tangled mass of dead wood, and I wanted to take the path instead of bushwhacking through the thick vegetation.

The walk along the path was pleasant and soothing, and the stillness around me was comforting and reassuring. I was nearing the deadfalls when a loud snap from the woods quickly caught my attention. The next thing I remembered seeing was the sky underneath my feet and the ground above my head. I was caught in a trap, dangling upside down in mid-air! A noose was wrapped around my left ankle, getting tighter each time I struggled.

As I hung there in mid-air, I couldn't help but be slightly amused. This small path must have been a game trail, and there might still be deer and other small animals inside the woods. Someone obviously set the trap to snag something to eat. *How can I be mad at them?* I asked myself. *They're probably starving, too.*

I tried reaching for the rope but couldn't even touch my ankle. The machete was on the ground and far away from my reach. I knew I was vulnerable. I had to call for Kara! Obviously my loud calls would also be heard by any infected who were in the area. But I had no other choice—I just hoped she could reach me before the infected did.

Before too long, Kara showed up. She smiled after seeing me. "What happened to you?" she asked, giggling.

"There's no time to explain," I said, trying to be serious. "You need to cut me down. There must be a tree somewhere that the end of this rope was tied to. Find it and cut the rope."

"You look good like this," she joked. After seeing that I wasn't amused, she quickly did a turnabout. "How do I know where to find it?" she asked, as if she was completely incompetent.

"Just follow this rope with your eyes, Kara," I said, annoyed.

"Found it!" she excitedly called out a minute later. I slowly turned around and saw her standing by a patch of trees about twenty-five yards away. "Good! Now come back and get the machete!"

After she came back, I felt the need to warn her. "Now, before you cut the rope, I need you to grab on to it. Then cut it slowly with one hand as you hold on to it with the other, OK? If you let go of the rope, then I will hit the ground really hard. Just slowly release the rope until I reach the ground. Got it?"

"I know that," she said sarcastically as she walked away. She gave me a look that made me feel bad. I didn't want her to think that she was completely incompetent. But I also didn't want to break my back from the fall.

I was anticipating a hard, painful drop to the ground. But it never came. I couldn't feel even the slightest touch or vibration on the rope.

After what seemed like a whole minute, I slowly spun myself in the direction of the trees, where Kara had walked. To my dismay, she wasn't there. It seemed she had vanished. "Kara?" I called. "Kara! Where are you?"

The silence was beginning to concern me now. Something must have happened to her! "Kara!" I called again. But there was still no response.

I tried reaching up for the rope several more times, but still to no avail. Then a scream rang out, but it was quickly muffled. I spun around to the trees again. My eyes widened as I saw three men coming out of the woods with Kara. One of them was holding on to her, covering her mouth with his hand. *They must have been hiding there the whole time!* I thought. They were probably waiting to see how many of us there were before they showed themselves.

I sighed deeply as they approached me. Despite my being upside down, I recognized who they were—the crazy Madsen brothers! Donald was the oldest and the leader of their fucked-up group, Casper was the middle brother, and Keith was the youngest. Keith was also a complete moron with the attention span of a flea.

The Madsens lived in the Central Sector and wreaked havoc throughout their neighborhood. They occasionally crossed over to the Western Sector, but they almost never ventured beyond Orbit Parkway. It was definitely a huge surprise to see them this far away from the shithole they called home.

I quickly pulled out my pistol, but I had to drop it after seeing that Keith had placed a small knife to Kara's throat. Donald was holding my machete, which he'd taken from Kara.

"Look who we got here, Donnie," Casper said. "We snagged ourselves a cop." He picked up my gun and handed it over to Donald.

I was hoping that Keith wouldn't recognize me. I had given him a well-deserved ass whooping a few months back for beating up an elderly couple on Orbit Parkway. I tried turning my face from him, but it was too late. That tiny brain of his was already set in motion as he gazed intently at me.

"Hey, I remember *you!*" Keith suddenly said as he released Kara and ran up to me. "*You're that cop that beat me up!*"

He punched me in the chest and immediately screamed in pain. The idiot had hit me square on the small metal plate in front of my ballistic vest. I pretended to be gasping for air to satisfy him. I didn't want him to hit me again.

Still holding his hand, Keith turned to Donald and pleaded, "I want to kill him, Donnie! I want to cut his belly open and show him his guts before he dies!"

"Easy now, Keith," Donald said calmly. Then he turned to me and gave me a look that instantly sent a chill through my body. "We're going to have a lot of fun with him first," he said. "Then, I'll let you kill him."

I knew Donald was speaking more to me than to Keith. I closed my eyes and took a deep breath. *These guys are probably going to torture me to death*, I thought. *And they will probably do far worse to Kara.*

Although my mind was fixated on the thought of my demise, I wasn't ready to accept it yet. I had just spotted the small black handle of the boot knife that was strapped around my right ankle. I slowly moved my right leg and wrapped my foot behind my left calf so they wouldn't see it. Now I still had a chance. They had taken my weapons, but not all of them. I was fortunate that the noose was around my left ankle. I could still bend my right foot down to retrieve the knife. All I had to do was try to come up with something to divert their attention from me.

I knew I had to be quick and say something to Donald before they tied me up. I had to get his attention and stroke his ego. After taking a deep breath, I began: "If I'm going to die anyway, Donald, may I first ask you a question?"

A sinister grin flashed across his face. "Go ahead, *Officer*," he replied. "Ask me anything you want."

"What is the purpose for the trap?" I inquired. "Are they for humans or zombies?""

He raised a brow as if he was surprised that I'd figured it out. "The zombies are too dumb," he replied. Then with a sadistic smirk, he added, "It feels so good to be God!"

I knew what he meant by that. They had probably done this to a lot of people already. It was unfortunate that it was now my and Kara's turn.

I knew what I had to do. Donald was the brains of the group—his brothers would follow him and do whatever he wanted them to do. He was a smart guy, but he did have a flaw that I could exploit. He was one of those sick, sadistic assholes who loved to torment his victims by rendering them helpless, then performing his criminal acts in front of them to get his high. If I could get him to do that to me, then I might be able to distract their attention away from me. But it was going to be at Kara's expense!

I tried to be as pathetically woeful as I could while I pleaded to Donald, "Do whatever you want to me, but please let the girl go." I wanted to let him know how precious Kara was to me, and that I couldn't bear to see her get hurt. His eyes were getting wider with each plea. I could tell that it was feeding his ego even more.

Donald laughed. "Truthfully, we're going to kill your little girlfriend too," he said. "But we're not going to kill her yet. We'll kill her in a few days when we're tired of her."

That's what I was waiting to hear. Now it was time for the bait. "You sick fuck!" I shouted as I swung my fists wildly at him. "You better not hurt her, or I'll kill you! I'll kill you!"

Donald continued laughing. "You hang in there, hero, and enjoy the show," he said. Then he turned to Kara. "Here's a preview of what we'll be doing to her."

He had taken the bait! As much as I dreaded it, I knew they were planning to rape Kara. I just hoped they didn't do it right in front of me—it would be too agonizing to watch. Then this whole act would have been a complete failure.

I was relieved when Donald gave Keith my machete and made him stay with me while Donald and Casper dragged Kara to a small clearing about twenty yards away. Kara was putting up a vigorous fight. But I knew she would soon be overpowered by the both of them.

I wanted to retrieve my knife right away, but Keith was still with me. He was holding my machete, and I didn't want him to strike at me with it. I also didn't want his attention to be focused on me. But I knew I would get my chance soon. He was already distracted as he kept glancing over at his brothers.

As I expected, Keith's attention was shifting. He was getting bored staying with me, so he began moving toward his brothers. Still, he continued to glance over at me every few seconds. I couldn't go for the knife yet.

Finally Keith was only a few yards from his brothers. He had forgotten about me and began cheering them on. I finally had my chance. Slowly, I bent toward my right foot to retrieve the knife from my ankle.

Again and again I tried reaching for the rope, but I couldn't quite get to it. I couldn't even touch my ankle, let alone the rope. After several failed attempts, I was getting extremely desperate. Kara was being attacked, and I couldn't do anything about it. *I have to try harder!* I told myself. *For her sake, I have to do this!* With every ounce of strength I had left, I pushed myself as hard as I could. Finally, I was able to grab hold of my ankle. Then I quickly cut the rope.

The fall was excruciatingly painful. My lungs were emptied, leaving me panting and gasping. My entire body felt numb, and I could barely move. *If those guys see me now, I won't be able to defend myself.*

After a few moments, I was able to breathe normally again. My strength was also returning. I quickly rolled over on my belly and glanced over at the Madsens. I was fortunate that the crash hadn't alerted those idiots to me. Keith was making too much noise calling out, and his brothers were too focused on Kara. They were oblivious to their surroundings. *Now it's going to be their turn! They're going to die today!*

With my knife in my hand, I snuck up to Keith and stood quietly behind him. He was still holding my machete, and I didn't want him to strike at me while I attacked him. I wanted to cover his mouth, stab him, and hold on to the machete, but then I realized I would need four arms to do that!

Just when I thought I was going to have to take the risk, Keith helped me out. He dropped the machete and began clapping his hands, laughing loudly at what was transpiring in front of him. Kara had kicked Donald in the face while he was pulling her pants off. *Thank God he hasn't raped her yet,* I realized, feeling relieved. *And he's not going to get that chance now!*

I quickly covered Keith's mouth and thrust the knife deep into his throat. Warm gushes of blood began to spew out as I moved the knife across his throat, slicing through his esophagus. He was gagging and his body began to shake. I wanted to hold on to him until he stopped moving. *But Kara is about to be raped. I have to save her now!* Although Keith was still alive, he was incapacitated and done for. I carefully placed him on the ground. Taking the machete, I quietly snuck up to his brothers, who were solely focused on Kara.

Casper was crouching over Kara's head, pinning her arms to the ground with his knees while smothering her mouth with his hands. Donald had his pants down, exposing his erect penis. He had ripped off Kara's panties. But she was still kicking out at him. He was having trouble prying her legs apart.

I struck sideways at Casper with the machete, taking off the top half of his head. He instantly went limp and fell on top of Kara. Donald was startled by it and quickly looked up. The bottom of my foot was the only thing he saw before he passed out.

I had never kicked anyone as hard as I kicked Donald. I surprised myself by sending him flying backward several feet. He was definitely knocked out for a moment as he lay motionless on the ground.

I ran up to him and kicked him several times in the chest. "Get up, asshole!" I shouted. "Get on your fucking knees!"

Donald slowly got to his knees. He was still dazed from the blow and was trying to figure out what had happened. Then, seeing the bloody machete displayed in front of his face, he began to cry.

I was taken aback—amazed at the complete turnaround. Here was this tough, sadistic asshole, now cowering and crying like a baby.

Noticing that he was moving his right hand down to his waist while pleading for his life, I followed his gaze: The butt end of my gun was peeking out of his waistline. I immediately struck down at his arm, and he let out a high-pitched scream. Glancing down, I saw that his forearm was dangling from his elbow by a small strip of skin.

"Please! Don't kill me!" he cried.

I had no intention of sparing his pathetic life. "You're going to die, motherfucker!" I shouted. "You're going to join your fucking brothers!"

As I raised the machete to strike him again, I paused when I spotted movement in front of me. Several infected were coming out of the woods! Then I heard laughter from Donald. He saw my facial expression, and he took a look behind him, too.

"Now you're going to die too," he said, taunting me.

The infected were about thirty yards away. I still had time to get back to the cave. *I want to kill Donald before I go, I told myself. But why should he deserve a merciful death? His death should be excruciating!*

"You're going to die first," I said, gazing down at him. "You're going to die screaming as they rip you apart."

With a swift kick to his face, I sent him back to the ground. Then I grabbed my gun from him and left him there—conscious but dazed and helpless, blood spewing from his arm.

Kara was sitting on the ground, dazed. Her pants were lying next to her. She didn't seem to notice that she was naked from the waist down. She simply stared at me, not registering what I was saying. Her body was trembling and unresponsive to my touch.

"Kara!" I shouted, slapping her on the shoulder. "Snap out of it!"

She quickly twitched as if I'd startled her. Then she looked up at me.

"We have to get back to the cave!" I said.

After pulling her up, I told her to run to the cave. I didn't care if she was still naked at that point—we didn't have time for her to put her pants on. I picked up her pants and followed after her.

After concealing the cave entrance with tree branches, I went inside and took out all of the boxes of shotgun shells and placed them on the ground in front of me. With my shotgun loaded to full capacity, I sat in the middle of the enclosure, anxiously waiting for something to come bursting through the entrance.

Kara was sitting a few feet behind me. She was still in shock from the ordeal. I handed her pants over to her. "Put them on," I said quietly.

As the seconds turned to minutes, and the minutes turned to an hour, my mind was still reeling with anticipation. I could still hear crackling noises from the branches and twigs outside. The infected hadn't made it up to the cave yet, but they were still lurking about. The shotgun was getting heavier and heavier, but I couldn't put it down. My tired, beat-up body was begging to rest. But I refused. *I won't rest until the night is over*, I steadfastly told myself. *We might not make it through the night. Our fate is in God's hands now.*

It wasn't until three hours later that the noises finally dissipated. My anxiety was at a more manageable level, and I welcomed the sound of silence. Suddenly, I felt a pair of trembling hands slowly reaching around me, grasping together in front of my chest.

"How are you holding out so far?" I asked Kara as she slowly leaned her head against my back. I was trying to be as comforting as I could.

"I'm still so scared," she whispered faintly.

"You're safe now. Try and get some sleep. I'll watch over you tonight."

"Thank you for watching over me every night," she said.

CHAPTER 24

The invigorating rays of the sun slowly pierced through the branches to abolish the darkness inside our rocky enclosure. I could feel my mind relaxing and my heart beginning to settle. I closed my eyes and took a deep breath. Even though the odor of booze and urine inside the cave seemed to be more pungent in the cool morning air, I somehow found it sweet and refreshing. The multiple mosquito bites that I'd sustained throughout the night were itchy and irritating, yet at the same time soothing. Things that I had taken for granted for so long—being able to see, smell, and touch—were now things I appreciated and was willing to fight vigorously for.

My back ached from leaning against the hard rocks all night. But that was not the worst of it. It seemed that every injury I had ever sustained had come back to torment me as well.

My tired body was begging to rest, and my eyes couldn't stay open. Still, I refused to give in. I couldn't risk another night in the cave. It was daylight now—we had to leave. We had to make as much progress as we could before it got dark again.

Kara was still sleeping a few feet away. Her head was propped on her backpack. Her gentle snoring was comforting and reassuring. As I thought about what this gentle creature had been through, I couldn't help but feel sad for her. *What wrong has she done to be thrown into this hell with me?* I asked myself. *Does she have the mental fortitude to continue on?*

"Wake up, Kara," I said quietly, gently nudging her. "It's time to leave."

She slowly sat up. "I'm still so tired," she mumbled, rubbing her eyes.

"I know," I said. "I'm very tired too. But we have to leave now. We have to go as far as we can before it gets dark again."

• • •

As I stood at the entrance, I couldn't help but marvel at the scene below me. The cave was high enough that I could see over and across the long stretch of treetops down to the river. The beautiful morning sun was still trying its best to melt away the thick, heavy mists, emitting a spectacular hue across the valley. The chirping of birds and steady hum of insects added another level to the picturesque view. It was truly a serene moment. At that moment, I could understand why I had fought so hard to preserve the life I had.

I sighed deeply as I stared far beyond the valley and over the river to the Hiawatha side. Freedom was so close, yet I couldn't reach it. I wondered if there were people over there looking across the river at us. What would they say to us? Would they tell us to keep fighting? Or would they tell us that we are doomed, and that they are praying for our souls?

We made it down to the bottom and began bushwhacking. The deadfalls and thick undergrowth were extremely hard on my tired body. But I didn't want to be on the small path again. There might be more traps there. I didn't want to be caught in one of them again.

We came to the site where we had left the Madsen brothers. A large pool of blood, along with some bone fragments, was all that was left of them. Kara began panting and shaking. I quickly held on to her. "It's OK," I gently assured her. "They're gone now. It's a fitting end to those assholes."

We made it to the trail and continued on for a while. Then I spotted something inside a heavily wooded area about a hundred yards away from where we were. Through my binoculars, I could see a greenish tent amid the trees and shrubs, well camouflaged near the river. *The Madsens' camp!* I wanted to ignore it and continue on, but we were very low on food. We needed to go scavenge for whatever was inside that tent.

Although Kara strongly objected to the idea, I insisted. For the Madsens to be surviving as long as they had, they'd probably stashed away plenty of food inside that tent. And there was no telling how long it was going to take us to get to South Park. I wasn't going to waste the opportunity.

I found a small path behind some tall bushes that seemed to lead to the tent. Knowing that the Madsens had probably set more traps in or around the path, I wanted Kara to stay at the trail. But the thought of the infected still somewhere inside these woods was too overwhelming for me to leave her behind.

"Stay behind me and step only where I've stepped," I said.

We were only twenty yards down the path when I spotted the first trap. It was another spring snare. I initially wanted to clear it and make it safe for us. But then an idea came to me: *This trap could be useful if the infected follow us down here.* I left it alone and continued on.

After a few more yards I spotted several more traps like the first one. Again, I decided to leave them and carefully walk around them instead.

Inching further down the path, I spotted a different type of trap. There were hundreds of wooden spikes hidden inside the bushes along the path. I dropped down to the ground and attempted to look for a triggering mechanism. Slowly crawling on my hands and knees, I finally found what I was looking for: Several fishing lines were strung across the path, approximately three feet apart from each other and about six inches off the ground.

I was amazed at the level of ingenuity the Madsens had put into their work. Using the fishing lines was a brilliant idea. I could barely see them while on my hands and knees. They were nearly impossible to spot if a person was just casually walking down the path. I was almost tempted to set off one of them just to see what it would do. But I knew that wouldn't end pleasantly.

After carefully maneuvering past the last trap, we finally reached the tent. The patches of dry, flaky tree saplings and dead vegetation that were plastered all over the tent were evidence that the Madsens had been staying in the area for quite a while. I couldn't help but wonder how much carnage they had caused thus far.

As I stood by the entrance to the tent, an eerie chill engulfed my body. I knew that all three Madsens were dead. But I couldn't stop the weird vibe from overtaking my senses. I felt as if someone was watching us.

I was hesitating to enter the tent now. Something gruesome or grotesque might be in there. I was even thinking about leaving. But we had just risked our lives to get there. We were going to leave with whatever I could scavenge from inside the tent. *Besides, I'd seen enough gruesome things already*, I told myself. *There's nothing in there that will faze me now.*

With the machete gripped tightly in my hand, I slowly entered the tent. What a freaking mess! But then, I remembered that the inside of the Madsen home in the Central Sector wasn't much better. The smell of cigarettes, booze, and body odor in the tent was overwhelming. Beer cans, cigarette butts, and piles of dirty clothes littered the floor. Several stained sleeping bags were spread out here and there. A large, medieval-style axe leaned against the wall behind the dirty pillows.

The southwest corner was where they stowed their food. Several cases of baked beans were stacked up, and a box of potato chips and a huge bag of smoked meat were on top of the beans. Knowing that the cans were going to be too heavy to carry inside our backpack, I took the potato chips and the meat with me.

Kara was outside, anxiously waiting for me. "There's nothing else inside except for these," I said, showing her the items.

She smiled after seeing the huge bag of meat. "Well, at least we'll have plenty of protein," she joked.

Suddenly, a strong gust of wind blew by us, bringing the familiar stench of death along with it. I immediately jumped into a defensive stance and quickly scanned our surroundings. The source of the smell hadn't shown up yet. We had to leave before it did!

"Let's get out of here," I whispered to Kara.

As we took a couple steps away from the tent, a loud moan quickly alerted me and I jumped back into a defensive stance again. The source of the smell had arrived! Now I had a dilemma. I knew we couldn't run across the path, and there was no way we could get by the traps without setting one of them off. *It was a dumb idea not to clear the traps earlier!* I scolded myself. *Now we have to stay here and fight!*

A minute went by, and still no one had appeared. The moans continued, but they were getting faint. As I tuned my ear intently on the sound, I thought I heard someone calling for help!

"Stay here," I whispered to Kara.

The voice was calling from the woods behind the tent. But as I made my way around, the voice stopped. The dense vegetation was impenetrable, and I couldn't pinpoint where it was coming from. Then, it called again. It was very weak and barely audible, but it was definitely someone calling for help.

A thick patch of bushes about twenty yards away grabbed my attention. I had no idea what was behind those bushes. But I knew that an infected shouldn't be able to speak.

As I made my way around the bushes to a clearing behind them, I shielded my eyes from the horrendous sight before me. A nude woman was lying on the ground. Her arms and legs were spread apart and tied to wooden posts at each end. Her face was badly bruised, as if she had been used for a punching bag. A deep laceration spread across her left cheek. The bruises on her neck were consistent with choke marks. Dozens of small cuts and burn marks were etched all over her body. I had to glance away when I noticed that one of her breasts was considerably larger than the other. Then I noticed a huge laceration below her right breast. *My God!* I said to myself. *The Madsens were trying to perform breast augmentation on her!*

I didn't care if she was an infected or a human. No one deserved to be tortured that way! I reached out a hand to touch her shoulder. The warmth confirmed that she was definitely human. I was almost in tears now as I thought about the hell that she had been through. I couldn't imagine the amount of pain that she had been forced to endure!

As I gazed at the poor woman, my breathing suddenly became rapid and unsteady. An intense feeling of rage was surging from deep within me, making its way up to my throat. My body shook as I tried to keep the rage from spilling out of my mouth. Finally, I couldn't hold it in any longer.

"*FUCKING MADSENS!*" I screamed at the top of my lungs. "Burn in hell, you fucking bastards!"

The woman must have heard me. She slowly opened her eyes. Then she began to tremble. Her quivering mouth was struggling to say something to me. She was terrified and was pleading for me not to hurt her.

I knelt down and gently caressed her mangled cheek. "Shhh… I'm not going to hurt you," I assured her as warmly as I could. "I'm here to help."

I quickly cut off the ropes that were binding her extremities. Then I called to Kara to bring a sleeping bag from inside the tent. As I held the woman in my arms, a cruel reality hit me like a punch in the gut. I was reminded of what Donald Madsen said to me the previous night. Kara would have suffered the same fate as well.

"What…what happened to her?" Kara asked, horrified by the sight of the woman.

"She's hurt, and she needs our help," I said as I wrapped the sleeping bag around the woman. "We'll keep her warm and try to find something to treat her injuries."

"Who did this to her?"

"Those assholes from yesterday did this to her. I'm glad they're all dead. I'm glad I killed them all!"

The woman began shaking more vigorously. I didn't know what else to do. So I continued holding her and tried my best to comfort her.

After a while, she stopped shaking. Then she began gasping for air like a fish out of water. I sighed deeply. I knew she was about to die.

I turned her face to direct her eyes to mine. She needed to find some comfort before she left.

"I'm sorry that this happened to you," I said softly. "I want you to know that the people that did this to you are dead now. I've killed them all." Reaching a hand to slowly caress her cheek, I quietly added, "You can go in peace now."

A few tears leaked out of her eyes. Then she slowly turned her face to gaze at a patch of clouds above us. A glimmer of joy flashed across her face, as if she already knew where she was going. Then she slowly closed her eyes. Her next breath never came.

Gently, I laid her on the ground. My heart was aching with an indescribable sorrow. But there was also a feeling of liberation: I would never be tormented by what I did to the Madsens. With their deaths, I'd brought closure for this woman and myself as well.

Kara was sitting by herself near a tree. I guessed she went there to deal with it in her own way. I couldn't imagine what was going on inside her head at that moment. *How long can she go on before she finally loses her sanity?* I wondered.

I went over and sat quietly with her for a long while. Finally, I reached over and pulled her toward me. "I'll never let this happen to you," I said softly, looking up at the sky.

Suddenly, I saw a huge object coming straight down at us. I immediately pushed Kara out of the way just as a large rock struck the ground between us, narrowly missing me by a few inches. I quickly rolled away a few times and then looked up. I couldn't believe my eyes—Donald Madsen was still alive! He was running at me with a huge axe in his hand. His right forearm was missing, but his left arm was still intact, holding the axe from the tent. I was bewildered: *How had he been able to escape the infected?*

"Run, Kara!" I yelled. She leaped to her feet and scurried away.

I noticed that my machete was still over at the tree and I began to panic. Donald was coming at me with the axe, and I was unarmed! Just as he was about to strike down at me, I rolled away, causing him to pause and refocus his aim. I waited until he was about to strike, and then I kicked him in the testicles. He winced and quickly backed away. I took the opportunity and ran for the machete.

As I held the machete in my hand, I felt an immense surge of energy pouring into my body, as if I had been transformed into a superhero! My body seemed so light, I felt I could glide across the field. The heavy machete felt like a plastic sword. Everything was in slow motion.

As I stared at Donald, I felt a sick, sadistic grin spreading across my face. All the rage that I'd felt earlier came rushing back to me. Yet I remained calm and collected. I was going to enjoy myself! I almost felt sorry for Donald now. He had no idea what I was about to do to him. Every ounce of pain that he and his brothers had inflicted on that woman, he would get in return. What an indescribable rush!

"You should have never shown yourself, asshole!" I shouted. "Now I'm going to take revenge for that woman! You're going to die very painfully! You will be screaming for days!"

Donald seemed unfazed by what I'd said to him. His eyes were still burning with intense hatred. He quickly ran up to me and swung the axe, but I jumped out of the way, and he missed again and again. I could tell by his awkward swing that I had chopped off his good arm. With only one arm, his handling of the heavy axe was unsteady and uncoordinated.

"Come on, *asshole*! You're not going to kill me like that! Swing *harder!*" I said, trying to provoke him to keep swinging until he tired himself out.

As he continued swinging, I kept moving from side to side, taunting him. He was getting frustrated and infuriated, and his swings were getting wilder.

Finally, he swung at me so hard that he lost his balance and fell to the ground. "Now it's my turn!" I yelled.

I struck the machete down toward his remaining arm, completely taking off his hand. After an agonizing scream, he began to plead for his life. He was vulnerable and completely at my mercy now. His crying almost enticed the humanity in me—I thought about chopping off his head and ending it all. But then, a quick death was not what I wanted for him. *This asshole has to pay for what he and his brothers did to that poor woman*, I told myself. *He is going to suffer excruciating pain.*

I stood over him and swung the machete down on one of his knees, nearly slicing it off. Then I hacked off the other knee. "Stop!" he cried. "Please, stop! Don't kill me!"

I knelt down to look into his eyes. Those demented and sadistic eyes that took so much pleasure in watching the horrific pain in his victim's faces were now pleading for mercy. I gave him a satisfied and sadistic smile. I wanted to give him the same smile he'd given to me the previous night—the smile he'd probably given to every one of his victims.

"You have your wish," I said. "I'm not going to kill you. But in a few days, you'll be begging for someone to come and kill you."

I left Donald to his slow, agonizing demise. I felt no guilt and no remorse for the unspeakable cruelty I'd inflicted onto another human being. It was like my conscience had abandoned me. There was no humanity left in me anymore. I was becoming a monster, and I knew it.

I found Kara hiding inside a thick patch of shrubs, shaking and unresponsive. It took me a few minutes to convince her to come out. I could tell from her facial expression that she couldn't bear it anymore. I reached out and held her tightly.

"It's all over," I said, gently. "Everything is over now."

As we walked back to the tent, I felt weak and lethargic. My hands still had the blood of the Madsen brothers on them. I needed to wash them off. I wanted to wash away the memories of the Madsens and never think about them again.

I went over to the river and crouched down. As I washed my hands, a thundering sound rattled my ears. Then my body immediately flew backward and landed on the ground. I felt like I had been struck by a car. My chest was in tremendous pain, and I couldn't breathe. *Did I just get shot?* I asked myself. I quickly rolled over onto my stomach and crawled toward a large log.

A hole was embedded in my shirt. The heavy metal plate on my vest, which I hated so much and often contemplated taking off, had just saved my life. Carefully, I peeked over the log. A boat was in the middle of the river. I was lucky that it was far away. If it had been any closer, the rifle round would have gone straight through me.

As the boat came within twenty yards of shore, a hail of gunshots rang out, striking the log and the ground around it. "Stay away from the river or we'll shoot you again!" shouted the voice on the megaphone.

"I'm *human*!" I shouted back.

"We don't care!" the voice replied. "If you come back to the river, we'll shoot you again!"

I looked over to Kara and was relieved to see her over at the tent. They hadn't shot her. Then suddenly, my eyes widened and my heart began to palpitate. Hundreds of infected were heading our way down the trail! I felt helpless. *What are we going to do?* I asked myself in desperation. *We're trapped between two hostiles, and there's no way out!*

My tongue was tied, and I couldn't yell a single word to Kara. So I got up and ran over to her. I grabbed the shotgun and our backpacks, and tried pulling her toward the river. But she resisted. "What are you doing?" she asked.

I cleared my throat. "Come with me," I said hurriedly. "Just come with me."

Confused, she tried to stop me again. "But they don't want us down by the river," she said. "They're going to shoot us!"

I didn't have time to explain. So I simply said to her, "Look behind you." She turned and screamed as she saw the infected.

I knew we wouldn't be able to outrun the infected through the woods—there were just too many deadfalls hindering us. I had to get back to the log and make my stance from there. At this point, I didn't care if the military shot us. I was actually hoping for it! At least we'd have a merciful death!

We crouched behind the log with our backs toward the river. I was waiting and hoping for a hail of bullets to pierce my back. But it didn't happen. The boat was still there, but there was not a single word coming from the megaphone now. I guessed the military was going to stand idle and watch us struggle to survive. If that's what they wanted to see, then I would give it to them! They would see how the people of this city struggled every day just to stay alive!

I took out the boxes of shells and placed them on the log. My shotgun was still loaded to full capacity. "Keep your head down, Kara! I'm going to kill everything that comes this way!"

The first wave of infected were caught in the snare traps and sent dangling in mid-air. Then I wondered about the trap with spikes: *What kind of carnage would that inflict?* Within seconds, my curiosity was satisfied as roll upon roll of spikes sprung out from the bushes, impaling their bodies, mangling and killing every one of them.

The traps did what they were supposed to do. They had stopped some of the infected. But the bulk of the infected were still coming. There was nothing else up there to stop them. Now it was going to be my turn. And hopefully, the military would shoot us when I ran out of ammunition.

I waited until the infected grouped together. Then I began to unload. Wave after wave they fell, but still more came. I continued shooting until the first box of shells was gone.

I was just about to reload when I heard several steady streams of gunshots coming from the boat. Thinking that the soldiers were shooting at us now, I put my shotgun down and closed my eyes as I anticipated a hard, painful impact to my back. But it didn't come. I opened my eyes and noticed that the shots were flying past me and hitting the infected. I quickly crouched down and covered Kara with my body. I guessed the military had seen what they wanted to see. My desperate fight for survival had compelled them to help.

• • •

When the shooting finally stopped, I raised my head to look at the woods. Fallen bodies were littered everywhere. A few infected were still alive, but their bodies were so badly mangled that they were unable to crawl over to us.

I turned to the river. The boat was leaving. I stood and held my hands up over my head as I approached the river. I wanted so desperately for them to take us. I even waded into the river. But they simply ignored me and drove away.

"Stay away from the river!" the voice said. "This is your last warning!"

CHAPTER 25

I knew that going back to the trail was no longer an option. We had to continue on through the woods. But after a few minutes of bushwhacking, I realized that it would probably take us all day just to get halfway to Asbury Park. I wanted so badly to be at the river's edge and follow the shoreline. But I knew that the military would not be so forgiving the next time.

The more I thought about our situation, the more depressed I became. Not only were we in constant fear of the infected, but we would have to contend with other humans as well. Everyone was in survival mode now. They would kill us for our supplies. As much as I dreaded it, I knew in my heart that I would have to kill some more humans along the way.

We hadn't gone far when my nose caught a whiff of the familiar stench of death. I instantly went on high alert and told Kara to hide. The woods were quiet. The rattling of the leaves on the trees was the only detectable sound.

The smell was getting more potent as I moved closer to a small clearing behind a patch of bushes. When I made it over there, I realized that I'd finally discovered the source of the smell that had accompanied the wind earlier when I was at the tent. The horror displayed before me left me stunned and speechless. Not that I wasn't used to seeing carnage. But this was beyond comprehension.

There must have been at least fifteen mutilated corpses inside a large pit behind the bushes. Judging from the various stages of decomposition, I could tell that the Madsens had been killing people for a while. What disturbed me most was that all the corpses had their heads and extremities chopped off. *Why did those assholes do that?* I wondered, scratching my head. *For what purpose?*

As I pondered the missing heads and limbs, the answer to my

question came to me at a fire pit about fifteen yards to the west. There must have been ten ragged, decomposing heads impaled on individual poles. The poles formed a circle together, surrounding the fire pit like some sort of demonic ritual. *It wouldn't be a huge surprise to me if those sick assholes were devil worshipers.*

When I came upon a large bloodstained log to the south of the fire pit, I started to make sense of it. Behind the log was pile of bones. Several long strips of meats were still hanging on a pole that was leaning against the log. I just couldn't believe it. But my suspicions were confirmed.

I tried to conceal my emotions as I walked back to Kara. "What happened over there?" she asked. "What did you see?"

"Just a couple of dead infected," I replied nonchalantly as I went to the bag of meat and quickly threw it in the woods.

"*Hey!* What are you *doing?*" she asked. "We need that food!"

"No, we don't," I replied. I had no intention of telling her that the meat was from the victims of the Madsens.

After an hour of bushwhacking, we only managed to gain about two hundred yards. I could still see the Madsens' tent from where we were. I was getting increasingly angry, and I didn't know why. Maybe I was frustrated by the slow progression. But I was also frustrated and pissed off at everything that was happening to us. It seemed there was always something hindering us every step of the way. And my mind was constantly plagued with questions that I had no answers for.

After a while of letting my frustrations run rampant, I was at a point where I wanted to look for a beautiful patch of land and just end my miseries right then and there. *I'm ready to give up!* I told myself. *There's no point in fighting for this life when I'm going to eventually lose it anyway. Why prolong this misery?*

But as I looked at the young woman beside me, I couldn't help but keep pressing forward. I thought of all she had been through, yet she still had the mental fortitude to keep trying. She still believed in me. She still had hope that I would get her home to her family. *I can't give up on her now! I have to keep trying!*

A few hours later, we finally made it out of the woods. The paved trail was cleared, and we started to make progress. My mind began to settle and my heart was filled with glimmers of hope.

A mile into the walk, the Pine Street Bridge finally came to view. What a magnificent sight! Starting from the cliff above, the bridge extended far beyond the valley, over the river and to the Hiawatha side. A mist from the river made its way up, creating a puff of cloud underneath the bridge, simulating a walkway in the heavens. My eyes lit up. My pace quickened. There was a deep urge within me to be over there.

Suddenly, a hail of gunshots rang out, killing all of my jubilation. "Take cover!" I shouted. We both ran to the embankment and hid behind a large tree.

I had no idea what was happening up ahead, but I knew that the gunshots meant that humans were out and about. Up until the Madsen brothers, I had welcomed the company of other human beings. But now, I feared humans even more than the infected. *Humans have the ability to think. They are also far more malicious!*

After a few minutes of silence and no one appearing, I was getting curious as to what was happening up ahead. I needed to find out. Our destination lay beyond that bridge.

"Wait here," I whispered to Kara. "I have to go check."

"Please don't go," she quickly pleaded.

"Don't worry. I'm not going far," I assured her. "I'm just going to go a little ways. I want to find out what is happening at the bridge."

I went back to the trail and walked until I lost my nerve and couldn't venture any farther. Knowing how cunning humans are, I feared I might walk into an ambush. So that was as far as I wanted to go.

As I started back, I heard the gunshots again. This time, they were coming from the top of the bridge. From where I was at, I couldn't see that far up. Then, an idea came to me as I saw Kara standing behind the tall, old tree. That tree was almost halfway up the embankment. And from there, its height was about level with the bridge. If I climbed to the top of that tree, I would have a view of the commotion on the bridge.

"What's happening over there?" Kara asked as I approached her. "What did you see?"

"Nothing," I replied softly as I took off my backpack and rummaged through it for the binoculars.

"What are you doing?"

"I'm going to climb this tree to find out what's happening on the bridge."

The climb was extremely difficult because I was deathly afraid of heights. Halfway through the climb, my body already had begun to tense up. My breathing was rapid and unsteady, and my equilibrium was off. I felt as if I was going to fall. I closed my eyes and kept climbing until I was almost at the top. Wrapping my legs around a large branch, I brought the binoculars to my eyes.

On the bridge, in front of the massive concrete wall, were piles of bodies. It was nothing new to me; I'd certainly seen things like that before. Noticing that there were no soldiers on top of the wall, I looked beyond it. A pile of bodies was behind the wall. The mountain of barbed wire and barricades fifteen yards behind the wall held more twisted bodies. It seemed as if the soldiers had left the area. They were probably setting up defenses at the other end of the bridge.

The area underneath the bridge was occupied by a huge mob. They were standing at the edge of the river and seemed to be focusing their attention on something in the water. I looked in the direction they were looking and spotted two patrol boats about thirty yards off shore. It seemed to me that the infected were afraid to go into the water. I guessed the soldiers already knew that and didn't have to fire into the crowd. How I wanted so desperately for those soldiers to shoot the infected and clear the trail for us! But that was just wishful thinking. The soldiers were content to just stay where they were.

I dreaded the idea of going back to the residential area to look for another way around. But I had no other option. Despite my disappointment, I could still find something positive from all of it. I was grateful for the early warning.

I was about to climb back down when I heard more gunshots again. I brought the binoculares back up to my eyes and scanned the crowd. Not noticing anything happening down there, I turned my attention to the top of the bridge and spotted a group of people moving farther down the bridge. I was astonished that they had made it past the giant wall and through the heavily fortified barricades.

At first I thought that they were infected. But when I noticed that they were carrying a large sign with them, I was elated that they were, indeed, humans. They even had a little girl with them!

I began focusing on the large, bold letters on the sign, which read: "WE ARE ALIVE! WE ARE HUMAN!"

The group was moving toward a giant dumpster that was placed in the middle of the bridge. Another heavily fortified barricade was twenty yards behind the dumpster. Several soldiers were behind the barricade with their rifles aimed at the group.

It was getting intense, and I was extremely worried for those people. As they got closer to the dumpster, the soldiers began firing shots at them. But the group seemed unfazed and kept pressing forward. I knew the shots were probably warning shots and if they continued, they were going to get killed.

Why won't they turn back? I wondered. *Why would they do this?* Maybe, like me earlier, those people had had enough? Maybe they didn't care about their lives anymore. They wanted a way out. It was going to be one way or the other.

"*Turn back! Please turn back!*" I pleaded desperately as more warning shots rang out.

The people were approaching the dumpster when several soldiers came out from behind the barricade. They were dressed in yellowish hazmat suits. Their rifles were drawn and aimed at the group.

My body was trembling. I couldn't help thinking that I was watching a prelude to an execution. The drama was too overwhelming, and I had to put the binoculars down.

After a moment with no shots being fired, I slowly brought the binoculars back up to my eyes. To my surprise, the soldiers were escorting the people to the barricade! I let out a huge sigh of relief and slowly lowered the binoculars. Those people were so lucky! They had made it! *Could I apply the same strategy?* I wondered. *Maybe we don't have to go all the way to South Park?*

I was about to climb down when I heard gunshots again. I quickly raised my binoculars again. I was horrified by what I saw! The soldiers were shooting at the people, gunning them down mercilessly. I almost passed out when I saw what they did next. *They even killed the little girl! Those inhuman bastards!* I lowered the binoculars. I couldn't bear to watch it anymore.

The rage inside me was so extreme that my body began to tense up and shake uncontrollably. I heard myself scream, though I had no idea what I said. I had never before witnessed such a cowardly and unconscionable act. I knew I would never forget it.

After the shooting stopped, I peered through the binoculars once more. The soldiers were gathering up the bodies and dragging them over to the dumpster. My heart sank into my stomach as I watched them tossing the bodies into the dumpster. Then they set the dumpster on fire. *That's enough! I've seen enough!*

I climbed back down to Kara. I tried to conceal my rage but my facial expression said it all. "You look so angry," she said. "What were you yelling about?"

Without a word, I just stared at the bridge for a long while. I was angry, all right! I was angry at the lack of compassion. I was angry at the total disregard for human life. I was angry at the lack of respect from those soldiers to be burning those bodies inside the dumpster like they were garbage. And what really made my blood boil was how they killed that little girl! Those soldiers were cowards! They were no different from the Madsen brothers. They all deserved to die!

"What happened up there?" Kara asked again.

"We have to find another way to the other side," I replied.

"What happened up there?" she persisted.

I took a deep breath and slowly let it out. I didn't want to snap at her. Then I calmly replied, "The military doesn't want anyone on the bridge. That's all."

CHAPTER 26

Kara and I made it to the Covington neighborhood, a quiet and peaceful area just north of the Asbury Park neighborhood. The houses in Covington were small but well maintained. I was always amazed each time I drove through it. It seemed as if the residents were trying to outdo each other for the best and most beautiful yard. The competition got even more intense during the wintertime, especially at Christmas when the residents decorated their houses and yards with thousands of Christmas lights and ornaments. When my children were young, I used to bring them to Covington at Christmastime to gawk at the magnificent decorations.

It was getting late into the afternoon. I knew that we had to find a place to stay for the night. Even though there were hundreds of houses to choose from, I couldn't seem to find anything suitable for what I needed. I wanted to be tactical and look for a house that could be easily defended from the inside.

After an hour, we finally came to a small house on Carter Avenue. The house was about mid-block between Chad and Virginia Streets. Kara hid between the garbage bins at the garage while I went up to the house.

The windows at the rear and the sides were high and small enough that it would be difficult for anyone to squeeze through. There were also several windows on the upper floor. The rear door was solid wood, with a deadbolt above the doorknob.

With a slight turn on the knob, I was pleasantly surprised to find it was unlocked. The door opened to a dim hallway. A faint odor of decomposition lingered inside, putting me on high alert. There was another door directly across from the first—the door to the basement, I figured. I pondered checking the basement first, but decided to leave it for later.

The kitchen was at the end of the hallway. The sticky floor was littered with trash and empty beer cans. The counters were stacked with dirty dishes and food wrappings. The sink was clogged to the top with stagnant water and overfilled with dirty pots and pans.

A narrow hallway led to the gloomy living room. The window shades were opened, giving me the assurance that the residents had probably left. *If people were still here*, I reasoned, *they would have closed the curtains and lived in the darkness.*

A staircase to the right of the living room led to the second floor. A door stood at the upper landing, blocking off access to the second floor. The uneven placement of the door told me that it didn't belong there—someone had obviously placed it there for safety reasons. *If the door is locked, then I'll leave*, I told myself. *I don't want to go in there and contend with whoever is inside.*

With a twist on the doorknob, the door opened slightly. A room was directly across from me. Another room was to the far left of me, toward the end of the hallway. The door to that room was missing. I could only assume that the missing door was probably this one.

The first room was neat and tidy, with two twin beds tucked in the corners. The lively posters of various teen idols and superheroes that were plastered on the walls above each bed told me I must be in the children's room. The silence and stillness were enough to convince me that no one was in there.

I made my way down the hallway and entered the second room, which was much larger than the first one. But it was not anywhere near as neat and tidy. The floor was littered with clothes and plastic food wrappings. A full-size bed was at the northwest corner, next to a large window. There was a large propane stove in the northeast corner, next to the bathroom. Someone had definitely been living in there at some point. But they had probably left.

I was ecstatic and satisfied that I'd found the perfect place. Not only did we have security, but we also had a bed to sleep in, and a stove to cook a hot meal on. I had been craving the small comforts of home for such a long time.

I was just about to leave to go get Kara when I heard a voice behind me. "You move and I'll blow your fucking head off!"

Stunned, I immediately dropped the machete and held my hands at my sides.

"Drop the rest of your weapons!" said the voice.

"OK," I said, compliantly. "Don't shoot."

After I dropped my shotgun and my pistol on the floor, I slowly turned around. The barrel of a shotgun was the first thing I saw. The rugged face of a middle-aged man with a long, fluffy beard was at the other end of the shotgun.

"You move and I'll blow your fucking head off!" he sternly warned again. "Now drop your backpack! And you better do it real slow!"

I slowly took off the backpack and dropped it to the floor. "Listen, sir," I said. "I'm not here to harm you or steal from you. I was just looking for a place to stay for the night."

"You come to the wrong place, asshole!"

"Please, sir. Please, just let me go, and I promise not to come back to your house again. Honestly, I was just looking for a place to stay for tonight, that's all."

"Shut the fuck up!" he shouted, poking me in the chest with his gun. "Now get back downstairs!"

I had no idea what he was going to do to me. But as we walked down the stairs, I felt a little relieved. It seemed he only wanted my food and weapons. He was going to kick me out of his house. I guess it was a fair trade, considering that I was the one who was intruding. I would look for another means to protect myself. And Kara still had the majority of the food.

"Thank you for letting me go," I said. "I promise not to come back here again."

"You're not going anywhere," he responded. "You're staying for dinner."

His response was both confusing and terrifying. My heart was in my throat as I feared him killing me for food. I'd seen what the Madsen brothers had done, and I was getting deathly afraid. My body began to tremble. My legs were getting weaker with each step. I felt like a lamb being led to slaughter.

I tried to prolong the walk to the kitchen as much as I could. I knew he was probably going to kill me once I reached it. "Listen, sir," I said. "My backpack has some food. Just take everything and let me go."

"*Shut the fuck up!*" he said, hitting me in the back of my head with his gun. "Is there anyone else with you?"

I didn't want him to know about Kara. So I told him that I was alone. I was desperately hoping that Kara wouldn't come in after me, because I had been there for quite a while.

We entered the kitchen and Kara suddenly appeared from the hallway. *Oh my God*, I said to myself. After noticing me, she stopped and gave me a pleasant smile. Obviously she didn't see the guy behind me.

"You were in here for a long time," she said. "I was getting worried."

"You fucking liar! You said that you were alone!"
As soon as I heard those words, everything went dark.

I opened my eyes and saw Kara crying over me. She was holding my head in her lap. Her tears were trickling down onto my face. I realized I had been knocked out. I was still lying on the floor. My head felt very heavy. Everything around me was in constant motion. I tried to speak to her, but the guy reached down to grab her hair and pulled her away. Then he turned to me and kicked me in the chest.

"Get up, asshole!" he shouted.

Still dazed from the blow to my head, I was a little slow to get up.

"Get the fuck up!" he said, kicking me in the chest again.

"OK, OK, I'm up," I said as I slowly pushed myself to my feet.

He shoved me down the hallway to the door that I had seen earlier but was reluctant to check. "Now open the door!" he ordered.

I opened the door and immediately got a whiff of the reeking stench. Right then, I knew that my luck had run out. *This is where he's going to shoot me!* I thought as I gasped. *And after he kills me, he's going to chop me up and then throw whatever is left of my body down into the basement.*

He laughed after noticing my terrified expression. "I saw you coming to my house," he said. "I purposely left the doors unlocked. I knew you were coming in here. You saved me a lot of trouble. Now with you and your bitch, I don't have to go out for a while."

I felt so defeated! I should have known it was too easy. I didn't know how I could get out of my predicament. The only thing I could do was plead for our lives. "Please, sir. Please don't do this. We have plenty of food in our bags. Take everything and let us go. There's no need to kill and eat—"

"Shut the fuck up!" he interrupted me. Then he laughed. "Do you think I'm going to *eat* you? Are you fucking *crazy*?"

I was surprised to hear that. If he wasn't not going to eat us, then why kill us? Why wouldn't he let us go? He had taken everything we had. "Then why do you want to kill me?" I asked.

He pointed to the basement. "My family is down there. I'm going to keep them alive until the government finds a cure for them. You're going to feed my family!"

My head hung low. There was no possible way out now! My demise was what I feared the most—to die an agonizing, horrific death by being ripped apart. "They're not your family anymore," I tried to explained. "They're not human. They're—"

"*Shut the fuck up!*" he quickly interrupted, hitting me in the back of the head with the barrel of his gun again.

"Look, the government is not going to..." I was about to tell him about the incident at the bridge when another blow to the back of my head stopped me.

"I said shut up!" he yelled. "Get down there or I'll kill you right now and feed your girlfriend to my family while she is still alive!"

"OK, OK. Please don't hurt her."

I moved to the edge and reached my foot down to the stairs, but couldn't feel anything beneath my feet. "There's no stairs," I said.

"You don't have to worry about that. Because where you're going, you're never coming back." After he said that, I felt a hard impact in my back, sending me flying down to the basement.

Fortunately, I landed on something soft to break my fall. I didn't know what it was, but as soon as I smelled the stench and felt the cold slimy liquid on my hands, I knew I'd landed on a corpse. I immediately got up and began scanning my surroundings.

The basement was eerily dark. The only light came from the two small windows at the southeast corner. The infected were somewhere in there. But I could barely see inside the room. I had no idea where they were.

As my eyes slowly adjusted to the darkness, I peered around. Silhouettes of corpses were scattered all over the floor. The darkness at the corners was nearly impenetrable. Then, I caught sight of something by the windows. A small person was standing in the corner. I paused as the figure slowly moved toward the light. The face of a boy, maybe twelve years old, slowly came to view. He stood there for a moment, just staring at me. Then he let out a growl. I knew he was about to attack me. I tried to brace myself for it. But just as things couldn't be getting any worse, I heard more growling noises coming from the same corner. A teenage girl, an elderly woman, and a middle-aged woman slowly walked up and stood with the boy. The whole family had revealed themselves.

I was hysterical! I was about to be attacked, and I didn't have any weapons to defend myself! I was terrified. *What should I do?* I wondered, panicking. My mind was a complete blank. Out of pure fear, I began screaming at the top of my lungs to release my anxiety.

Then, I noticed more light was coming through the basement door. I realized that the father had been standing at the doorway the whole time. It wasn't until he heard my screams that he was finally satisfied and walked away.

I looked back at the infected. They were still standing there. *Why haven't they attacked me yet?* I wondered. As I frantically glanced around for anything I could use to defend myself, I realized that there was nothing down here. The father must have thought about that and cleared out any possible weapons.

Now I was desperate. Everything was rushing back and forth in my mind, and I couldn't sort anything out. I was going to die if I didn't force myself to calm down! *Think! Think! Think!* I said to myself, forcing myself to relax.

Then I realized that I wasn't that useless without my weapons. Of course! I used to be a fighter! I used to fight many Muay Thai matches back in the refugee camp when I was young. I was trained by my father when I was eight years old. Although it had been over thirty years since I last fought in the ring, I still knew how to fight. Those monsters were not going to beat me!

I began to relax and focus on my breathing. Then I put myself into a fighting stance. If those monsters wanted to kill me, then they were going to have a hell of a time doing it! They should prepare for a fight! I was going to give them everything I had. I would fight until my last breath!

The boy was the first one to take action. He let out a scream as he took off running toward me. I could tell he was a fast mover. I waited until he came into range, and then I swung my right leg forward and gave him a hard front kick to the face. The impact sent him flying to the ground, momentarily stunning him. Noticing that he was trying to get up, I quickly went up to him and began stomping on his head until he stopped moving.

I quickly got back into my fighting stance and waited for the others. I could tell by their movements that they were all slow movers. I wasn't scared anymore. I knew it was going to be a lot easier now.

I stayed in the middle of the room to allow myself enough space to maneuver. I waited for them to come into range. With continuous knee jabs, kicks, and elbow strikes, I sent them all down to the ground. Then, I went around to each of them and stomped on their heads until they all lay motionless. I breathed a sigh of relief: I was fortunate not to sustain any cuts or bites.

I went back and stood at the bottom landing. The basement door had been left open, but the top landing was too high for me to reach. There was a rope on the floor of the top landing. One end of the rope was tied to a metal hook at the corner and the other end was dangling from the landing. *This is probably how that guy gets in and out of the basement,* I thought.

I tried jumping for the rope but couldn't reach it. I glanced around but didn't notice any furniture or large objects that could assist me. The father had been very thorough: he left nothing down there.

After several failed attempts, I was feeling hopeless. I tried again and this time, I was able to touch the rope. The next two attempts ended in failure, but I was able to touch the rope again and draw it a little lower.

Then the sudden sound of growling put me in a panic mode. *The infected are probably waking up*, I thought. *I don't have much time left.* I took a deep breath and focused only on the rope. Then, gathering all of my leg strength, I leaped up and finally grabbed a hold of the rope. I hopped on it and quickly pulled myself up before the infected got to me.

I was very fortunate that the crazy guy hadn't closed the door. Maybe he had become too complacent because every victim he had thrown into the basement never made it back up? Or maybe he wanted to bid goodnight to his family after they had fed on me? For whatever reason, he was going to pay for his carelessness. He was going to pay for what he did to me, to Kara, and to all of those people that he fed to his family.

I found a large butcher knife inside one of the kitchen drawers and took it with me. The living room was cleared. The sound of yelling confirmed that Kara and the guy were on the upper floor.

Slowly, I walked up the stairs. The door was slightly ajar, and I hesitated to open it. But after hearing the voices, I knew they were at the far bedroom.

I finally made it to the room and cautiously peeked inside. The guy was standing in the middle of the room with his back toward the hallway. Kara was on the bed and completely nude. She was crying and covering her face with her hands as if she had just been raped. The asshole was still yelling profanities at her, telling her to go into the bathroom and take a shower. I was so furious! I wanted to run up and stab him in the back right then and there. But he was still holding the shotgun. I needed to control my emotions or I'd get myself killed.

My focus was solely on him now. The asshole was so focused on Kara that he was oblivious to his surroundings. A mistake he would pay for dearly with his life.

I quickly approached him from behind and placed the knife to his throat. "Remember me, *asshole*?" I said. "Drop the gun or I'll slice your fucking throat open!"

He immediately dropped the gun and raised his hands. I could feel his body tense up and begin to shake. The rush of complete dominance overwhelmed me: Now it was my turn to torment him. "You're not so tough anymore, are you?" I asked. "Why don't you try to do something about it now? Give me an excuse to cut your fucking throat from ear to ear!"

"I'm not going to do anything stupid," he said, shakily. "Please don't kill me."

I nearly passed out from the rush of blood shooting up to my head after he said that. How dare he beg for his life when he never showed me or any of those other people the same courtesy! I was so furious that I wanted to slash his throat and watch him bleed to death. But something was stopping me from doing that. A deeper urge was telling me to give this guy the same courtesy he had given to me and to all those people that he'd thrown down the basement to feed his fucked-up family!

"Kara!" I called to her. She was still covering her face and wouldn't look at me.

"Kara! It's me!" I said again. Upon hearing my voice, she slowly put her hands down and gazed at me. She seemed shocked to see me again and couldn't speak a word.

"Come over here, sweetie," I said calmly.

She got up and came over. She was still nude. But I don't think she even noticed it at that point. "Take his gun and follow me," I said.

I was pressing the knife so tightly against the guy's throat that I could feel his blood dripping down from the blade onto my hand. "If you're thinking about purposely falling down the stairs, this knife will go right through your fucking throat! And if you survive the knife and the fall, I will take that gun from her and blast you in half!" I sternly warned him before we descended the stairs.

"I won't do anything stupid," he quickly replied.

As we approached the kitchen, he began weeping. He realized what his fate was going to be. I was amazed at how tough this piece of shit was earlier. Now he was crying like a baby—just like that fucking Donald Madsen. For a moment, I even had some compassion for him. I almost gave in and thought about tying him up and leaving him inside the living room. But after what I had seen in the basement, I knew he deserved to die. *He needs to pay for what he did! I want justice for every one of those people!*

Approaching the basement door, he went into full breakdown mode. He was crying hysterically as he pleaded for his life. "Please! Please don't do this!" he begged. "Please let me go! Show some compassion."

I finally lost it when he mentioned "compassion." How dare he ask me for that! Every one of those bodies down in the basement had once been a living person. He had deprived them of their lives and showed them no compassion. And now he was asking for compassion? *Fuck him!*

"Show you compassion? How dare you ask me that!" I shouted in his ears. "Did you show me any compassion earlier when I was begging you for my life? Did you show any compassion for all of those innocent people you threw into the basement to feed to your family?"

I pushed him to the doorway. "I will show some compassion," I said. "Your family is down there, and they are very hungry. I will show them compassion by feeding them."

I pushed him as hard as I could and sent him flying down into the basement. After a loud thump, I heard him scream out that his leg was broken. Moments later, he began screaming in agony. I stood by the doorway until the screaming had stopped, giving way to the eerie sounds of crackling bones.

After I was satisfied that the guy was no longer alive, I cut off the rope and threw it behind the rear door. Then I closed the door.

Kara was inside the kitchen. I could tell by her teary eyes and quivering lips that she was on the edge of losing it. There was no answer to any of this. So I just gently embraced her. Then she finally broke down and cried.

After a long while, she pulled back to look intently at me. "I thought you were dead," she said, still panting.

"No," I said calmly. "I will not die until I see that you're safely out of this city." Looking straight into her eyes, I gently added, "Did he rape you?"

"No," she replied quietly. "He wanted me to take a shower first."

CHAPTER 27

The morning inside the gloomy bedroom was somber, just like the previous three mornings. Outside, the sun was up and the sky was clear and blue. It was going to be another beautiful day, but I took no comfort in it. It was just another day of nothing to do except watch the time slowly tick away until nightfall. Then we would stay in the darkness and hope that we'd make it through to another day.

Kara was over at the stove cooking breakfast. Her spirited energy was very comforting. I was amazed at how quickly she had gotten over the ordeal. *Of course, if we ever make it out of here,* I told myself, *she'll probably be in therapy for the rest of her life.*

As I wrote down the events of the past several days in my journal, I couldn't help but think about those men—those despicable men that I had killed. A psychiatrist once asked me, "Do you believe people are born evil?" My answer at the time was that I believed all people are born good. It's what they were exposed to that made them evil. But then as I sat there writing I thought, *Maybe I'm wrong.* Maybe some people *are* born evil. And no matter how much good they were exposed to, they would always be evil. If that's the case, then was I born evil too? I wanted so badly to believe in my original answer. But only an evil person could be capable of doing the things that I had done.

I was still deeply enthralled in my thoughts and didn't realize that Kara had come over with two bowls of ramen noodles. I had been fortunate enough to find two boxes of noodles inside the bedroom. They had sustained us for the past three days.

"Are you still keeping that journal?" she asked as she set my bowl in front of me on the coffee table.

"Yes," I said softly as I closed it.

"What are you thinking about doing with it?"

"I don't know. I'm just writing down my thoughts."

I quickly stuffed a forkful of the noodles into my mouth and slurped them down without realizing they were still very hot. The burning sensation on my tongue was painful, but I found it soothing. I guess the comforting feeling of eating a home-cooked meal had somehow drowned out the pain.

Kara chuckled. "You should be more careful. It's still very hot."

I smiled warmly and continued eating. My mind was set on leaving that day, but I wasn't sure how to approach Kara with it. I knew she was deathly afraid to go back outside again. But we had been in the house for the past three days. I couldn't postpone it any longer.

I sighed deeply and glanced over at her. "We're more than halfway to South Park," I said gently. "We'll have to try to make it to the other side of Pine Street today. Once we get over there, we have to go as far as possible before it gets dark."

She ate quietly for a moment. Then she looked at me. "Why can't we stay here?" she responded. "We're safe in here. We have a comfortable bed to sleep in. We have a stove. Honestly, it almost feels like home in here."

I could understand why she felt that way. After what she had been through, it was natural to never want to venture back outside again. I reached out to gently clasp her hands. "I want to stay here too," I said. "But if we stay here too long, we will die when the military destroys this city."

"We'll die out there anyway," she said. "What's the difference?"

I had to admit that she was right. We had been very lucky so far; it was just a matter of time before our luck ran out. But there had to be a reason why we were still alive. There had to be a reason why we had stayed alive through so many atrocities. Maybe we were meant to survive and go home to our families?

"I know that you're scared," I said, "but we've made it this far. We're going to go home to our families."

"We're not going to go home. We're—"

"Yes we are," I interrupted. "I promise you that I will not let anything happen to you for as long as I'm alive."

"What happens if you die?" She began to sob. "What will happen to me then?"

I reached a hand over and gently lifted her face to meet mine. With sincere conviction, I gave her my oath: "I promise you that I will never die. I will get you back to your family."

"You say that, but what if you turn into one of those monsters? What will I do then?"

"I've protected you this far. My only goal from now on is to protect you and get you home."

"What if you're wrong about the military?" she said, suddenly shifting gears. "Why can't we stay here and wait for them to come for us?"

I knew that her courage was hanging by a thread now, and I didn't blame her one bit. What she had been through would have weakened any tough guy. She wanted so desperately to believe in a miracle. The hope that the military was coming for us was just that—a miracle.

"If the military was going to help us, then they would have taken us into their boat when we were at the river," I explained.

"But what if you're wrong?" she quickly responded.

I could tell that she wasn't going to budge. She was still holding dearly to that false hope because it was the only thing she had left. I had to tell her about what I saw at the bridge. At least then she could decide for herself.

"Listen to me," I said, looking straight into her eyes. "Do you want to know what I saw at the bridge when I was up in the tree?"

"Yes."

Her facial expression slowly changed to utter despair as she listened to my account of what I'd seen. She took a moment to gather her thoughts. Then she let out a sigh. "I'm sorry," she said faintly. "It's just that I'm so tired of being scared all the time."

"I know," I replied. "If you want to stay here for another night, then that's fine. We'll leave tomorrow morning."

After we finished eating, I opened my journal and began writing again. Kara came back to me and asked if the guy who lived in the house we were in was in the military.

"He might have been in the military at one point," I replied. I looked at her curiously. "Why do you ask?"

"Well, when he was up here with me, I saw a radio hooked onto his belt. There was a sticker on the radio that read, 'US Government Property,'" she replied.

"Shit! I didn't even check him!" I said, more to myself. He was wearing a large shirt, and I completely missed the radio. "Did he take the radio off when he was up here?"

"No, it was still on his belt when you grabbed him." Then she squinted her eyes and gave me that worried look she always gave me. "You're not thinking about going back down there, are you?"

"I have to. It's the only way to find out what the military is planning to do. If they're coming to save us, then we'll stay here. But, if they're planning on something else, then we have to leave."

I could tell that Kara was very reluctant to let me go back to the basement. But I desperately needed that radio. "Don't worry about me," I assured her. "I've seen what I'm up against. I've handled them before without any weapons. And this time, I have weapons with me."

With the shotgun in my hand and the machete strapped onto my duty belt, we walked down the hallway to the door. I cracked it opened and peeked down the dark staircase. The silence was encouraging, but I was still reluctant to venture out. Fearing someone was inside the living room, I threw a shoe down the stairs and listened carefully. After a long moment of silence, I was satisfied.

"I want you to close this door and lock it," I said. "If you hear anything downstairs, do not open it. Wait until I come back and ask you to do it."

"What about you?"

"I'll be all right."

The gloomy living room was empty, but it was so much more pleasant being down there than upstairs. The dull lighting and the warm décor around the room gave me a deep sense of home. If it wasn't for the fact that there were some undead lurking about beneath me, I would have loved to stay in that room until nightfall.

As I crept through the narrow hallway and into the kitchen, my anxiety was building. The basement door was just a few feet away and I could smell the stench seeping through the cracks. I was beginning to have second thoughts. But I really needed that radio.

I opened the door and the stench immediately rushed at me, choking every ounce of air out of my lungs. Gagging and coughing, I quickly closed the door and ran into the kitchen. I thought I was used to the smell of decomposition. But that odor was so extreme. I honestly wondered how I'd been able to handle it before. Maybe it was the adrenaline rush and sheer terror that had helped me to cope with it.

I was reluctant to go down there now. With the smell being so bad, I just might pass out. Besides, what if the radio had broken from the fall? The risk I was about to take was just too great. And I wasn't sure if it was worth it.

I knew that if I kept thinking like that, I would lose all my courage. So, I quickly shrugged off the thought and stayed focused on my task. The radio was more important to me than anything at this point. I had to take the risk. I had to go down there to get it.

But how was I going to get down there? It was going to be way more difficult than I thought. I couldn't just jump straight down there because I might get hurt from the fall. Even if I retied the rope and used it to get down there, I had no idea where the infected were. They might be at the landing, waiting to attack me while I was still hanging on the rope.

I needed a diversion—a way to draw them away from the bottom landing. I began searching the kitchen for some sort of object to use, but I couldn't find anything. Then I saw an orange box tucked behind a garbage bag at the rear door. I was elated at what was inside: road flares! Exactly what I needed! The bright sparks would light up the room. Plus, maybe the sulfur and magnesium fumes would help with the smell.

I lit up a flare and tossed it down to the landing. I immediately heard high screeching voices, followed by the shuffling sound of footsteps. My spirits lifted a little—the flare did have some kind of effect. I lit up several more flares and tossed them down. Again I heard more noises, but this time, they were farther away from the landing.

I retied the rope to the metal hook and slowly descended into the basement. The fumes from the flares did help drown out the smell to the point that it was bearable. As my eyes adjusted to the brightness, the true sickness inside the room revealed itself to me.

My heart cried out. That man's actions were right up there with the Madsens. He was truly a *monster*!

The squishy floor was littered with body parts and corpses. Some of the corpses were so badly mauled and mutilated that they looked like one big pile of flesh. Some of them were reduced to just piles of bones with small bits of flesh hanging off of them.

Just when I thought that I had seen enough, I was wrong. I nearly broke down crying when I spotted a torso of a little boy lying a few feet away from the headless and dismembered body of a woman. I could only assume that she was his mother. Unlike the woman's body, the boy's belly was not disemboweled for some reason. However, his arms and legs were ripped off. Although half of his face was missing, I could tell that he had been a beautiful little creature. How his life could be taken away in such an atrocious way was just too much for me to bear.

My blood began to boil inside as I thought of nothing else but revenge. I wanted to chop those monsters into tiny bits and pieces as I sent them to hell. *They will pay for what they've done to that little boy. They will all die today!*

With my focus now solely on killing the infected, I began scanning the room for them. They were scattered about the room and had me surrounded. But I was behind the flares, and they were afraid to approach.

I picked up a flare and tossed it toward the boy. After a high-pitched screech, he quickly backed away from the flare. Now I knew how the father had gotten in and out of the basement. He must have discovered that the monsters were afraid of the bright sparks.

I was elated by what I saw. Then an idea quickly came to me: instead of fighting them from all sides, I was going to use the flares to corral them together into a corner. Then, I would chop them down with the machete.

I picked up another flare and tossed it toward the old woman. She slowly backed away. I repeated this process until I finally had all of them bunched up at the southeast corner. They were too afraid to go past the flares, so they stayed huddled together.

I stepped toward them with the machete. The boy was the first one that I wanted to kill. Raising the machete, I prepared to strike down at him. But then I paused as I saw the expression on his face. His look of fear woke up a deep-rooted sense of humanity within me.

As I thought about it, I began to accept it. This boy was a victim too. They were all victims. They didn't know right from wrong; they were killing out of instinct. They were already in hell! And I could accept that. I slowly backed away and let them be.

Knowing that I only had a few minutes left before the flares burned out, I looked around for the father. A pair of bloodstained blue jeans near the northeast corner caught my attention and I went up to them. The bottom half of the body was still inside the jeans, with a large pool of blood and moist entrails spilling out of the pants.

I couldn't see the radio on the body, so I followed the trail of blood to the other half. It was definitely the father. His head was still intact and his face seemed untouched. I guessed his family didn't like his face either. Both of his arms were missing though. And his torso was ripped opened. Parts of his internal organs and entrails were pulled out and scattered around him. *What a horrific way to die.* But I couldn't say I felt sorry for him. He'd condemned so many people to die the same way. It was fitting for him to die in the same manner.

Although I had found him, I couldn't find the radio. I was running out of time and turned to go back. But as I approached the landing, I tripped on something. The radio! It must have fallen off the guy when he landed. It didn't appear to be broken. The red light next to the dials began flashing when I turned it on.

The top half of a severed head was lying a few feet away, inside a yellow hazmat helmet. The dark residue embedded on the outside of the helmet told me that the person had been shot in the head. Then I realized that he was a soldier. He was wearing a helmet similar to what those soldiers at the bridge were wearing. Now I knew how the father had obtained the radio.

I climbed back to the top, cut off the rope, and threw it down to the basement. Then, I went back to Kara.

CHAPTER 28

The midday sun was relentless as usual, causing the temperature inside the bedroom to become uncomfortably hot and humid. Every movement required an extra effort. Although I was just sitting and writing, I could barely move my fingers to form a word. There was really nothing I could do about the heat except wait it out until nightfall when it cooled off a little. Still, the feeling of home was something that gave me comfort, and I needed to savor it as much as I could.

It was at Kara's persistence that I agreed to stay for one more night. Truthfully, I didn't want to go back out there again. I was just as content to stay inside as she was. *Who knows where we will end up at nightfall if we leave this place?* I asked myself. *Can we really survive another horrendous ordeal?*

Although I was comfortable in the house, a hopeless feeling was still plaguing me. Now that I had the radio, maybe there would be some answers. I turned it on, but nothing was being broadcasted. The beeping noises indicated that it was still working, but the battery was low. After a few minutes of silence on the radio, I turned it off. I needed to use it sparingly and make the battery last a while longer.

Desperately seeking some relief from the heat, I went downstairs to re-inspect the doors and windows. After I was satisfied with everything, I moved a small table into the hallway to block the kitchen. Then I placed some pots and pans onto it. I went into the living room and placed some heavy books onto the coffee table. Then I slid it over to block the front door. I wanted an early warning. If someone came inside, they would trip over the tables. I would hear it from upstairs and would be able to prepare myself.

I came back into the bedroom and tied a rope to one of the bedposts. Then I threw the other end out the large window. The rope almost touched the ground. My idea was to use it to make our escape if the infected made it to the upper floor. After I reeled in the rope, I placed it next to the bed. I was satisfied that I'd thought of everything. It was time to relax.

The silence outside was peaceful and exuberating. But the heat was exhausting. My only refuge from it was to spread my body out on the bed and sleep till nightfall.

I was abruptly awoken to a sound outside, a familiar sound that I hadn't heard for a long while—the sound of a car. I quickly sat up and looked out the window. The view to the front was blocked by a tree, so I leaped out of the bed and I ran across the hallway to the other room. Kara was saying something to me when I ran by her. But I was too focused on getting to the other room and didn't hear a word she said.

Through the window in the other room I had a direct view of the street. A green military jeep had stopped just a few yards away from the house we were in, and four people got out of it. They were heavily armed and dressed in the same bright yellow hazmat suits that I'd seen at the bridge. Soldiers!

The soldiers were heading our way with a purpose that instantly put me on high alert. I was dumbfounded as to how they even knew that we were inside. My intuition told me that they hadn't arrived for an insignificant rescue mission. They were obviously sent our way for something much more important. *Are they here for the radio?* I wondered.

I ran back to the other bedroom and frantically tried to gather up our things. Kara was standing in the middle of the room. She was just staring at me as I stuffed everything into my bag. "We have to go, Kara," I said, panicking. "There are soldiers outside. If they find us in here, they'll kill us."

I was speaking quietly but desperately, so she would be alerted to the seriousness of the situation. But she was nonchalant about it and made no attempt to help with the packing. "Kara, we have to go!" I whispered harshly. "There are soldiers outside! They will—"

"They're here to rescue us," she quickly interrupted. "We're saved. We're going to go home today."

I had to pause to look at her. Noticing that I was begging for an answer, she smiled sweetly and calmly explained everything. "I spoke to a guy on the radio while you were sleeping. He asked me how I got the radio. I told them that we had found it inside this house. Then he asked me for the address. I didn't know where we were at, so I couldn't tell him. Then he told me to press the little orange button on the radio. He said that the button would give out our location, and they would send help for us."

"Damn it, Kara! You've led them to us!" I said quietly. "We have to go now! We have to get out of here before they get inside!"

The pounding at the front door had begun. I went to the bed and threw the rope out the window. Then I turned to Kara. "Let's go," I said, almost in a plea. "We don't have any time to waste."

"No!" she said defiantly. "*I'm not leaving!*"

The pounding was getting louder and more intense. It was just a matter of time before the door gave in. "Please, Kara, listen to me!" I begged. "They're here for the radio! They will kill us after they get the radio! Please come with me!"

"No!" she said, still being defiant.

Kara's stubbornness was absurd. I'd never seen this side of her before. I was almost in tears after I took her hand and she violently jerked it away.

The pounding had stopped momentarily. Then several gunshots rang out. I knew they were shooting at the locks. "Please, Kara. Please come with me. They will kill you if you stay here."

"No," she said again. Then she began sobbing. "I want to go home!" she cried. "I'm tired of being scared. I'm tired of running. I can't do this anymore."

I felt so powerless at that moment. My pleas to her were futile. I knew that I had to leave without her. I looked at her intently, as if I was looking at her for the last time. Then I let out a deep, painful sigh before I spoke my next words to her: "OK, Kara. I really hope that they're here to help you. I want you to know that I'll be going east in the alley. Then I'm crossing the street to the other side."

I went over to the bed and pulled off the red bedsheet. Then I ripped a portion of it off. "I'll be tying a small strip of this cloth to a house or an object that stands out among the rest. If you make it out of this house, then look for it. You should be able to find me."

After a loud crash downstairs, I knew the soldiers were inside and had tripped over the coffee table. I gave Kara a final embrace. Then I climbed out the window and down the rope.

As I ran from the house, my eyes were tearing up. I missed her already. We had been through so much together. I felt that I had known her my whole life. Although I wasn't certain about my own fate, I was pretty certain about hers.

I was four houses away when I heard gunshots. My heart sank at the thought of Kara's passing. "Good-bye, Kara," I said quietly.

As I kept running, I heard more gunshots. They had become rapid and steady, as if the soldiers were in a battle. The infected had probably arrived as well. I took comfort in knowing that those soldiers were going to die, too. But their deaths were going to be agonizing.

I was two blocks away and could still hear the ongoing battle. Hordes of infected were running down the street, heading in the direction of the gunshots. I hid underneath the rear porch of a small grayish house and waited for the infected to pass. *The soldiers are doomed now*, I thought. *They might be able to kill a lot of infected. But they won't have enough ammo to kill the hundreds more that I've seen.*

Although I knew that Kara was most likely dead, I was still holding on to the tiniest bit of hope that if she somehow made it out of the house, she would remember what I told her. So before I continued on, I went to the alley and tied a strip of cloth to the metal chain-link fence—the only fence in the area.

After one more block, I came up to the rear of a yellowish house. It was the only house on the block that wasn't white. There were several rows of bushes in the front yard. That seemed the perfect spot to cross over. I tied a strip of cloth to the small tree in the alley and went to the front.

The street was quiet and empty. All the infected in the area were probably drawn to the house where the soldiers were. It was the perfect time to run across. But I decided to wait, hoping Kara might show up. I wanted her to be with me so we could cross it together.

But after a while, I finally decided to continue on. I tied another strip of cloth to a bush that was directly across from the tree in the alley. I wanted to make sure that she could see it when she reached the tree in the rear.

I darted across the street and hid behind the bushes in the front yard of a small brick house—the only brick house in the area. *It should stand out among the rest*, I thought, *and make it easier for Kara to spot the ribbon on the bush in the front yard.*

As I continued sprinting from alley to alley, hiding behind garages and houses, I could feel hopelessness taking over. I just wanted to run down the street and keep on running. I didn't care if I was spotted and chased by a million zombies. Now I finally knew how Kara felt. *I'm tired of being scared! I'm tired of running! I want it all to end!*

I was losing my mind, and I knew that. So I took a moment to collect myself. I would die if I kept allowing it to happen. I wasn't in the right state of mind to continue on. So I hid inside a garage for a while.

• • •

It was about an hour later when I finally reached Asbury Parkway. I was relieved that I made it that far. But I was also dreading what lay beyond the street on the other side.

A huge strip mall occupied the entire area south of the street. The giant building stretched for several city blocks. To the east end of the mall were several apartment complexes and townhouses. The west end of the mall was occupied by a huge department store and a supermarket. There were also numerous restaurants, coffee shops, and fast food places scattered throughout the area. The huge parking lot in the front of the mall presented another problem. Fortunately, there were several abandoned vehicles that I could use for cover.

From afar, the mall looked like one continuous building. But there was a break in between. George's Hardware Store, an old and ugly brick building that stuck out like an eyesore between the two newer mall buildings, was going to be my next destination. The George building was built back in the late 1860s. It had been the first General Store in the area. Because of its historical status, the city couldn't tear it down. So instead the city constructed the two mall buildings next to it.

I knew there was an alleyway between the George building and the east mall building. That alleyway was narrow and had just enough room for two or maybe three small people to squeeze through. There was also a driveway between the George building and the west mall building. The small driveway had barely enough room to drive a vehicle through to the small private parking lot at the rear. Unfortunately, that parking lot was enclosed by a huge twelve-foot brick wall. The access to the driveway was also enclosed by a tall iron gate with a lettered locking system on it.

I couldn't help but think back to the old Thao Oriental Market. How these two buildings could be so strikingly similar amazed me. *Maybe the George building will be my salvation, just like the other building?* I pondered.

Pete, the owner of the George building, was a friend of mine. He and his wife, Marsha, lived on the upper floor of that building. He had given me the combination to the gate lock a while back after his store was burglarized through the rear door while they were on vacation. Ever since that incident, he wanted the police to have access to the rear. I still remembered the combination, and I could use it to open the gate if I needed to.

Now with plan B in place, I could concentrate on plan A: to get to the narrow alleyway east of the George building. I knew that if I made it to the alleyway, I could go through to the alley road at the rear and continue on from there.

CHAPTER 29

A gain, my plan was to get to the east side of the George building and go through the alleyway to the rear. From there, I would continue down the alley and try to go as far as I could before it got dark. It was a simple plan. But then, nothing I'd done thus far was simple. I didn't even know if I would make it across the street without being seen.

To the west of me, a mob was converging in front of the Park's Family Restaurant. They were a block away and wouldn't be able to catch up to me before I got to the George building. The area to the east of me was surprisingly deserted. On the street ahead of me were several stalled and burned-out vehicles that I could use as cover.

I reached the first vehicle without any issues. The second vehicle wasn't an issue either. The last vehicle was a burned-out Expedition. I hid behind it for a moment as I pondered how I was going to get through the parking lot and to the mall building. There were three vehicles inside the lot that I could use for cover. Once I reached the mall, I would parallel it until I got to the George building.

I took one more glance toward the infected—they still seem preoccupied with the restaurant. The sprint through the parking lot and to the mall wouldn't be an issue now. As I walked around the vehicle to the front, an oily spot suddenly took my feet out from under me. Thankfully the backpack broke my fall. But my foot accidentally kicked the side of the vehicle. A wave of high screeching noises immediately came from the car. Who would've thought the alarm was still working on the stupid thing?

The noise alerted the infected, and they rushed in my direction. I made no attempt to hide behind the other vehicles as I passed by them in the lot. I didn't try to get to the mall buildings either. Getting to the George building was my only priority as I sprinted across the lot in full view.

I finally made it to the George building and went straight to the alleyway. But upon entering it, I quickly stopped. The infected were in the alleyway! They had obviously heard the alarm, and they were coming to the front. But they were all jam-packed in the alleyway as the fast movers in the back forced their way past the slow movers in the front and couldn't get through. I quickly backed out. Now I had to go for plan B.

I ran to the gate and quickly entered the lock combination. But it didn't work! I began to panic as I glanced behind me and saw the infected approaching the parking lot. They had seen me at the gate, and they were headed my way. I felt as if my heart was going to leap out of my chest as I turned to work on the lock again.

"*Goerge! Goerge! The combination was G-o-e-r-g-e! Why is this fucking thing not working?*" I yelled out as I feverishly tried the lock again and again.

I kept trying to no avail. The damn thing wouldn't unlock! I spun around to check on the infected. They were inside the lot now and closing in on me. I would have to leave and go in the opposite direction. Then a feeling of defeatism overwhelmed me as I spotted another group coming in from the east. *I am done for!* I thought. *There's no use running now. I'm trapped. I have to fight them from here!*

I raised the shotgun and aimed it at the infected that were closest to me. Knowing that I only had seven shots, I had to take out as many of them as I could. Then I would use the pistol and the machete. I would keep fighting them until they overpowered me.

I was just about to shoot when I looked up and saw the sign above the building. No wonder the lock wasn't working: I'd spelled the name wrong! I quickly entered the right combination. After a click, the gate finally opened. I quickly locked it behind me.

A few infected were reaching their hands out to me through the metal bars of the gate. But the gate stood firm, hindering them from getting any further. I knew if more of them continued arriving, they would soon overpower the gate. I had to use the time I had to look for a way out.

I ran to the rear and stopped at the giant brick wall. Again, a feeling of defeat overwhelmed me as I steadily gazed up at the wall. It was just too high for me to reach the top. There was a large balcony on the second level of the building. But it was even higher than the wall.

As I glanced around for something to assist me, a large wooden crate at the end of the driveway, directly in view of the gate, was the only option. The crate seemed to be at least five feet in height. But it was too far away from the wall. If I could push it to the wall, then I could use it to get to the top.

I went to the crate and tried pushing it. But no matter how hard I pushed, I couldn't get it to move, not even an inch. There had to be something inside that made it so heavy! *Now what am I going to do?* I wondered.

Trapped and frustrated, I went to the rear door. I tried pulling on the metal handle, but to no avail—the door was tightly secured. Kicking the door in wasn't an option, because it opened outward. Shooting it was not an option either: it was a metal door and the pellets wouldn't penetrate it.

Then, a realization hit me like a ton of bricks. I was really going to die in there! *How ironic that I thought this place was going to be my salvation earlier*, I remembered. *Instead, I've found my demise here!*

The loud banging at the gate was getting more intensified, and a squeaking sound was evidence that the gate was about to give in. There was no way out of my predicament. I had to prepare for the inevitable!

I went over to the wooden crate and stood behind it. Taking several deep breaths, I began to calm myself. Then I emptied out all of the ammo from my backpack and placed it on top of the crate. I placed my machete there too so I could reach for it when I ran out of ammo. The shotgun and the pistol were loaded to maximum capacity. There was nothing else to do but wait.

As I prepared myself for the onslaught, my mind started to wander off. Memories of my childhood began replaying in my mind like episodes of a TV drama. I guess when death is inevitable, everyone has a story to tell. I felt compelled to tell my story.

My name is Wahuabmua Hua. I am Hmong! My people fought for the Americans during the Vietnam War. The dreadful memories of my childhood are something that I've always wanted to forget. But yet, they seem to be the only thing on my mind right now. Perhaps by telling them, these memories will never haunt me again.

I was born in a little village inside the Xiangkhouang Province in central Laos during the Vietnam War. What a childhood I have lived!

I was only five years old when I had to contend with death. My father was off to war, leaving my mother and me to fend for ourselves. Our village was attacked by the enemy. Most of the villagers were slaughtered. My mother and I escaped into the jungle with some other villagers. We stayed in the jungle for weeks, surviving on anything we could find. We were starving, dehydrated, sick, and exhausted. Most of the people who had escaped with us had died. But we survived when death was all around us.

My mother and I followed a group of Hmong people on the Trail of Death through the impenetrable jungle. It was a grueling, and at times insurmountable, trek. We had to force ourselves to ignore the cries of small children, elderly men and women, the sick, and the injured. They were too weak to keep up. So they were all left behind to their demise. So many people died along the way. But we survived when death was all around us.

My mother and I made it to the Mekong River. With only a log keeping us afloat, we paddled our way through the rough, turbulent tides until we were able to reach the other side. Most of the people with us had drowned. But still, we survived when death was all around us.

We made it to the refugee camp in Thailand. The weather was always unbearably hot and humid. Our only refuge from the scorching sun was a small tarp that my mother purchased from a Thai merchant who sneaked into the camp at the risk of his own life. Food and water were very scarce, and for many days, we went without it. Many people died from starvation, dehydration, sickness, and disease. Still, we survived when death was all around us.

As I thought about my current life and struggles, I had a single question that only God could answer: *What was the purpose for you to let me live through all those atrocities?*

I guessed that I would have my answer in a little while. If I was not meant to survive the upcoming battle, then I would have to accept my fate. After what I had done and what I was about to do, I hoped that God would understand my desperation and have mercy on my soul.

A thundering sound rattled the ground and quickly brought me back to reality. The gate had finally collapsed; the infected had made it to the driveway. Thirty yards separated us. I was fortunate that the driveway was narrow, because only a few of them could squeeze through at one time. With the spreads from the shotgun rounds, I could hold them back and prolong my life for a little while longer.

The first wave of infected was blown to the ground, hindering the ones behind them as they stumbled and fell on top of the bodies. I fired a few more shots to slow them even more. Noticing that this might work to my advantage, I waited until the ones in the back made it through. Then I began firing again, adding more bodies to the pile.

I was on my last box of shotgun shells when the advancement of the infected had slowed down almost to a stop. With only one or two of them getting through every few seconds, my spirit was a little uplifted. And for a moment, I thought I might survive.

My goal was to use all the ammo to delay them as much as I could. Then I'd use the machete to kill the ones that made it through. Although I had no idea how many of them were still out there, I was going to continue to kill them until they stopped coming.

As I reloaded my shotgun, I caught a glimpse of the rear door opening. I quickly paused to look closely. *It was Marsha!* "Marsha! Wait!" I screamed as loud as I could.

She stopped and gave me a surprised look. I quickly gathered up everything from the crate and raced to the door. "Hua, what's happening?" she said as I approached her.

"Just get in!" I said, still breathing heavily. "I'll explain everything."

Immediately after we locked the door behind us, the infected began pounding vigorously on it. But I didn't care. All of my despair had been lifted. I was almost in tears! I could never thank Marsha enough for saving my life!

CHAPTER 30

Marsha George Cohen was a descendent of Karl George, the first owner of the store. She and her husband, Pete Cohen had been married for over fifty years, and they had three children together. Marsha inherited the business from her father, and she and Pete had run it for almost thirty years. They lived in the apartment above the store and were planning to retire and move down south for warmer weather. But none of their children wanted to take over the business. Pete talked about selling the store all the time, but because of the family's history, he couldn't bring himself to do it.

"Hua, what's happening out there? Why is everyone going crazy?" she asked.

Is she completely unaware of what's been going on for the last month? I wondered. "Marsha, where is Pete?" I asked gently. She and Pete always seemed to be together. It was rare to see one without the other.

She lowered her head and replied in a tone that immediately made my heart sink. "He's upstairs."

I gently lifted her face to meet mine. "What happened to him?"

She held back for as long as she could. Then she lowered her head again and finally broke down. "Pete is sick," she replied, sobbing, with her face between her hands. "He's really sick, and I don't know what to do."

"What happened to Pete?" I asked again, placing my hand on her shoulder.

With teary eyes, she slowly explained: "He was attacked by those crazy people three days ago. He became very sick. I couldn't do anything to help him. I tried calling for an ambulance, but the phone isn't working. He told me to chain him to the bed and lock the door."

My heart cried out to her. This was probably the first time that she had been parted from her husband. I gently held her. "I'm so sorry, Marsha."

We went upstairs and as usual, the living room was neat and tidy. There was a pillow and a blanket on one of the couches. It seemed she had been sleeping on that couch. *Why doesn't she sleep inside one of the other bedrooms?* I wondered. *It would be a lot safer for her.* I wanted to ask her but decided not to.

The living room seemed to be a lot larger than I had remembered. Marsha told me that since the children weren't living with them anymore, they took out one of the bedrooms and expanded the living room. They kept the other bedroom as a guest room.

She was talking almost in a whisper. But I didn't think much of it. I knew she probably didn't want to disturb Pete. Although she did tell me that Pete was chained to the bed and locked inside their bedroom, I was still uneasy about it. I had no idea what Pete was doing in there at the moment. He could break out at any time.

"Marsha, is Pete still chained to the bed?" I inquired.

"I don't know," she replied. "I haven't been in there since I made that promise to him."

"What promise?"

She whimpered. "After Pete was attacked, he told me to chain him to the bed. When I refused, he became very angry. He slapped me and told me he didn't love me anymore. It was the first time he'd ever hit me and said those words to me. After I chained him to the bed, he made me promise to never go into our bedroom again, no matter what I might hear coming from in there."

"I'm so sorry, Marsha."

Again, I was still uneasy about it. The only thing on my mind was to go in there and kill Pete before he broke out. But I couldn't do it in front of Marsha. To her, Pete was and would always be her husband. I couldn't do that to her. I would have to be very vigilant and hope that the door held up.

We went to the kitchen, where I noticed that there was no food on the counters or inside the cabinets. The refrigerator was also emptied. "How long has it been since you ate, Marsha?" I asked, concerned.

"It has been a few days now," she quietly replied. "We were starving, and that's why Pete decided to go out. I begged him not to, but he said that we would die if he didn't."

I let out a deep, agonizing sigh as I thought about what Pete had done. For him to decide to leave her, they must have truly been starving. I noticed a small propane stove on top of the counter. I took off my backpack and pulled out three packages of Ramen noodles from it. "I'll make us something to eat, Marsha."

As the noodles began to soften inside the boiling pot, I glanced at Marsha. Joy and gratitude could be seen in the way her eyes perked up as she patiently waited. A touch of sadness came to me as I thought about how she had suffered. *That poor woman*, I said silently. *She saved my life. Now it's time for me to save hers.*

Although I was very hungry, I took only a few forkfuls of the noodles onto my plate and left the rest for her. As I watched the elegant and classy woman before me aggressively and unselfconsciously devour the noodles, my heart began to soften. An overwhelming feeling of satisfaction filled my soul. I smiled and I discreetly looked away.

We came back into the living room and sat on the couches for a while. I knew that Pete had probably become infected, but I tried not to speak about it just yet. I wanted to think of something positive to say, but all I could think about was Pete and what had happened to him. I remained quiet and let my eyes wander about the room and down the hallway, toward the bedrooms.

"How is your wife doing?" she suddenly asked.

Tears welled up in my eyes, because I was so desperate to know, too. Glancing away, I quietly replied, "I'm sure she is probably worried sick about me right now."

Silence filled the room. Then Marsha began to speak. "Pete and I were in here for a long time. We wanted to leave and go be with our children. But every time we went outside, those people would run at us, trying to attack us. Their faces were filled with so much anger. We couldn't understand why they hated us so much. We couldn't understand what wrong we had done to them. We tried calling the police, but the phone wasn't working. I was so scared that they might burn down our store."

"It's not anything like that, Marsha," I assured her. "Those people out there don't hate you. They were infected. I'm not sure what they are anymore."

Noticing her confused expression, I tried explaining it to her. "It's a virus, Marsha. I don't know where the virus came from. All I can tell you is that a person who was infected with it bit several people. Then they became infected and bit more people. Soon after that, the whole city was infected."

"Are the police doing anything to stop this?"

"We tried to, but there are too many of them. I'm probably the only police officer left in this city."

She paused for a few seconds. Then she slowly nodded her head. "So that explains it," she blurted out.

"Explains what?"

"I understand now," she said. "About a week ago, we heard a woman screaming for help. We looked out the window and saw that she was being attacked right outside our store by a group of people. Pete wanted to go help her. I begged him not to, but he just couldn't let it happen. He took a baseball bat with him and managed to fend them off her. She was badly injured when he brought her inside. I tried calling for help, but the phone was still dead. We took her up here and put her in the other bedroom. I tried cleaning her wounds as best as I could and bandaged her up. The next day, we went to check on her. She was up and about but she was so angry at us. She tried to attack me, but Pete stopped her. After he threw her on the bed, we left the room and closed the door on her."

My eyes suddenly widened. "Is she still inside that bedroom?" I quickly inquired.

"Yes," she replied. "She's quiet now. But she'll start banging on the door again soon. For many days now, I've tried not to talk or do anything that would disturb her. I was so scared. Without Pete, I don't know what I would do if that lady gets out."

"What kind of lock is on the door, Marsha?"

"It's just a simple knob lock," she replied. "You know, it's one of those locks that when you turn the knob, the button in the middle pops out, unlocking it. But we didn't lock the door. It doesn't matter if we did. If she grabbed onto the doorknob and twisted it, it would unlock itself anyways."

I knew then that I had to go inside the room and kill the woman before she broke out. I really didn't know the level of intelligence those monsters possessed. But I knew that if she accidentally grabbed onto the knob and twisted it, the door would open.

I was just about to ask Marsha about the lock on her bedroom door when we were both startled by the loud poundings. "There she goes again," Marsha whispered.

With only one purpose in mind, I took the machete and went over to the door. As I pondered how I was going to enter the room, an idea came to me: I would wait until she was standing directly in front of the door. Then I would kick it open. The force from it should stun her momentarily, giving me enough time to go in and get ready for her.

I stood by the door and I began to speak loudly to her, enticing her to come to the door. I noticed that every time I called to her, she growled louder and pounded harder on the door. I knew then that she was standing right in front of the door. My chance had arrived.

I thought about a hard front kick to the door. But the kick might not be powerful enough to knock the door open, and I might get injured doing it. The only kick I could think of was a powerful side kick, Bruce Lee-style.

I continued talking as I took a few steps back. Then I ran up and thrust my right foot toward the door, hitting it as hard as I could. The door immediately blasted open and a loud thump followed. I quickly entered the room. The woman was lying motionless on the floor near the opposite wall. I was amazed that I'd sent her across the room.

The woman seemed to be unconscious. This was my chance to kill her before she got up. But when I went over to her, I couldn't believe what I saw. "My God," I gasped. "It's Brook from the coffee shop!"

Brook Fisher was just about Kara's age. She worked at the coffee shop on Pine Street. She was kind and thoughtful. She always gave me a free cup of coffee whenever I stopped by. She was very chatty and was a joy to talk to. She was always excited to tell me about her daughter, who was going to start kindergarten in the fall. It pained me so much to know that she would never see her daughter again.

I was extremely conflicted as I thought about what I should do. I really didn't want to kill her, because I knew her for who she was. Still, I had to kill her for what she had become. My emotions were still running rampant inside me when Brook suddenly opened her eyes. I was hoping that she would recognize me. But after she let out a growl, I knew she was no longer the person I'd known.

She was still flailing and trying to get up as I held her down with my foot. I was thinking about chopping off her head. But I couldn't do that. I couldn't bear to look at her and kill her that way. I put the machete down on the bed and withdrew my pistol. As I aimed the pistol at her head, I felt compelled to say something to her. "I'm so sorry, Brook," I said. "Please go in peace now."

After it was over, I pulled the sheet off the bed and wrapped her in it. I couldn't leave her in the room. After a few days, the stench would be too overwhelming. So I dragged her out to the balcony. The infected were still inside the lot, gazing intently up at me. "Good-bye, Brook," I said. Then I tossed her over the balcony.

I came back to the living room and sat on the couch. Marsha was sitting quietly on the other couch. I wasn't sure if she had fully grasped the situation or my actions. And although I had done similar things many times in the past month, I myself couldn't fully grasp my actions either. Everything that I had done thus far was taking a toll on my mind, body, and spirit. I didn't know how long I could continue before I went insane.

I desperately wanted to get out of there! But what could I do? I was trapped. My shotgun ammo was down to half a box. I still had a few magazines for my pistol. But the pistol wouldn't stop a horde of infected.

As I tried to figure out how I was going to get by without the shotgun, I suddenly remembered that Pete owned a couple of 12-gauge shotguns. We used to go hunting together every fall until I stopped going three years back. *Maybe he still has some ammo stashed away somewhere in here?*

"Marsha, does Pete still hunt?"

"Yes," she replied, glancing over at me.

"Does he still have some shotgun shells left?"

"I don't know. He stowed all of his guns inside the closet in our bedroom. Why do you ask?"

"I need some ammo for my shotgun."

"Oh, in that case, feel free to take anything inside the closet."

We walked over to Marsha's bedroom and quietly stood by the door. Although I knew Pete was in there, the silence worried me. I had no clue what he was doing. If only there had been sounds coming from in there, I would have an idea where he was and what to expect.

I noticed that there was a deadbolt on the door. I took the key from Marsha and unlocked it. She stayed outside while I entered the room. With the sunlight from the windows, I could clearly see that Pete was still in the bed. He was silent and motionless. For a moment, I thought he was dead.

The huge closet was at the southeast corner of the room, next to the bathroom. I let out a sigh as I pondered what to do. The bed was also over there and I needed to walk past it to get to the closet.

I quietly walked to the bed with my pistol aimed directly at Pete. After a quick glance at him, I began to relax a little. His eyes were closed. He looked like he was in a deep, peaceful sleep. His arms and legs were spread out and still chained to the bedposts.

I approached the closet and tried to open it as quietly as I could. But a sudden loud squeak from the hinges gave me away. I quickly turned to the bed. Pete was awake and gazing intently at me with his red, fiery eyes. I tried not to look at him, to avoid provoking him. But it didn't work. He let out a low, raspy growl and began violently jerking his arms.

I turned to the closet and focused my attention on finding the ammunition. Then, I heard a loud cry behind me. I quickly spun around. Marsha was inside the room. She had seen Pete, and she could no longer hold back her emotions.

Wanting to be with her husband, she stepped toward the bed. I immediately ran up to her and held her tightly. "Pete is gone," I said gently. "This is not Pete. This is something else."

Even though I had assured her that it wasn't Pete anymore, Marsha was still sobbing as she gazed passionately at her husband. Pete was crazed and still violently struggling to break free. Then Marsha looked up at me with pleading eyes. "I don't want him to suffer any longer," she said softly.

It must have taken all her strength to say that, I told myself. I, too, didn't want Pete to suffer any longer. So I slowly nodded and told her to leave the room.

As I stood next to the bed and gazed down at Pete, tears flowed down my cheeks. This was going to be the second time that day that I had to kill someone that I'd come to know, love, and respect.

Finally Pete stopped struggling and just lay there, quiet and motionless. As our eyes met again, there was an expression of peace and gratitude on his face. I'm guessing he knew what I was about to do. I really don't know if he was capable of thinking. But this was the second time I had seen this kind of awareness in an infected's face. The first time was from the boy in the basement at the other house.

"I'm so sorry, Pete," I said gently. "You will suffer no more. You will be with God soon."

He didn't even flinch when I placed a pillow up over his face. Then I brought my pistol up to his head. With a squeeze on the trigger, his body slowly went limp, quiet, and still. I stood by his side for a while, bowing my head. Then I covered him with the blanket.

I left the room with five boxes of shotgun shells that I had found inside the closet. Marsha was sitting quietly on the couch with her eyes fixed on the floor. She stood up and looked at me as I walked over to her. Without a word, I gave her a simple nod of confirmation.

A few tears leaked out from her eyes. Then she closed them. "Thank you," she whispered.

CHAPTER 31

The sun selflessly spread its magnificent beams across the vast, endless sky. The darkness inside the room was slowly being chased away as the brilliant light made its way across the floor. It was morning again—my third morning inside this refuge.

Slowly, I rose from the couch. I sighed deeply as I looked out the window. It hadn't changed much from the previous few days. The infected were still out there and hadn't wandered far from the store.

As I pondered my situation, I could once again feel despair and hopelessness overtaking me. *I'm still trapped in here*, I told myself. I couldn't think of a plan to get out. The little food I had inside my backpack was diminishing. I couldn't play the waiting game with the infected much longer.

Marsha was in the kitchen with a bowl of noodles waiting for me at the table. I went over and settled myself across from her. Although the mood was somber, we both managed to give each other a smile.

"It's a beautiful morning isn't it?" she said, trying to stay cheerful. "It sure looks like it's going to be another beautiful day."

I smiled faintly and continued eating quietly. Of course it was going to be a beautiful day if I kept looking up at the sky. But if I looked down at the streets, it was just another day of despair. I wished it would rain. The rain could truly reflect the pain and sorrow we were both feeling.

After the meal, I went out to the balcony. I wasn't surprised at what I saw. It was exactly the same as the previous days: The infected were still in the lot, looking up and growling at me.

As I continued scanning, I finally noticed a possibility. The top of the twelve-foot wall was just a few feet below the balcony. The length of the wall extended all the way to the west mall building. The roof of the mall building was probably about the same height as the balcony, and I could probably reach it. The width of the wall was about a foot. If I could get down to the wall, maybe I could walk on it to the other side.

Although I was happy that I'd found a possible way out, I was reluctant to try. I was still deathly afraid of heights. And with the infected on both sides of the wall, my demise would be agonizing if I fell off.

I came back to Marsha. I could tell from her sad, desolate expression that she already knew what I was going to say to her. I was extremely conflicted. I wanted to take her with me. But she was well into her seventies. With her frail body, she wouldn't make it across the wall, let alone make it to South Park with me.

My emotions were running rampant as I pondered what I should say to her. After taking a deep breath and slowly letting it out, I spoke: "I have to go."

"I know," she quietly responded. Then she smiled sweetly and added, "You don't have to worry about me. I've lived a full and wonderful life."

I took my bag with me as I went into the kitchen. Then I opened it and took out five packages of ramen noodles and placed them on the kitchen table.

"No!" she said as she came into the kitchen. Then she quickly picked up the packages and placed them back into my bag. "You'll need these," she said. Tears began streaming from her eyes as she quietly added, "I'm going to go lie next to my husband and sleep. When I wake, I'll be with him again in the next life."

Those words made me so emotional that I couldn't keep the tears from forming in my own eyes. I knew I would never see this wonderful woman again. It broke my heart to know that her life would end in such a sad and lonely manner. I quickly embraced her. "God bless you, Marsha. I hope to see you again in the next life."

As I walked out of the kitchen, I turned back to take one final look at her. She quickly wiped away her tears and managed to give me a smile. I tried to implant that smiling face deep inside my heart so that I would always remember her that way. Then I slowly turned around and left her behind.

Standing on the balcony, I tried to gather up my courage for the precarious walk along the wall. Hundreds of fiery eyes were gazing up at me from both sides, waiting and anticipating. One hundred feet was the distance that I needed to travel. But, being deathly afraid of heights and walking on top of a foot-wide brick wall, it was going to be dauntingly difficult. I wasn't sure if I would make it.

With the machete strapped to my belt and the shotgun slung over my shoulder, I carefully climbed down the balcony. As I took my first step on the wall, I immediately dropped to my knees. The infected were snarling and growling as they reached up for me. They were so close, but they couldn't quite touch me. I tried to stand back up. But each time I tried, I couldn't balance myself and had to go back down on my knees.

After a few failed attempts to stand, I finally gave up and decided to sit on the wall and scoot myself forward a little at a time until I reached the other side. To lessen my anxiety, I closed my eyes and tried to imagine a beautiful, lush meadow with a peaceful-running stream. And I was getting closer and closer to the stream to bathe in its refreshing, life-giving water.

It was a long, agonizing process. My thigh muscles strained and ached from having to push myself slowly along. I didn't know how long I would be able to withstand the pain. But as I kept thinking about the meadow and the stream, the pain subsided.

After a long while, I finally made it to the other side. Using the mall wall for leverage, I slowly stood up and reached for the roof. It wasn't as high as I initially thought, and I was able to grab onto it. With a huge leap, I pulled myself over the edge and onto the roof.

Standing on the roof, in the middle of the building, my eyes were sheltered from the chaotic streets. The beautiful, lush meadow in my mind came into view as I looked far and wide at the miles of treetops. The cool morning breeze blew through my clothes, gently brushing against my bare arms and drying my nervous sweat.

It was such an exuberating feeling to be out in the open and not have to worry about death. The tranquility began to overwhelm me, and my mind began to soar. But then, a gush of wind blew by me and I immediately opened my eyes. The stench of death that came along with it quickly reminded me of the reality I had to face.

I located an access door at the southwest corner. The door was unlocked, and it opened to a stairway. The bottom landing was dark, but the silence was encouraging. I thought about lighting up a flare and tossing it down the stairs to scare off whatever might be down there. But as I searched through my backpack, I realized that I had left the flares back at the house when I was frantically packing to leave.

Using my flashlight, I looked down at the landing and saw two doors parallel to each other. As I reached the bottom, I noticed that one of the doors was an exit door to the alley, and the other was to the Asbury

Tobacco Shop. I was very low on food and I needed to go to the tobacco shop to scavenge for whatever I could find in there.

With the machete held in front of me, I slowly opened the door and peeked inside. The place was completely ransacked. The cash register was on the floor, opened and emptied. *What were those people thinking when they took the money?* I wondered. *Who needs money at this point?*

Looking around the overturned counters and display cases, I was able to gather up a few bags of potato chips and a couple candy bars. I felt fortunate to have found something. It was not enough, but at least it would sustain me for a day or two.

The door to the manager's office was next to a huge display case. As I stood by the door and listened for a moment, a faint moan quickly alerted me to someone inside. I knew whoever was in there was probably infected. I hesitated. *But that room was probably where the supplies were stowed*, I reasoned. I needed anything I could find in there.

The door opened to another sight that stunned me. I should have been used to it by now. But the person I saw in there was someone I knew. There, on the floor, amongst the blood, guts, and feces, lay the mutilated body of Irena, the store owner. One of her arms was ripped off at the shoulder and lying on the ground next to her. The other arm was still attached to her shoulder but badly mauled. The bottom half of her body was torn off and lying on her desk.

Incredibly, Irena was still alive and was looking at me. She hissed at me, and I could tell she wanted to come over to me. But she could barely lift up her remaining arm to pull herself over. I couldn't bear to look at her as I thought about the person she once was. She had come to Minnesota from Ukraine about ten years earlier and had started this business by herself. She was very kind, always giving me an extra can of chewing tobacco every time I stopped in to buy a tin. I also had written three police reports for her in the past two months, and she even called my commander to brag about the wonderful job that I had done.

I didn't know if she could feel pain. But if she could, then she must have been suffering tremendously at that point. I had to put an end to her suffering.

Taking a few steps forward, I sighed deeply as I stood over her. Then I crouched down and placed the machete across her throat. She tried to reach for me but still could barely lift her arm.

"Irena," I said. "I'm so sorry this happened to you. You will suffer no more. You can go in peace now." I pressed the blade deep into her throat until I felt a snap. Then her eyes slowly closed. Her suffering had ended.

CHAPTER 32

It was late in the evening. I had settled inside a small house in the Asbury Park neighborhood. It was a comfortable little rambler with two bedrooms—a nice starter home for a young family. The rear door opened to the kitchen. An informal dining room was between the kitchen and the living room. There was a small window inside the kitchen and one more inside the dining room. A larger window was at the west wall of the living room, facing Oxford Street. The thick curtains at the windows easily concealed my presence from the outside world.

Although the place gave me a sense of comfort and security, it had nothing else to offer. The cabinets and the refrigerator were completely emptied of food. I guessed the occupants of this house had stayed for as long as they could until starvation finally forced them out. There was one thing, however, that this place had plenty of: scented candles.

As I sat inside the dimly lit living room writing in my journal, my mind hadn't stopped wandering, and my heart hadn't stopped longing. The two small flickering flames dancing on top of the large scented candles had become my companions. Everyone that I had known was gone. I had either left them behind or had killed them. I was truly alone now. And for the first time in my life, I began to understand what it meant to be human. *What makes us human is our need to be with one another.*

I often wondered if all of this was God's work. How could he be so cruel and merciless? I had to admit that before all of this happened, I hadn't been a spiritual person. I had never relied on hope or faith. I honestly thought that I could determine my own fate. But now that I was faced with such uncertainty, I had learned that all I could do was to hope and to have faith. And my fate could only be determined by God.

With that thought heavily implanted in my mind, my attention shifted back to Robbie at the bridge, before all this had happened. Then memories of my childhood suddenly came rushing back again. Everything was starting to make sense to me. It wasn't God who had done this to us. We had doomed ourselves. God was just standing by, watching us and trying to save those who were worthy.

Tou Xiong was Robbie's real name. I wasn't sure when and why people started calling him Robbie. I wasn't sure he even knew.

Robbie's life story could have been made into a movie and displayed on the big screen; then people would understand the tragedy and atrocity of warfare. Having grown up during the Vietnam War and its aftermath, I had learned to understand the evil that men were capable of. I had endured my fair share of suffering, but not to the extent that Robbie had. Unlike him, I was fortunate to have both my parents with me.

Robbie was born in a small village inside the Luang Prabang province in central Laos. He had lost his entire family. He made it to the refugee camp in Thailand when he was only ten years old. Being an orphan, he survived mainly on begging and occasionally stealing food. Sometimes he would come to our tent at night. My mother would give him a little bit of food to help sustain him a little while longer.

Robbie came to America when he was thirteen years old. He lived with a distant uncle, a cruel, selfish asshole who beat him regularly. Everyone in the neighborhood knew that Robbie was being abused and deprived of food. But because Robbie was slightly mentally challenged, no one did anything about it. They didn't want to end up with the burden of taking care of him.

Robbie ran away from home at the age of sixteen. No doubt he could no longer endure the abuse. He reverted back to the life he once knew: begging and stealing. At first, the Asian community was sympathetic to him. They provided him with food and shelter. But after a while, he was becoming a pest.

Robbie moved to the Asbury Park neighborhood when he was in his twenties. He slept in the parks in the summer. During the winter, some of the convenience store owners would allow him to sleep inside their stores after closing time.

Robbie was able to earn some money by doing odd jobs for the store owners and cutting grass around the neighborhood. He also received a disability check every month. But instead of getting a place to stay, he usually spent the money on booze and drugs. It was like he just wanted a nonexistent life.

I had always felt bad for Robbie, because he was so messed up. He never had a family. He never had a home. And he never had a sense of belonging.

• • •

Growing up in the same housing project with Robbie, I had heard a lot of far-fetched stories from him. Most of them were outrageous and ludicrous. However, there was one story that he was always consistent about. And that was his story about the Yellow Mists.

The last time he'd told the story to me was a few years back. It was consistent with the story he'd told me when we were young.

Robbie said that while his father was away fighting the war, his mother took him to a small village up in the mountains. She had grown up there, and she wanted to be with her family.

While there, Robbie saw an airplane flying over the mountain, spraying a trail of yellow mists into the jungles. After a few days, the animals in the jungles started dying. Fish were floating in the ponds. Some villagers went out to gather the carrion and brought it back to the village to be consumed.

A few days later, those villagers became sick. Their bellies became bloated, and they couldn't defecate to relieve themselves. Then they began regurgitating dark liquid. The vile odor was so bad that it seemed as if they were rotting from inside. Their skin became dry, itchy, and flakey. Then lesions appeared and would not heal. After a while, their skin began to rot away and peel off. Those people were in such excruciating pain that they screamed nonstop for days.

After the villagers died, a huge hole was dug at the edge of the village for a mass burial. During the funeral ceremony, the villagers came back to life. But they were not themselves anymore. They began attacking the other villagers and consuming them.

Robbie and his mother ran from the village and hid in the jungles. They survived by eating anything they could find. After three days of walking, they finally made it to another village down in the valley.

When his mother told the village chieftain about what had happened, the chief sent a couple of his people to her village to find out what was going on. After they returned, they said that all of the villagers were dead. They said that all of the bodies had been tossed into the large hole and burned. They also said that most of the villagers had been shot in the head. Some of them had been completely decapitated.

Robbie's mother became sick a few days later. After she died, she came back to life and tried to attack some people. She was restrained by the villagers, and then they killed her by chopping off her head. Because Robbie was with his mother, the villagers feared that he might turn into something like her. So he was banished from the village.

• • •

Of course I didn't believe Robbie at the time. Everyone knew he was crazy, and they quickly dismissed his stories. Maybe that was the reason why he was so messed up? No one believed him, and no one cared. The drugs and alcohol were probably his only way out. Maybe he did it so that he would no longer remember.

I didn't know if Robbie was exposed to the mists or not. But he and his mother were in the jungle for days, eating anything they could find. His mother died in the same manner as those villagers. Maybe Robbie was exposed too? But by eating something in the jungle, his body had somehow developed an immunity to the virus.

I think that Robbie was a carrier of that deadly virus all his life. Maybe after years of drug use, heavy drinking, and paint sniffing, his immune system had gotten so weak that the virus was able to overtake his body.

I now knew that Robbie had been telling the truth. One thing that I had completely overlooked from the story was that the villagers were shot in the head. It didn't dawn on me until now that those villagers were still living a primitive lifestyle. Not one of them had a gun. Those unfortunate villagers were experimented on. I just didn't know which government had done that to them.

I was still deeply enthralled in this conspiracy theory when three quick beeps alerted me to the radio. A message was being broadcasted:

> "All personnel, the package will arrive in seventy-two hours. Proceed with the operation at 0900 hours and fall back to the safety zone."

The message repeated itself over and over. I turned off the radio to save the battery.

I had no idea what "the package" meant. But I could only assume that it wasn't going to be beneficial to the residents of this city. I also had no idea what they were talking about when they said, "Proceed with the operation at 0900 hours." I just knew that I wasn't going to stick around to find out.

I thought about leaving. But it was too dark out. Besides, where would I go? That same uncertainty had been plaguing my mind, body, and spirit ever since the ordeal had begun. The only thing that I was certain about was that death would come to us all.

CHAPTER 33

The uncanny silence outside assured me that I would be safe inside my refuge. The small flames from the candles provided just enough light for me to see vaguely inside the living room. The couch was soft, and my body sunk comfortably into it. I was tired, but I couldn't sleep. As always, my mind was still reeling with questions that I had no answers for.

I turned to the radio to help alleviate some of my despair. But all I got was the same message repeating over and over again. Hopelessness and helplessness set in. The event that was about to unfold in the morning terrified me. *Will tomorrow be my last day on earth?* I wondered.

Then a sudden scream from outside startled me and I quickly jumped to my feet. A few more screams alerted me to the rear. From the high-pitched sound, I knew it was definitely a woman's screams.

The thought of self-preservation didn't even register anymore as I grabbed the machete and ran to the door. I had no idea how many infected were out there. But I didn't care at that point. If I was going to die anyway, then at least I would die with some honor.

The backyard was dark. But the moonlight revealed several people in silhouettes. I wasn't sure which person needed help. But after listening carefully, my ears were drawn to a figure on the ground. Her desperate cries were enough to assure me.

I ran up and began swinging the machete at every person standing. After few more groans and moans, the last person fell to the ground. Still breathing heavily, I stood guard for a moment, waiting to see if more were coming. The long silence was enough to convince me that those were the only ones there.

I turned my attention to the woman on the ground. She was curled up into a ball and weeping softly. "Hey, you're safe now," I said quietly, reaching out a hand to touch her.

"Please! Don't hurt me!" she begged.

"Shhh…You're going to draw more of them to us," I said quietly. "You're safe now. Come with me."

Upon hearing my assurance, she took my hand and got up. The darkness was still concealing her face from me. But I didn't care what she looked like. I was just happy to have a companion with me.

Through the kitchen and through the dining room, her face was still concealed by the darkness. Then the dim light inside the living room finally revealed a face that I knew, a face that I had missed, a face that I had longed to see. "Oh my God! Kara! It's you!"

When she noticed who I was, she quickly hugged me and began sobbing. "I thought I would never find you again!" she cried.

After a long embrace, I gently pulled back to look at her. I couldn't believe she was still alive! I couldn't believe that she'd made it out of that house! And what just blew my mind was that she had made it down *here*, and even managed to find the house I was in! She was definitely a survivor and was by far the luckiest person I'd ever known.

"What happened back there at the house?" I asked gently.

She was still panting as she tried to explain. "After you left, I heard shooting again downstairs. The shooting went on for a while, and then I heard some loud crashes. After that, I heard lots of screaming. Then the shooting stopped. I was too afraid to go check, so I climbed out the window to come after you."

She paused to wipe her tears. "I didn't know what to do. So I just kept running until I saw a ribbon on a tree. Then I remembered what you had told me. I continued looking for the ribbons until I reached the mall. But there was a lot of shooting over there, and I was too scared to go any farther."

She paused again to regain her composure. "After I made it past the mall, I didn't see the ribbons anymore. I didn't know what else to do, so I snuck around and hid inside garages for days."

"You did a good job," I said softly to comfort her. "You're safe now."

I noticed that she didn't have her backpack with her. Maybe she'd left it outside? If she did, then I would have to go back for it. "Where is your backpack, Kara?"

"I left it back at the house," she replied quietly. "I'm sorry. I was so scared at the time. It wasn't until later that I realized I didn't have it with me."

That was not what I wanted to hear. I was upset, because most of the food was in her backpack. Now it was going to be twice as hard for us because we would have to share the little food I had left. But I couldn't stay mad at her for long. It was a miracle that she was still alive.

"So have you eaten anything since?" I asked gently, trying to conceal my disappointment.

After she shook her head, I was completely astonished. My anger immediately dissipated. "My God," I said. "You're way tougher than me, or anyone I've known."

I went to my backpack and took out all the snacks that I had scavenged from the tobacco shop and gave them to her. I smiled amusingly as I watched her devour the food. I was going to tell her to slow down. But I would have done the same thing if I had been starving for days.

I couldn't help but admire this young woman's strong will and tenacity. I didn't think anyone could survive out there as long as she had without food or water, and completely unarmed.

"Are you feeling better now?" I asked, noticing that she had finished the last bag of chips.

"A lot better now, thank you," she replied, almost cheerfully.

"How did you make it down here?" I asked. I was truly intrigued.

She let out a soft sigh. "I was hiding around for days," she replied. "I tried to look for you, but I didn't know where you were. I didn't know what else to do. So I just kept heading south, trying to get to the park where you told me you were going to be."

Tears began to form in her eyes as she continued her story. "It was getting very dark, and I was getting tired. So I hid behind a garage and tried to sleep. When I saw some people running toward me, I got up and ran. They kept chasing me, and I was getting so tired. When I got to this house, I just couldn't run anymore." Her voice cracked, and she broke down, sobbing. "I didn't know what else to do. So I finally gave up. I was just waiting for them to kill me. But then you came out to help me again."

"You did good, kiddo," I said as I embraced her. "You did a good job."

I went to the other couch and sat on it for a while. I didn't want to ask Kara any more questions. She was still too emotional, and her cries might be heard from outside. So I took out my journal and began to write.

After a while, she came over and sat next to me. I slowly closed the journal and gave her a polite smile.

"I'm curious," she said.

"You're curious about what?"

"I'm curious about what you wrote in your journal after you left the house."

I looked away. "It's something that I will never want to read again," I said sadly.

"What did you do?" she inquired.

I took a deep breath and let it out. Then I slowly turn toward her. "I've done things that will haunt me for the rest of my life."

After a moment of silence, she shifted gears. "What are we going to do now?" she asked.

"I don't know," I replied. "But we'll find out in the morning at nine o'clock."

She looked at me. "Why? What's going to happen then?"

"I don't know. But something big is going to happen. After that, I'll know what to do."

CHAPTER 34

My body was spread out weakly on the couch as I stared at the beam of light that was slowly making its way across the kitchen table. I let out a deep, painful sigh and turned back to the darkness inside the living room. Morning had come. *This might be the last morning that I will ever see,* I told myself.

Kara was still sleeping on the other couch. I had missed her gentle snoring. But it didn't give me any comfort this time. The deep sorrow I felt was mostly for her. She had survived so many trials. She could not possibly survive the next one. She would not be going home. She would not be seeing her family again. Our fates are about to be revealed. Our journey will end here inside this tiny house.

It was almost nine o'clock. The moment was arriving. I made no effort to prepare to leave—there was nowhere to run to. I just lay motionless on the couch. Gone were my anxieties, my pains, sorrows, guilt, and regrets. A peaceful feeling of acceptance flowed through me. I was finally liberated from my struggles.

I didn't want to wake Kara. She would get the chance to die peacefully in her sleep. I closed my eyes and calmly waited for what was about to come. I basked in the tranquil moment—the quiet before the storm.

Suddenly, an earth-shattering sound rattled the ground beneath the house. I immediately knew what the military was doing: they were bombing the city. It was just a matter of time before death arrived from the sky.

Kara was quickly awoken by the sound and ran over to me. Trembling, she huddled next to me. "What's happening?" she asked, panicking.

"It has started," I replied calmly. "There's no way out of this now. I'm so sorry, sweetie."

Several more blasts occurred nearby and the house began to shake. I continued holding on to Kara, anticipating a huge, fiery inferno at any moment. Then the blasts suddenly stopped. Loud splashing sounds from the river finally revealed to me what the message on the radio was about: the military had blown up the Asbury Bridge to the north of us.

I was relieved that I had been wrong about the bombing campaign. But that didn't make me feel much better. My suspicion about the other half of the message had just been confirmed. The military had probably blown up all the bridges to this city. They were planning to keep everyone confined inside the city while they fell back to the safety zone. The package would be coming. It was going to be total annihilation then!

"We have to go, Kara," I said, calmly.

"What's happening?" she asked, still perplexed.

"The military just blew up the Asbury Bridge," I explained. "We have to get out of here. We don't have much time left."

"Why would they blow up the bridge?"

"They don't want anyone leaving this city. They blew up the bridges to keep everyone trapped in here."

"But we're already trapped in here! Why would they want to do that now?"

"They planned to leave. They wanted us to stay behind. But I think they will still be patrolling the rivers until the package arrives."

"What package?" she inquired, confused.

"They're sending in a missile or some type of weapon of mass destruction to destroy this city," I revealed. "I'm guessing we have about seventy-two hours to get to South Park before it arrives."

"How do you know all this?"

"I heard the message on the radio yesterday."

She was about to ask another question, but I cut her off. "Let's go," I said quickly. "We don't have any more time to waste."

Suddenly, the sound of footsteps outside alerted me to the front of the house. Looking through the living room window, I could see hundreds, if not thousands, of infected coming up the street. They had also heard the blasts, and they were heading toward the bridge.

As more and more infected appeared from everywhere, I was getting increasingly desperate. I was hoping to get to Asbury Park by nightfall. But now, we would have to stay put for another night. And it was not going to be a pleasant night either.

I came back to the couches and sat with Kara. There was nothing else to do but to wait it out. But after a while, I became increasingly paranoid. The commotion outside was sending my blood pressure through the roof. The thought of the infected bursting through the door at any moment was raising my anxiety to an unbearable level. The thumping sound of my heartbeat was so amplified that I feared the infected might hear it from outside. It was psychologically killing me. And I didn't know how long I could withstand it.

It was well into the afternoon before everything finally began to settle down. Most of the infected had left the area. There were still some slow movers straggling about outside. But they were gradually leaving, too.

It seemed like forever before I watched the last of the infected make their way up the street. Then it was our chance to leave. I returned to the couch and quickly gathered my things together. "We have to go now, Kara," I said. "We have to get to Asbury Park before dark."

We left through the rear door and went into the backyard. The carnage that I had caused the previous night was displayed before my eyes. I had killed a man, a woman, and three children. They were a family. *I had killed an entire family!*

The sorrow I felt after seeing the headless body of a young girl was indescribable. My knees quickly buckled beneath me. Tears leaked out of my eyes. "I'm so sorry," I cried. "I'm so very sorry!"

After a moment, a hand gently touched my shoulder. Kara was standing behind me. Wiping away my tears, I slowly stood up. I had come to terms now with what I had done. The reason for my actions was standing behind me.

CHAPTER 35

A fter hours of sneaking around, we finally made it to Grand Hill. River Road was on the other side of that hill. Asbury Park was about a mile beyond that.

We made it to the road and down to the woods. With the protection of the trees, I was confident that we would make it to the park before nightfall. But after bushwhacking for a long while, I was feeling dejected. The slow pace was consuming time and energy. And to make matters worse, I could still see the road from where we were at.

It took us a few hours to reach a clearing, at the northern edge of Asbury Park. My eyes willingly took in the amazing, picturesque scene before me. Far from the chaos, this place seemed harmonious and beautiful, as if it had been untouched by the foul hands of hell. The cloudless summer sky splendidly complemented the vast open field. The golden sun smiled charmingly above the horizon. Its bright orange rays shone brilliantly onto the majestic field, turning the luscious greens into a magnificent golden pond. Here and there a patch of wildflowers appeared in the golden field like an oasis in the middle of a desert. The trees around me swayed back and forth with the breeze. Birds flew above me, circling and singing beautiful melodies. Their spirits were undaunted by my presence.

As my eyes wandered around, I almost smiled. I could almost picture gleeful children running across that field and hear happy parents laughing and mingling. But my heart ached as I silently marveled at the scene. *How could I have missed such beauty before?* I wished I had not taken so many things for granted, for the simplest things in life back then were now the things I yearned for the most. I sighed deeply as I watched several busy bees flying hurriedly from one patch of flowers to another, as if there was still hope for another day. I looked up and admired the birds above me going from tree to tree and gliding across the field to the other side as if they were on just another mission. Sadness finally consumed me as I thought about their peacefulness. I was briefly jealous as my mind drifted off into the horizon. *I wish I had wings. I guess only those with wings can truly be at peace.*

As I wondered where we were going to hide for the night, I spotted the obvious choice: the large pavilion at the end of the parking lot. I remembered that Bobby, who used to be a park ranger before he became a cop, had a master key to all the facilities inside the park. He had given me a copy of it a year earlier when I had gotten locked inside the park once while patrolling it during afterhours. One of the restrooms at that pavilion would be our safe haven for the night.

Roughly two hundred yards of open field lay between us and the pavilion. There were no infected anywhere in sight. I was quite confident they hadn't been there yet.

We quickly covered the first hundred yards. I was exhausted, but my spirits were still high. Then, as we approached the parking lot, I increased the pace. A group of infected were appearing from the woods behind the trail fifty yards to the east. They had seen us and were coming our way!

"Run faster, Kara!" I shouted.

She sped up after hearing that. I was hoping she didn't see the reason we were hurrying. But when I heard a quick scream, I knew she'd seen the group. "Damn it, Kara! Stop screaming!" I scolded her.

"I'm sorry! I'm a screamer!"

"Just keep your eyes fixed on the pavilion," I said, to direct her attention away from the infected. "Focus only on getting over there!"

We reached the pavilion and went around it to the front. But as we turned the corner, we quickly stopped. A small group of infected were standing near the picnic tables. Surprised by our sudden appearance, they just stood there and gazed at us, bewildered.

We can't outrun them now, I said to myself. *We're too exhausted from the sprint.* We had to stay and fight. I would have to kill them before the others arrived. I quickly took out the set of keys from my pocket and gave it to Kara. "Use these keys to open the door while I hold them back!" I said.

It appeared the infected were still trying to figure out what to do. I was hoping that Kara would get the door open before they rushed toward us. Finally, one of the infected decided to come at us. Soon after that, all of them rushed toward us.

I fired two quick shots at them, and they went down to the ground. A couple of them stayed motionless. But the rest were trying to get back up. Two more shots and they finally stayed down.

More infected quickly appeared from the northwest corner of the pavilion. I fired until the shotgun was empty. Then I slung it over my shoulder. Taking out my pistol, I continued firing at anyone who came close enough for a shot to the head.

After the first magazine was emptied, I glanced over to Kara. She was still fiddling with the keys. "*Hurry up*, Kara!" I shouted. She was saying something back to me, but I couldn't understand it. My focus was solely on the infected.

Halfway through the second magazine, I glanced over at Kara again. I couldn't believe it! She was still playing with the lock! "Kara!" I shouted, panicking. "What the hell is taking you so long?"

"Which key is it?" she shouted back. "You're not answering me!"

"It's the biggest key in the ring!" I shouted angrily. Was she completely incompetent? I couldn't believe she couldn't figure that out by simply looking at the size of the keyhole. She was trying all the damn keys on the ring!

I was on my last magazine when Kara finally unlocked the door. We rushed inside and slammed the door shut. The vigorous pounding at the door was unrelenting. But I paid no attention to that. The fact that we might be trapped inside had crossed my mind. But I didn't care. I was living in the moment. Again and again, I was just thankful to be alive.

After a long while, I finally allowed my eyes to explore the inside of our new refuge. The gloomy room seemed larger than I'd expected. The walls were made of concrete. The small windows at the south wall were set almost at the top. The metal door at the front seemed sturdy enough to withstand quite a lot of beating.

I took a deep breath. The noxious odor of urine was mixed with the minty smell of the urinal cakes.

"What are we going to do now?" Kara asked, still panicking from the commotion at the door.

"We wait," I replied calmly. "We'll stay here for the night. We'll leave tomorrow when they're gone."

I tried to be optimistic and reassuring with my response. But I knew that we were probably doomed. I just didn't want her to know it, too. The infected would remain out there for days. We didn't have enough food or time to wait it out. We were probably going to die in there.

• • •

It was almost midnight. The pounding at the door still hadn't subsided. I didn't know how long the door would be able to withstand the vigorous impact, but it seemed to be doing its job so far. My hands were still firmly gripping my shotgun. My mind, body, and spirit were spent.

The room was dimly lit by the two scented candles that I had taken from the house. It was getting cold, and the hard cement floor was uncomfortable. Still, I felt fortunate to be there instead of out in the woods.

Kara was sleeping soundly as usual, lying against my backpack. She seemed oblivious to the noise and the smell and didn't even flinch after a loud bang startled me. I wondered if she could still dream. Could she still have wonderful dreams? I was sure I couldn't dream anymore. Heck, I wasn't even sure I could sleep anymore. Every time I closed my eyes, the faces of all those people that I had killed kept staring back at me— tormenting me and reminding me of the hell that was waiting for me.

Being in the pavilion and knowing that my demise was almost inevitable, there was really nothing else to do except reflect on my life. *The wonderful memories of my life before all of this happened will always stay with me*, I reassured myself. I would take them with me when I perished from the earth. And although I didn't want to take the sorrows, they would have to come along too.

But each time I thought about my wife, the wonderful memories became secondary to the sorrows. Although her face was fading from my mind, her love would never leave my heart. I wished my spirit could fly out of Riverdale and over to see her one last time. What would I say to her? Would I be able to tell her to move on without me? Would I have the strength to encourage her to find another man that would love and cherish her as much as I had?

I thought about my mother, and I felt even sadder. For years, she was living in the poorest, most run-down part of the city. I had finally bought a house for her in Oakdale. But who would pay the mortgage now? I wished I could tell her that she had raised me well. I wished I could tell her that I would try to survive, even though death was all around me.

I wished that things hadn't changed so much. I wished…

CHAPTER 36

I didn't remember falling asleep. But when I opened my eyes, the sun was already peeking through the windows above me. My head felt ten pounds heavier; I could barely lift it. As I stared lethargically inside the room, something seemed odd, though I couldn't make out what it was. I was sitting with my back against the wall, still holding on to the shotgun. The distinctive odor from the urinal cakes was still lingering. The scented candles were still burning, and Kara was still sleeping a few feet away from me. Everything seemed to be in its correct place. So what was wrong?

Then, it finally occurred to me: the silence. The poundings at the door had stopped! I had no idea if the infected had given up and left—I could only hope so. But I did know that they would not go far away. They were still out there somewhere. Our situation hadn't changed much. We were still trapped inside the pavilion restroom.

As my eyes wandered about the room, my mind became fixated on the thought of my passing. I'd never imagined that this place was going to be my tomb—that I was going to die inside a *bathroom!* How glorious was that? I had always pictured myself dying an admirable, heroic death. But I guess when it came right down to it, everyone wants a peaceful, painless death.

As my eyes continued wandering, a small beam of light on the floor of the last toilet stall suddenly caught my attention. I got to my feet and started toward it. As I opened the stall door, a jubilant feeling quickly revived my tired body. There was another door on the wall behind the stall!

The lock on the door required a key to turn it. *If the master key works on the lock, then that is going to be our way out*, I thought. But as I checked my pockets, I realized the keys weren't inside. Then I remembered I had given them to Kara to open the door the previous day.

I went back to Kara and gently nudged her. "Kara, wake up."

"Is it time to go?" she mumbled.

"Where are the keys that I gave you yesterday?"

"I thought you had them."

As soon as she said that, I knew that the keys were probably still hanging from the lock outside the door. We had been in such a hurry to get inside that I hadn't even thought about taking the keys.

I went to the front door and slowly cracked it open. The infected were still outside. But they had moved back toward the picnic tables. As I expected, the keys were still dangling from the lock.

With the door slightly opened, I reached for them. The master key was slightly bent and appeared to be stuck inside the lock. After a few gentle tugs, I realized that I had to pull harder. With a quick, hard yank, the keys suddenly shot out of the lock, slipping out of my hand and landing on the floor a few feet away. The clanging sound immediately alerted the infected to me. I dashed out and grabbed the keys. Within seconds after shutting the door, the poundings resumed.

Feeling a glimmer of hope, I ran to the rear door and placed the master key into the lock. There was some resistance as I tried turning it. I was worried that if I turned it too forcefully the key might break off. So I held my breath as I carefully added more force each time I twisted on the lock. After I felt a click, I finally let out all the air in my lungs. The door opened slightly.

But my high spirits were quickly dampened after I peeked out the door and saw the infestation. Even with the commotion at the front, the ones in rear were still there. They seemed unfazed by the noises, which were probably nothing new to them.

There's no way I can kill them all, I told myself. *It will take a miracle to get out now!* I closed the door and went back to Kara. She kept glancing at me, silently begging for a plan. But I didn't have one for her. I was at my wits end. I was just as desperate as she was. I turned away and quietly looked around the room.

As the poundings intensified, I could tell that Kara was getting increasingly anxious. She was dying to say something. But she understood my frustration and remained quiet. My mind was too cluttered to think of anything at that point. So I decided to do something else to distract us for a while.

I took two packages of ramen noodles out of my bag and handed one over to Kara. Bewildered, she silently took it from me. She must have thought I had lost my mind to be thinking about food at that point.

"Let's eat," I said calmly. "We're going to need all of our energy to get out of this."

The noodles were dry and hard to swallow. I chewed slowly and drank some water to flush it down. Even though I felt like I was eating plywood, it was still satisfying. I tried to savor it as much as I could. It could be my last meal if I decided to leave.

The meal did help boost my morale. My mind was distracted from the commotion long enough for me to come up with an idea: I had to create a diversion. I needed to draw all the infected to the front. If I could do that, then we could escape through the rear door.

I explained my plan to Kara, and her eyes widened a little bit more with each word that came out of my mouth. I told her to go open the front door and let the infected inside. When the shooting began, the rest of them would be drawn to the front. When the rear of the pavilion was cleared, then we'd leave through the rear door and run like hell to the woods.

Obviously, this plan wasn't going to put her mind at ease. I wasn't sure if anything I came up with at that point would put both our minds at ease. But she seemed to be taking it well. Without a word or an objection, she simply nodded.

After a long while, I finally built up enough courage to begin. Kneeling in the middle of the restroom, I placed a box of shells on the floor in front of me. With the shotgun loaded to full capacity, I aimed it at the door. After several deep breaths, I became relaxed and ready for the onslaught.

Kara was at the door waiting for my signal. "Kara, after you unlock that door, I want you to run straight to the rear door. Wait for me to tell you when to open it. You got it?"

Paralyzed with fear, she just stood there staring blankly back at me, as if she was in a trance. "*Kara!*" I shouted. "Do you hear me?" She quickly snapped out of it and nodded.

After unlocking the door, she immediately ran to me and hid behind me. Startled by her action, I yelled to her to go to the rear door. She scurried to the stall and crouched behind the rear door.

The front door swung opened and the onslaught began. I fired a round directly at the doorway, sending the ones in front of it to the ground. But they were quickly replaced by others behind them. A few more shots and the doorway began to pile up with bodies, giving me time to reload.

After I reloaded for the second time, I was pretty confident that all the infected had been drawn to the front. So I called to Kara to open the rear door and check. "They're still out there!" she shouted.

"How many are still out there?"

"A lot!" she replied.

As the battle continued, I noticed that there were fewer and fewer infected at the doorway. It seemed as if they were leaving. I paused as I thought I heard some loud popping sounds out there. *Could that be gunshots?* I wondered. *Yes, those are gunshots out there!*

Someone else was out there doing battle with the infected! I was relieved and felt extremely thankful for the help. But as I continued listening, I realized that the shots were being fired from automatic rifles. My upbeat feeling suddenly turned to fear. It had to be the military out there. And they had probably arrived to exterminate everyone!

After realizing that the infected had abandoned the doorway, I quickly ran to Kara. I wasn't sure which side was winning the current battle. But it didn't matter. We were still doomed if we stayed where we were. Our chance had come to make a run for it!

Peeking through the door, I saw that the area was cleared. The gunshots were coming from the front. "This is our chance, Kara," I said. "We have to get to the woods. Do not stop until we get to the woods!"

We were about thirty yards from the pavilion when I heard a man's voice calling for us to stop. I knew we had been spotted—we had to get out of rifle range! So I told Kara to run faster.

Another twenty yards, and I could still hear the voice calling to us. I quickly glanced behind to see how far we were from him. I was expecting to see a soldier pointing his rifle at us. But instead I saw a guy in a blue uniform waving to me.

As we walked back to the pavilion, I couldn't believe my eyes. It was Kevin! He had made it all the way there. "You have no idea how much I've missed seeing you, kid," I said, almost giving him a hug.

"It's good to see you, sir," he said, smiling.

"Are you by yourself?"

"The guys are here, too," he replied. "Even Jack came along."

"Really? How did you manage to persuade him?" I asked. I was really curious.

"Well, it wasn't that hard when we were starving," he replied. "I told Tommy and Bobby about what you were planning to do. Then Bobby told everyone else about it. Jack didn't want to come, but he didn't have a choice. Liam was coming with us. I guess Jack didn't want to be alone."

"Did you guys go over to the bridge when you were near the freeway?"

"We got about a hundred yards from it. When we saw the soldiers shooting at people, Jack was finally convinced."

As we were speaking, the rest of the guys started appearing from the pavilion. "Hua! We finally found you," Bobby said as he approached me.

"Hi Tubby. Thanks to your master key, Kara and I are still alive," I said with a genuine expression of gratitude. "How did you guys know we were at the pavilion?"

"When we got here, we heard the gunshots. We knew it had to be you," Tommy replied.

"Hi Jack, I'm glad to see that you came," I said after seeing him approaching.

"Well, I didn't have any choice," he said. "You better be damn sure that cave of yours is still there."

"I'm pretty sure I can still find it," I said, trying to sound confident. "It's a good thing you guys decided to come. The military just blew up all of the bridges yesterday. Now they're planning to destroy this city in less than two days."

"How do you know that?" Jack asked, still skeptical.

I knew I had to provide proof in order to convince Jack. So I reached into my backpack and took out the radio. I turned it on. But the message had stopped broadcasting. Nothing else was being broadcasted either.

"Where did you get that radio, sir?" Kevin asked.

"From a crazy guy inside one of the houses at Covington," I replied. "I think he killed a soldier and took his radio."

"Do you mean the house with a military jeep parked in the front?" Bobby asked.

"Yes," I replied, surprised. "Did any of those soldiers survive?"

"Were they the ones in the yellow hazmat suits?" Tommy asked.

"Yes."

"We only saw bits and pieces of them," Mo said.

"We thought about driving the jeep," Kevin said. "But the streets were filled with abandoned cars. It wasn't an option."

"Yeah, we checked the jeep and found a bunch of ammo for our guns," Bobby added. Then, he reached into his pockets. "Look what I found," he said, as he proudly displayed two grenades in each hand.

"Bobby! Put those away, you idiot!" I shouted, quickly snatching the grenades from him. "You're going to blow all of us up!"

"So, what are your plans now, sir?" Kevin asked.

"Well, all of the bridges are probably destroyed by now," I replied. "I think the military is still patrolling the river, so we can't cross it. We have to get to South Park."

CHAPTER 37

The walk on the trail was becoming more enjoyable now with so many pairs of eyes looking out for danger. It was such a liberating feeling not having the burden resting solely on my shoulders. My mind was actually focused on going home. The thought of my wife wasn't accompanied by sorrow like it had been. For the first time in a very long time, I could hear her sweet, angelic voice calling to me, telling me to wake up. I could see her sitting at the dining table, smiling that gorgeous smile at me as she watched me enjoy the meal she had prepared.

An hour later, however, my gleefulness came to an abrupt end. There was something up ahead that worried me. A huge cloud of dust was rising from the valley floor, up to the cliffs of Crosby Boulevard. *Something dreadful happened over there*, I thought.

Through the binoculars, I could see that the once magnificent Crosby Bridge was now a gigantic pile of rubble. Hundreds of infected were milling around amongst the debris. Thirty yards off shore, two patrol boats were stationed. My suspicions were confirmed: The military was still patrolling the rivers until the package arrived.

It was no surprise that Liam wanted to go over and do battle with the infected. His way of thinking was just suicidal. We would not win that battle. We didn't have enough ammo to fend them off. The massive pile of steel, concrete, and boulders would hinder us from getting to the other side. And if the military got involved, then we would be in even more trouble.

"We have to go up to the residential area and find another way to South Park," I said to them.

"Are you *crazy*?" Liam retorted. "There are probably thousands of those monsters up there! We have to—"

"Well, Liam, it's better than your suicidal idea!" I interrupted. Then

I glanced at the others. "If anyone has a better idea, now is the time to share it."

After a moment of silence, I reiterated my decision. "Kara and I are going up to the residential area to look for another way to the park," I said. "If any of you guys want to stay here and try to get to the other side, then that's fine with me. If you guys happen to get to the park, then go to the marina. The caves should be at the cliffs about two hundred yards to the east. We will be there by tomorrow."

"I'm going with you," Bobby said. Kevin, Tommy, and Mo also agreed. Liam was still pessimistic—as usual. But he reluctantly agreed after Jack decided to come with us, too.

We backtracked until we came to a small path that led up to River Road. After ascending up to the road, we were now in the Niles neighborhood, by far the richest neighborhood in the city. The property taxes alone could probably pay for the salaries of the entire police department.

After a few hours of sneaking between yards, garages, alleyways, and houses, we finally made it to Otto Avenue. The street ended at a cul-de-sac on top of a steep hill overlooking the Crosby Park neighborhood. If we followed the street up to the cul-de-sac, Crosby Boulevard should be directly at the bottom of the hill. Everyone was enthusiastic about getting to South Park. But the sun was beginning to set. We had gone as far as we could. We had to find a place to rest for the night.

We settled inside a large brown house in the cul-de-sac. It seemed a perfect location for the final push to South Park in the morning. The woods in the back would provide excellent cover for the descent to Crosby Boulevard. Pillsbury Road was going to be the primary objective from there. The road began at the south side of Crosby Boulevard and extended for five blocks, ending at a large grassy field. Beyond that field was the north entrance to South Park.

As I stared out the window at the Crosby Park neighborhood, I couldn't believe how much the area had changed over the course of time. When I started my job, the whole area had been like a ghost town, filled with abandoned companies and warehouses. Then ten years ago, the city embarked on a very progressive project. They tore down all of the deteriorating buildings and replaced them with hundreds of high-end apartment buildings and townhouses. After that, hundreds of shops, markets, and businesses sprouted up alongside Crosby Boulevard. Now, the Crosby Park neighborhood was one of the busiest neighborhoods in the city. When it came to population density, the neighborhood rivaled Charlestown. But the crime rate in Crosby Park was nowhere near that of Charlestown.

After securing the windows and all points of entry, we gathered inside the living room. The light from the two scented candles was barely enough to penetrate the darkness. But it was enough to reveal our faces to one another as we started in on dinner.

The eight cans of cat food that Bobby found in the basement were perfect for the occasion. The slimy texture and pungent fishy smell was enough to make me vomit. *But food is food*, I reasoned. And when you're hungry enough, the taste is irrelevant.

"So how are we going to get to the park tomorrow?" Liam asked me.

"We have to get across Crosby Boulevard," I replied. "Pillsbury Road is on the other side. It's only five blocks long. Once we reach the end of the road, we go across the grass field. The north entrance to South Park is about a hundred yards after that."

"I know I haven't been down here for a long time now," Bobby said, "but isn't that area just as crazy as Charlestown when it comes to the number of people?"

For the first time in a long time, Bobby was right about something. The other guys were north guys, and they rarely came into this neighborhood. I was hoping they didn't pick up on what Bobby was saying. "Yes," I replied discreetly, "but it's not as crazy as Charlestown. We will have to go through shops and apartment complexes. But it's only five blocks."

I was expecting a few grumblings. But the silence was encouraging. Even Liam was surprisingly quiet. I guessed with me sugarcoating it, it was a little easier for them to bear.

After dinner, I went into the kitchen while the others stayed in the living room. I thought about the plan again, and quite honestly, I didn't think it was going to be viable. Pillsbury Road would provide us with a direct route to South Park. But that whole area was so compact, there was no way we would get through without being spotted. There were probably thousands of infected down there. We would have to fight our way through to the park. And I wasn't sure if any of us would make it.

Seeking relief from this revelation, I took out the radio. I was hoping to hear something that would spark a new idea. I turned it on and sure enough, a new message was being broadcasted.

"All personnel evacuate your post by 0900 hours and fall back to the safety zone."

A glimmer of hope came to me as my mind went straight into overdrive. Then a new plan emerged. "Change in plans, guys!" I called to them as I went back to the living room. "Come over here!"

After they all gathered around, I turned on the radio and let them listen to the message. "The original plan isn't going to work," I explained. "Crosby Park is way crazier than Charlestown. At least in Charlestown, people are somewhat spread out. There's a very high concentration of people within those five blocks. We will be fighting thousands of those monsters. I don't think we'll make it."

"So what is it that you're proposing?" Jack asked.

"I'm thinking about going back to the Crosby Bridge in the morning," I replied. "The military will be leaving at nine o'clock. No one will be patrolling the river then. If we can find some ropes in here, we can use them to tie some logs together to make a raft. There's got to be a car somewhere over there in Hiawatha. We'll use it to get as far away as we can before they bomb this city."

"And I know how to hotwire a car," Tommy quickly added. Noticing our raised eyebrows, he quickly added, "Not that I used to steal cars. But I grew up in the 'hood."

"I knew it!" Liam snorted loudly. "We should have stayed over there! Now we have to go all the way back there again!"

"Shut the fuck up, Liam!" I snapped. I'd had it with him. "What are your fucking ideas, then? Tell everyone what you are planning to do!"

After a moment of silence from him, I decided to shut him up for good. "Shut the fuck up, and talk only after you come up with something constructive!"

He quickly walked away.

"Hey," Jack said to me. "Don't think too much of it. Liam was just venting his frustration."

"I know," I said, exasperated. "We are all frustrated. But his attitude is detrimental to everyone's spirit."

"Well, at least this new idea of yours will give all of us the much-needed uplift."

Jack's approval meant a lot to me. He had always been a take-charge type of guy. For him to follow me with no objections was new, and it was encouraging. Sure, it would take us two to three hours to get back to the river. But the military would be long gone by then. The current would be strong and turbulent, but if we built a raft, we could make it across the river. Plus, Tommy wasn't the only one who could hotwire a car. *I also grew up in the 'hood.*

It was almost midnight, and I still couldn't sleep. Tired bodies were stretched out all across the living room floor. Jack and I got the couches because we were the oldest, and seniority still counted. I had to poke Bobby several times with a broomstick to stop his obnoxious, trumpeting snores.

Even though I hadn't slept for more than three to four hours the previous two nights, my body still wouldn't succumb to the fatigue. There was so much to write down in my journal. I wanted to finish writing everything before I forgot it all. But then, how could I forget? I knew I would never forget, even if I tried.

Thinking back to that heinous first day up to the present, I didn't think I would ever be able to fully comprehend or justify all of my actions. I didn't think I would ever be able to truthfully speak to anyone about the hell that I had been through. What would I do when I woke up screaming in the middle of the night, drenched in sweat? What would I say to my wife? What would I do when I encountered someone who acted differently? Would I run from them? Would I kill them? I didn't think I would ever be normal again.

Slowly, my eyes began to close. Then my body gradually succumbed to the fatigue. And…

CHAPTER 38

Standing on a summit, I marveled at the grandeur of the vast starry sky. My heart danced blissfully as I watched the golden rays of light slowly appear on the horizon and split into a perfect division of light and darkness.

As the magnificent rays rose and spread a blanket of light, the splendor of a spectacular, picturesque valley below slowly revealed itself to me. The majestic fields of green, the lush trees, the crystal-clear ponds, and the endless array of flowers were all vivid and inviting. However, there was an uncomfortable urge in my heart that did not wish to go down there. It felt almost like a warning; that such a beautiful Garden of Eden-like display should remain untouched and unspoiled.

A gust of cool wind shot up from the valley and gently brushed against my face. Suddenly a chorus began to sing a hypnotic, soothing hymn. I closed my eyes and inhaled a deep breath of air. It was at that moment that I realized I had never felt so content and peaceful.

A sudden distant rumbling of thunder rattled my ears and drowned out the comforting hymn. I instantly opened my eyes to a bitter struggle between light and darkness. A smoky mushroom-like cloud began to spread slowly across the sky. Then, the light began to fade as darkness prevailed.

My heart was palpitating so hard. I could feel a raging storm coming my way, and there seemed to be nowhere for me to run for shelter. I could feel the ground beneath me begin to rattle as the thunder echoed. Lightning bolts shot violently across the sky. The angry wind ceaselessly shoved itself against my weak body. Its loud cries deafened my ears with its eerie howls. I prayed for God to hold me and keep me safe.

Then suddenly, a flash of light appeared and the darkness faded. The sound of raindrops softly filled my ears. I then tilted my head to peek up at the sky and noticed that it wasn't rain. Instead, millions of small flames dropped from the sky, scorching the valley below and turning it into an inferno. I could hear countless voices crying out to me and begging me to take my place *among them. I closed my eyes and covered my ears, but to no avail. Nothing I tried could drown out the desperate voices.*

"Make it stop!" I cried. "Please make it stop!"

Suddenly, everything went silent. A cool breeze gently brushed against my face again and playfully enticed my eyes to open. I squinted a little as I tried to open them, and I could see a reddish-orange ray of light slowly piercing through the darkened clouds. The crimson sky then quickly turned into a bright, clear, sunny day.

However, a dark, ominous cloud hovered over the valley below and obscured my view of it. As my heart longed to know what had become of the magnificent fields of green, the lively flowers, the thousands of trees, and the breathtaking ponds, I heard a soft, soothing voice asking me a question, as if someone had been observing me and knowing all along what my heart desired. "Is your heart yearning for a place down there?"

I was taken aback by the words it asked, so I just stood there silently for a minute or so. But then I couldn't help but wonder how I could possibly get down there, even if I wanted to.

"How can I get down there through the thicket?" I asked.

"Jump," the voice replied.

"What?"

"Just jump," it said again.

"…and die?" I asked with a concerned tone.

"Trust me, you will not die."

I was confused, but it said to trust it. No. I hesitated. "What if I die?" I asked myself.

I looked around and was sure that I was alone—but then who or what was that voice? Should I just take my chance and trust it? I gathered up my courage, took a deep breath, and leaped off the summit. To my surprise, I wasn't falling. A feeling of euphoria overwhelmed me as I noticed that I was floating gracefully in mid-air as I made my way down. The dark clouds slowly opened to make way for me and to reveal a grisly remnant of a city—the rubble of buildings, the charred trees, the solidified residue of the ponds, the parched streets and scorched earth—I saw it all. Nothing stood. Nothing remained.

My mind couldn't comprehend as my eyes surveyed the poisoned land. Suddenly, the ground rattled with an earth-shattering sound. Thick puffs of dust rose and shot up into the air. A chorus of voices filled my ears and overwhelmed me with their despair.

As the dust settled and stilled the air, amid the ruined and the scorched earth I could see endless piles of bones. In disbelief I let my eyes wander, and yet my heart refused to accept what I saw and heard. The voices were now whispering to me from among the bones. Each voice had a story to tell and wanted to be heard.

My heart suddenly felt despairingly alone as I thought about my family. Were they among the voices? Were they calling to me, too? "Where is my family?" I finally managed to utter, almost silently. But there was no reply.

"Where is my family?" I shouted out. Still, there was no reply.

Frustrated, I began to weep. "I guess I'm alone in this world." I said to myself. "Why am I here to see this?" I cried.

"The time has come," the voice suddenly replied. "Your world will be ending."

"Why show me this if this is the end of me?"

"You are the first one."

"What do you mean?" I asked.

"You will be the first of your kind."

"What will become of me?"

"You will live to see the end. And you will live to the beginning."

"I don't understand."

"Those around you will die and wither away. But you will not. You could never love, you could never fully live, and you could never find peace."

"Please, stop!" I cried. "Please make it stop!"

I opened my eyes to a beam of light cutting sharply across my face. I'd awoken from a dream! And not a wonderful dream by any means. It was a nightmare within a nightmare. How ironic that I'd wished so many times to be able to dream. But if my dreams were going to be like that one, I didn't want to ever dream again.

I quietly got up and walked over to the window, letting out a painful sigh as I gazed out at the view. I wondered if I would ever see that majestic sight again. The glorious rays cast a shimmering glow onto the Mississippi River. The thick morning mist still hovered over South Park. The Coral Cliffs of Antiman City stood far beyond the park and the river, stretching for hundreds of miles. I wondered what would become of all of it. *After today, there will be nothing left but the searing remnants of it all,* I told myself. *If today is my last day, then at least I will have the memory of this view to take with me wherever I may go.*

It was a somber morning. We gathered around to start in on a meal of crushed ramen noodles mixed with the last four cans of cat food. There was no levity or enthusiasm as we ate quietly. I guess we all knew it was probably going to be our last meal. Everyone was trying to cope with it in their own way.

"If I make it out of here, I promise to take my wife on that vacation that I've been promising her for so many years," I said, trying to alleviate the gloominess that was engulfing the room.

Kara quickly glanced over to me. "If I make it out of here, I promise to seek a lot of therapy. Then I'm moving to the country. I want to be as far away from society as possible," she added.

"If I make it out of here," said Kevin, "I promise to marry my girlfriend. I don't know why I didn't marry her. I love her."

"If I make it out of here, I promise to stop screwing up and do something right with my life," said Tommy.

"If I make it out of here, I promise to move to Mexico with my wife," said Mo.

"If I make it out of here, I promise to stop living in my van. I'm going to find a decent woman and move in with her," said Bobby, and we all laughed.

"Well," Jack said. "I have four daughters. I want to grow old and be a grandpa."

We all looked at Liam. He glanced away and remained quiet. "Liam?" I said. "It's your turn."

He slowly looked back at us. "I've been a cop since before I was old enough to drink. My life still hasn't changed much. I've never been married. I have nothing to go home to." He took a deep breath and continued. "I promise all of you that I will do whatever I can to help you make it out of here, so that you all can fulfill your promises."

I was moved by Liam's words. I'd never seen this side of him before. He had always been cocky and self-centered. Maybe I was wrong? Maybe there was a compassionate side of him that was never displayed to anyone until that moment.

Silence filled the room again. Our spirits were still dampened by the uncertainty that lay ahead.

Then Kara suggested we say a prayer. Although I had never prayed before, it was only fitting that I conduct my very first one.

I spoke honestly from my heart, as if I was reciting my last rites to God:

> *"Dear Heavenly father, please forgive me, for I've never prayed to you before. I pray to you now because we are in desperate need of your guidance. Give us the courage and the strength to embark on this seemingly insurmountable task. Be merciful and forgive us for what we are about to do. Outside, there are thousands of lost souls that cannot pray to you now.*

Please forgive them and be merciful with them, too. If all our lives are to end this day, then please welcome us into your heavenly kingdom. Amen."

It was nearly eight o'clock. We were packed up and ready to go. Bobby came to the living room with two coils of climbing ropes. I was amazed at how the guy could find nearly anything he was asked to look for. Now that we had everything, I figured we would be back to the river around eleven o'clock, provided we had no issues.

I took out the radio and turned it on. I needed to be sure the military was definitely leaving at nine o'clock. I wanted to get to the river long after they had left. But something else was being broadcasted. My heart dropped as I heard the new message:

"All personnel fall back to the safety zone by 0900 hrs. The package will be arriving at 1200 hrs."

I buried my face between my hands. I had never felt so defeated. We had only three hours to get back to the river, build a raft, cross the river, hotwire a car, and get far enough away to avoid being engulfed by the blast. It couldn't be done! Just getting to the river would take nearly all the time we had. And we still had to contend with the infected along the way.

"We don't have the time!" Liam snorted as he paced about the room. "*We don't have the time!*"

"Let me think, Liam!" I shouted.

"So what are you planning to do?" Jack asked. "Liam is right. We don't have time."

"We have to get to the caves before the blast," I quickly replied.

"Wouldn't we die too?" Mo inserted himself. "Even if we make it to the caves, the blast will still kill us."

"We might die," I replied. "But if we get to the caves, there's a corridor that gradually descends all the way down to and then below the river. We might be about fifty to even a hundred feet below the river. If we stay underneath the river, the water might protect us from the heat. There's a chance that we could survive the blast."

"That's bullshit!" Liam shouted. "We're going to drown!"

"Well, Liam!" I shouted back. "Tell me your ideas, then!"

"That's enough!" Jack finally put an end to the bickering. "We're going to the caves!"

CHAPTER 39

The trees at the bottom of the hill concealed us from the hundreds of infected that were gathering outside Truong's Vietnamese Bakery. They were just a block away to the west. But they were preoccupied with that small building. A few pockets of infected were wandering about a few blocks away to the east. Pillsbury Road was just ahead of us on the other side of Crosby Boulevard.

"Do not use your guns unless you absolutely have to," I warned everyone. "When we get down to the caves, we'll make our stand from there."

The sprint across Crosby Boulevard to Pillsbury Road went quickly. I barely breathed hard at all and was having no issues with the pace. After a block, I was still doing fine keeping up with everyone. But after one more block, I was beginning to feel the strain. Kevin and Tommy were like gazelles as they glided effortlessly across the pavement, leaving everyone in their dust.

After the third block, my body was beginning to fail me. I was lagging further and further behind. Bobby noticed it and had to come back for me. "I'm dying, Bobby," I said, panting, struggling for air. "I don't think I can run anymore. You keep going. I'll try to catch up."

Bobby continued glancing back at me every few yards or so as he ran ahead of me. But with his last glance, his facial expression suddenly changed. Noticing this, I looked behind me. Then with a sudden jolt of adrenaline, my pace increased immensely. Hundreds of infected were coming out from between the buildings behind us. I quickly ran past Bobby, passing Jack and the others and almost catching up to Tommy and Kevin.

We were almost a block away from the field when the sound of gunshots suddenly halted us. Bobby was shooting at the infected. The asshole would doom us all! "Bobby! You fucking *idiot*!" I shouted. "Why do you have to do that?"

"I'm sorry! But they were getting too close!"

Suddenly, choruses of screams were coming from every direction. The pounding sound of footsteps rattled the pavement. It seemed the entire Crosby Park population was heading our direction. "*Run!*" I shouted.

We were at the last block when we had to stop again. A huge gathering was at the end of the road. The two large apartment complexes on both sides of the road had cut off our escape routes. The infected behind us were a block out but closing in.

"Shoot the ones ahead of us!" I shouted. "We have to blast our way through them!"

I was completely mesmerized as I watched the guys tearing up the crowd with their AR-15s. At that moment I wished I also had that rifle. I was just too old-school and had always been used to the shotgun. I guess this change the department made was a good idea after all.

The infected behind had arrived. We were boxed in—trapped between the buildings, with the infected on both sides. Now we had to shoot in both directions to fend them off. There were just too many of them. We were not going to have enough ammo to keep up the fight. So I yelled to the guys to keep shooting the ones in the front to clear the road while Bobby and I defended the rear.

"I'm out of ammo!" Liam shouted. "Follow me!"

I glanced behind me and saw that Liam was running toward the thin line of infected at the front. With his head down and his rifle held in front of him, he charged at the crowd like a bull on steroids. "Liam! No!" I shouted.

Liam didn't seem to hear me, nor did he care. He charged into the crowd, knocking them down, clearing a small path for us to go through. "Go!" he yelled as he held them down. "Get out of here!"

Everything was like a blur to me. I didn't remember going through the crowd. The next thing I recalled was running across the field. I was halfway across when I noticed that Jack wasn't running next to me anymore. I looked behind me and saw that he was running back toward the crowd.

"Jack!" I called. "*Jack!*"

He quickly stopped and turned to look at me. "Go!" he shouted. "Get everyone out of here!"

"Come back, Jack!" I pleaded. "We have to leave together!"

"*Get the fuck out of here!*" he shouted.

I didn't know what else to do except turn around and leave him behind. His and Liam's extraordinary acts of bravery were something that I could never do. I was going to miss them, and I would never forget what they'd done.

Finally I caught up with the others at the entrance. No questions were asked. Jack's gunshots and the desolate expression on my face were enough for them.

The steep cliffs on both sides of the entrance assured me that there was only one way into the park. The infected would have to come in the same way. The small paved road from where we were descended all the way down to the marina. The cave was two hundred yards beyond.

A few infected were already on their way toward us. We had to get down to the marina. We were just about to leave when I noticed that Mo was limping. So I told the others to continue to the marina and wait for us there.

"C'mon, big guy," I said gently. "Let's get out of here."

"You go on ahead," he said quietly. "I will hold them off from up here."

I didn't want to hear that. I wanted him to come with me. "Let's go, buddy," I said. "We're going to make it together."

"I'm done," he said. Then he slowly rolled up his right pant leg to show me the reason.

I was devastated when I saw a huge chunk missing from his calf. Obviously he had been bitten when we were going through the crowd. "We'll find some medicine to fix that," I said, trying to encourage him.

He placed his hand on my shoulder. "You know that's not going to happen," he said. "I will turn into one of *them* soon." Then he gave me a faint smile. "I'm going to miss you, old man."

I managed to give him a faint smile in return. "Good-bye, Mo. I'm going to miss you, too."

I reached the marina and found the others hiding in the back. Still breathing heavily, I sat on the ground and leaned my back against the wall for a moment. I could tell that they were desperate to know what had happened to Mo. But before I could tell them, a barrage of gunshots at the top of the hill answered their questions.

"We have to go now," I said. "We have to get to the cave."

As I gazed at the marina, an option quickly came to me. I thought about the docks at the river. They were only twenty-five yards south of the marina. Maybe there was still a boat over there that we could use to make our escape.

"Stay here," I said to them. "I'm going to go check the docks. I'll be right back."

I was ten yards from the docks when I knew there was no need to go any further. It wasn't a surprise to me: The docks and boats had been the first things the military destroyed, to prevent people from leaving. Now we really had to get to the cave.

I quickly ducked behind a tree when I saw a group of infected coming out of the woods. Obviously Mo's gunshots had enticed them to come out. I held my breath as I watched them stepping out into the parking lot. There were so many of them! They were looking around, trying to figure out where the shots had come from. But the gunshots had stopped. I had to be very careful not to make a sound.

As I quietly backtracked to the marina, an infected suddenly appeared in front of me. He was partially eaten and moving very slowly toward me. He wasn't much of a threat. I didn't want to take the risk of making noise when I killed him. So I carefully moved around him and continued to the rear.

The guy was still following me to the rear of the marina. I was just about to tell the others not to shoot him because of the other infected at the front of the building. But then, a gunshot suddenly rang out from behind me, and the guy's head instantly exploded. I quickly spun around and saw Bobby aiming his rifle at me.

"Bobby! You fucking idiot!" I screamed as I reached over and slapped him on the side of the head.

"I'm sorry, but he was going to kill you!"

"I could have easily outrun that guy, you dumbass!" I said, still fuming. "Now the others are coming!"

Within seconds, the entire area was filled with the sound of growling and high-pitched screams. The crackling sounds of twigs and branches were getting closer to the marina. "Run!" I shouted. "Get to the caves!"

The sprint across the field didn't seem to bother me much as I kept my eyes focused on the three giant boulders that were marking the cave entrance. Glancing behind me, I saw that the infected had reached the marina. But they stopped there. We were too far away, and they had lost sight of us.

My spirits were high after noticing that. Something had actually gone right for me. I felt a new pair of legs beneath me now. My pace was beyond everyone else's. I found myself encouraging them to keep up with me. The boulders were just a few yards away. We were almost there!

As we passed the boulders, my spirits immediately dampened as I gaped at the sight in front of me. A huge metal door was blocking the entrance. It had been such a long time since I'd visited that spot. I had no idea how long that door had been there.

There were no locks on the door. It was probably secured from the inside. *There has to be a secret entrance somewhere around here*, I said to myself. *But where? It could be back at the marina. Or it could be somewhere at the top of the cliff. Who knows where it is?*

"What do we do now?" Kara asked, adding more drama.

"I'm going to shoot the door," I quickly replied. "Get back behind the boulders!"

I knew the noise would definitely bring the infected over to us. But it was the only thing I could think of. I raised my shotgun and fired two rounds at the door. But it didn't have any effect. The pellets only managed to make a couple of dents. Then I told Kevin to come over and shoot it with his rifle. The bullets from his rifle went through the door. But that also didn't matter. The door was still tightly secured.

I had to consider other options. Glancing back at the marina, the infected were on their way toward us. Another group of infected were also approaching from the woods at the river's edge. There was no way we could get to the river now. Shooting that door was a bad idea!

I was at a loss and couldn't come up with any other ideas. Then Bobby suddenly blurted out, "Why don't you just use the grenades to blow up the door?"

Of course! I had taken two grenades from him the previous day and placed them inside my backpack. "Bobby!" I said gleefully. "You've said a lot of stupid things. But this is the smartest thing I've heard from you. I forgive you now, you idiot."

I held a grenade and waited for everyone to tuck themselves safely behind the boulders. After pulling the pin, I carefully tossed it toward the door and immediately ducked behind the boulder. BOOM!

My ears were still ringing as I peeked at the door. After the smoke and dust settled, I saw that the door was lying on the ground. "Quick!" I shouted. "Let's go inside!"

With the door being blown off, Kevin, Tommy, and Bobby stayed at the entrance to fend off the infected. Kara and I hurried farther into the cave to search the labyrinth of corridors for the specific one that led down to the river.

I had no idea where to start. I hadn't been there for more than thirty years. But back then, I had done something that I was proud of: I spray-painted my initials on the top of the entrance to that corridor.

"Look for the letters 'JH' on the entrance, Kara!" I called.

The gunshots were getting less and less intense now. I was getting desperate after not locating the corridor. The guys wouldn't have enough ammo to sustain the onslaught for long. And we were still dinking around!

"Kara, did you find anything?" I called.

"No!" she replied.

After a short while, Kara excitedly called to me. "I found it!" she yelled. "I found the corridor!"

I ran over and was astonished that my initials were still there, in bright yellow paint. I was so glad Kara found it. I had been looking in the complete opposite direction.

Kara stood by the entrance while I went back to the guys. After seeing what they had done, I couldn't be more proud of them. The entrance was littered with piles of dead infected. There was barely enough room for the ones outside to squeeze through. The attack had slowed down considerably. But the infected were still trying to squeeze through.

"I'm almost out!" Kevin said as he inserted his last magazine into his gun.

"Me too!" Tommy added.

"Follow me!" I said to them.

As we ran back to the corridor, I found myself in a dilemma. The infected were still coming. Even if we got inside the corridor, there was nothing that would keep them from following us. We had to kill them all. But we were running out of ammo.

Somehow, Bobby also knew the dilemma we were facing. So he told me to go without him.

"We all go together, Bobby!" I insisted.

He turned to me and lifted his left shirt sleeve to reveal a bite mark on the back of his triceps. "I was bitten when we were up there," he said. Then he reached out his hand to me. "Give me the grenade," he said. "I'll hold them off for as long as I can. Then I'll blast the entrance."

An extreme rush of sorrow overwhelmed me as I gave Bobby the grenade. "I'm so sorry for calling you an idiot, Bobby," I said softly. "You're really a very good friend. I will never forget you."

CHAPTER 40

Bobby's gunshots were still ringing in my ears as I crawled down the dark, narrow corridor. I was trying to get as far away from the entrance as I could. I didn't want to be caught in the cave-in when the blast came.

As I struggled to gain distance, I was still thinking about Liam, Jack, Mo, and Bobby. They had died deaths that I could have only imagined myself dying. They would always be heroes. I was determined to never let any one of us forget about their sacrifices.

The gunshots finally stopped. A brief moment of silence instilled a deep panic within me. The blast was going to happen at any moment, and I had to increase my pace. Then a deafening noise rattled the corridor. A strong gust of wind quickly caught up to me, knocking me off of my knees and down to the ground. The stinging sensation from the sandy debris felt like a million needles, pricking my arms and legs. The sound of falling rocks was getting louder. *I have to keep going!*

After crawling for a long while, the only sound that prevailed was the fading sound of falling rocks from the ceiling. I waited for a moment to ensure that no one was following me before I continued on.

The temperature was getting colder as I continued. It seemed like I was crawling forever inside the dark, confined corridor. I had no idea where the guys were. But I wasn't too worried: there was only one way they could go.

After a while, I saw a light up ahead. My spirit was quickly lifted—the guys were probably over there. The narrow corridor widened, then opened into a small enclosure. Sure enough, there they were, huddling around a small lamp.

"Where's Bobby?" Tommy asked.

"He didn't make it," I replied quietly. "He did what Liam, Jack, and

Mo did. They bravely sacrificed their lives so that we could get away. We will never forget that."

We sat there for a moment. But I felt unsettled. We had to go farther down. We had to keep going until we were far underneath the river. Although I was thinking that the water might shield us from the extreme heat of the blast, in truth, I had never been in a blast as powerful as this one before. The theory of possibly surviving the blast might have boosted the others' morale, but it wasn't making me feel any better.

The temperature kept dropping as we went farther. It was getting so cold that the damp dirt on the ground was getting icy. My mouth was quivering. My speech was beginning to slur. My body was shivering so much that I couldn't concentrate on anything else except getting warm.

After I heard a loud splash up ahead, Kevin quickly called out, saying he had fallen into a small pond. "How deep is it?" I called to him.

"It's up to my chest!"

"That's good! We'll stay in that pond and wait!"

I took out my journal from my backpack and placed it inside a plastic Ziploc bag, which I had taken from the house that we stayed in the night before. Then I placed it back into my backpack. The machete was strapped onto my duty belt, in case I needed the weight to help me stay submerged in the water. My shotgun would never be parted from me.

The water was extremely cold. All we could do was to huddle together to stay warm. I looked at my watch: five minutes to noon. Trembling and lethargic, I stared anxiously at the limestone walls. I had no idea how deep we were below the river. I just hoped the walls were strong enough to withstand the impact.

Everyone was shivering so badly, we couldn't say anything to each other anymore. I knew if we stayed in the water too long, hypothermia would set in. But we were too close to the time of the impact. I didn't want to be out of the water when it happened.

As I watched the seconds slowly ticking away on my watch, I couldn't help but wonder which death was going to be worse: to be immediately engulfed by the fire or to slowly drown when the walls caved in.

With a minute to go on my watch, I found myself nervously counting down the seconds. I bit my lip and closed my eyes, taking slow, deep breaths. "Ten, nine, eight . . .one! Get ready!" I shouted.

We covered our heads as we braced ourselves for the impact. But there wasn't one. "What happened?" Kara asked, her eyes wide.

"I don't know," I replied, looking as dumbfounded as everyone else. "Maybe my watch is too fast."

Suddenly the ground began shaking violently, as if we were in an earthquake. The cold, damp walls of the corridor quickly heated up, turning everything into steam. The boiling water droplets from the ceiling began to trickle down on me, seeping through my clothes and burning my skin.

Thinking that it was just a matter of time before the fire engulfed the entire corridor, I told everyone to submerge themselves in the water. "Hold your breath for as long as you can!" I said. "Do not lift your heads out of the water until it's over."

I stayed under the water and watched as a flash of light illuminated the dark enclosure, making it bright as day. The pond instantly heated up, turning the freezing water to almost an unbearably hot temperature.

After a few seconds, everything became dark again. I stayed submerged until I could no longer hold my breath. Slowly, I lifted my head out of the water. The hot steam from the evaporating water had filled the entire enclosure, turning it into a sauna.

I choked as I took in a quick breath of air. "Breathe slowly," I said, coughing and gagging.

"Is it over?" Kara asked, panting. "Did we make it?"

"Well, we're still alive," I replied. "But I'm not sure if it's over yet."

CHAPTER 41

I don't know how long we stayed inside the enclosure. It might have been for hours or even days—I really don't know. My watch had stopped working. Time was distorted by the darkness. The small lamp had been blown away by the force of the hot wind. Our flashlights were destroyed by the water. The two scented candles I'd kept in my backpack were our only source of light. The temperature was getting increasingly colder—a sign that maybe it was safe to leave now.

As we started down the corridor, the passageway was getting narrower, forcing us to crawl again. The jagged rocks cut painfully into my hands and knees. As the rocks piled up higher inside the corridor, all we could do was to squirm our bodies over and around them like snakes. I couldn't stop the despairing thought of being trapped down there if the entrance at the other side was blocked off by fallen rocks. What a miserable way to die.

The process was slow going, and it seemed as if we had been at it for hours. But my spirit was uplifted a little after noticing we were finally ascending. We were close to the cliffs. But the process was even slower now that the rocky flooring was unsteady. Every movement had to be careful and methodical.

After a long while, I finally saw light in the distance. The entrance was just ahead! "That's it!" I said. "We're almost there!"

But as we got closer, I could see that the entrance was actually blocked off by piles of rocks. There was no other way to get through except to try to blast a hole through it. I fired several rounds at the rocks, trying to soften them up to make it easier for us to push through. But I was pleasantly surprised to find that I'd blasted a hole through the rocks and let in more light. There were no large rocks or boulders blocking the other side. The small rocks and debris were easily moved out of the way to widen the hole.

• • •

We emerged into a world of complete and utter devastation. The scorched earth extended far into the distance. Shock and despair seemed to hit everyone deeply as we gazed at the smoldering destruction. No one could make even the slightest sound as we looked around in total disbelief. Thick flakes of ashes floated everywhere like droplets of rain falling from the broken sky. Tears trickled down my face as I silently sent God another prayer. The once great and abundant city of Riverdale was now an endless pile of charred rubble.

I guess it wasn't a surprise to me after all. Though I had hoped for a better solution, my gut instinct was not wrong. My heart had predicted this mayhem weeks ago, and I already feared learning the truth after my nightmare the night before. Even though not everything was exactly the same as how I remembered in my dream, the scene before me was an eerie déjà vu. The only thing missing was the voices.

"What do we do now?" Tommy asked.

As I looked at Kara, I knew that only Tommy and Kevin would be going home. "You guys go home," I replied.

"What do you mean, 'You guys go home'?" Kevin asked, puzzled. "Aren't you guys going home too?"

"No," I replied. "We have something else to do. You must never reveal any of this to anyone. The government will never leave you alone if you do. They do not want anyone leaving the city alive. If they find out about you, you will be hunted and killed. Now go home to your families."

As I watched Kevin and Tommy walk farther and farther into the distance, tears once again began to form in my eyes. I would never get to walk that direction. I would never see my family. Kara would never see her family either.

I turned to Kara. She was pale and sickly. I already knew what was happening to her. I gently lifted her right hand and looked at it. A tiny gash on the edge of her palm confirmed it. "It was when—" she said.

"I know," I interrupted.

I knew there was only one possible time that she could have been bitten. It probably happened as she was trying to get through the crowd when we were up at Crosby Park. It puzzled me why she hadn't turned yet. Maybe the gash was so tiny that the virus hadn't made its way through to her bloodstream yet. Or maybe the cold water helped slow down the progression. I wasn't really sure.

"I want to go home," she said sobbingly. "I want to see my family."

"Shhh… I know," I said gently as I pulled her toward me.

Kara stood with her back to me. I aimed my pistol at the back of her head, and tears began streaming down my cheeks as I thought about what we had been through together. I was going to miss her so much. Her tenacity and strong will had inspired me so many times when I had lost all hope. It was so unfair that she had made it out of Riverdale, but would never get to go home.

"You won't feel a thing," I said.

CHAPTER 42

It was a few days later when the president finally had enough courage to address the nation about the eradication of Riverdale. The bastard blatantly lied to the whole world, saying that the government had exhausted every option they had, and that nothing else could be done. As I watched him continually lying through his teeth, it took all my energy not to shoot the TV.

"Mr. President!" said Sam King, the reporter that I had sent a copy of my journal to. "Are there any survivors?"

"No," replied the president. "I was assured that no one had made it out of the city."

"Mr. President," Sam shouted over the other reporters. "I have with me a copy of a journal written by a lone survivor. In his journal, he said the government had done nothing to help the people of Riverdale. He explained in great detail about the suffering that the citizens endured. He also witnessed many murders carried out by the military. He even has proof of a conspiracy to cover up biological experiments conducted by the government during the Vietnam War."

"Who is this person?" asked the president, his eyes wide. "Where is he?"

"He's in hiding with the proof."

I turned off the TV, letting Sam expose the lies to the whole world. Kara had asked me several times what was I planning to do with my journal. It wasn't until my dream that I finally realized what I must do with it. I had to be the voice of all those people—all those souls. Every one of them had a story to tell. They would never rest, and they would never relent. They would continue to haunt me unless their stories were told.

• • •

It has been seven months since the eradication of Riverdale. I found myself on the run. Although I had changed the names in my journal to protect everyone, I don't know how the military was able to obtain our true identities. I heard Kevin and Tommy were captured and taken to a secret facility. I never made any attempt to contact my family. But now, their whereabouts are also unknown to me.

I am a marked man. Several times, I have encountered federal agents. But I was able to elude them every time. I don't know how long they'll be pursuing me. But their persistence has made me into someone far beyond my own control.

Inside an old farmhouse in southern Minnesota, I watch as two federal agents make their way through the soggy field and slowly approach the front door. What I like about federal agents is that they sit behind their desks the majority of the time. Their habits are like those of a rookie cop—they're unsure and very predictable. They have no idea what is waiting for them in here. This house is rigged with booby traps. No one escapes with their lives!

Hiding quietly inside a small space between the walls, I watch the agents slowly make their way down the dark hallway. I can see them clearly, but they can't see a thing. I chuckle at the awkwardness of their movements in the darkness. The stupidity of someone not to use a flashlight while coming down this dark hallway is beyond me. I almost feel sorry for them. Their demise is inevitable.

Suddenly, one of them lets out a high, screeching scream. His ankle is caught inside the jaws of a steel trap. The other quickly turns in the direction of his buddy. That is his last movement. The machete slices through his neck and takes off his head.

The remaining one is oblivious to my approach. The shock from the pain keeps him incapacitated. A slight glimmer from the machete is the last thing he sees.

I drag their bodies and throw them down in the basement. I've removed the stairs to prevent anyone from escaping. It was a tactic that I picked up during my time in Riverdale. Moments later, the flapping sound of a pair of feet quickly approaches. Soon after that, the eerie sound of feasting begins.

Shining my flashlight down at the landing, a pair of fiery eyes stares intently back at me. That once beautiful face that I had known and loved is now something that I often see in my nightmares. "Goodnight, Kara."

I've become a monster. I have kept Kara alive with the hope that someday I will find a cure for her. I once promised her that I would take her back to her family. I will never rest. And I will never die until I fulfill that promise.

I also cannot be with my family. I've changed, too. But unlike Kara, I still have my humanity. I've become something else. I've become stronger—much stronger. My senses of sight, touch, and smell are greatly enhanced. My body regenerates itself every time I sustain an injury. I don't know what I've become. But in my dream, *I was the first of my kind.*

www.ingramcontent.com/pod-product-compliance
Lightning Source LLC
Chambersburg PA
CBHW030306200626
46816CB00002BA/786